THE CLINIC

Also by David Jester

An Idiot in Love
An Idiot in Marriage
This is How You Die
Forever After

THE CLINIC

A Thriller

DAVID JESTER

Skyhorse Publishing

Skyhorse Publishing books may be purchased in bulk at special discounts for sales promotion, corporate gifts, fund-raising, or educational purposes. Special editions can also be created to specifications. For details, contact the Special Sales Department, Skyhorse Publishing, 307 West 36th Street, 11th Floor, New York, NY 10018 or info@skyhorsepublishing.com.

Visit our website at www.skyhorsepublishing.com.

10 9 8 7 6 5 4 3 2 1

Library of Congress Cataloging-in-Publication Data is available on file.

Cover design by Lilith_C

Print ISBN: 978-1-5107-0437-4
Ebook ISBN: 978-1-5107-0444-2

Printed in the United States

To my mother,
I hope your warmth and empathy lives on in me,
just like your short temper and foul mouth has.

1

The rhythmic fluctuations of a heavy snore crept through the house like mist through a graveyard, interrupted sporadically by the chugging of a strained breath and spaced, almost melodically, between the mechanical machinations of a large grandfather clock.

Inside the living room, a veil of dust hovered, its gentle flow caught in the moonlight that spilled through a hastily opened curtain.

The living room had been overturned. The drawers were opened and emptied, their contents piled on the threadbare carpet. Ornaments had been hastily checked and repositioned, a box of painkillers had been studied and discarded, a box of papers, receipts, old newspapers and lottery tickets, had been skimmed and then rejected.

Next to the living room, through a short hallway, the kitchen was still. The back door was ajar and rocking in the light breeze, the night outside peeking in. A large pan, an assortment of cutlery and a single plate were stacked in the sink; a half-eaten cake sat uncovered on the counter.

On the other side of the living room, beyond the kitchen and through the disturbed sheet of dust, stretched a short hallway. Three sets of cautious footsteps skulked in the darkness, taking each stride with purpose, careful not to step on any of the worn and creaky floorboards that lined the L-shaped hallway. Scuffed jeans brushed the carpeted floor, threatening the silence.

One intruder stopped at a closed door, waiting patiently as the sound of snoring punctured the otherwise silent house. A second stopped at a door that stood slightly ajar, eager to go inside. The final intruder paused outside an open doorway, through which, aided by a sliver of moonlight, they could see the noisemaker: a fat man lying on his back, his chest rising and falling with each chaotic breath.

The first intruder opened the closed door, glided inside and shut the door behind, making sure it didn't click in place. They quickly moved around the room; opening drawers and wardrobe doors. There was little for the second intruder to find. They scuttled around the room, took an interest in a few objects and quickly left. The third intruder was slower, more cautious. They advanced slowly, opened dresser drawers and took the objects that glittered in the moonlight: rings, earrings, a diamond necklace. They took a wallet and a watch from the top of the dresser and a smartphone from a bedside cabinet beside the snoring man.

The three intruders met in the hallway, paused and then broke away, this time heading in the same direction and moving with haste. They moved noisily across the thin hallway carpet and then over the linoleum kitchen floor, before filing out through the back door.

Giggles and hushed breaths of excitement cut through the night air, filtering through the blackness, not penetrating the drawn-curtains and sleeping suburban exteriors.

They wound through a back alley, their feet stomping heavily, visible in the blotches of light shed by the streetlights that lit either end of the long alleyway. They moved into a park, cut through a line of trees and stopped in the center of a copse.

In the house, the snoring stopped, transformed into a wet chortle, and then a choke. The strained sound spat into the dark room and then a veil of silence descended. After a few breathless moments, the obese snorer gasped in a large lungful of air and bolted upright in bed, his body struggling against asphyxiation.

He mumbled to himself, snapped on a bedside lamp, and rubbed his eyes. He checked the digital display on the bedside clock and pushed off the edge of the bed, his bulbous feet slapping on the floor. He slipped into a pair of slippers and slogged his heavy backside across the room, the hallway, and then into the bathroom. He whistled to himself as he struggled to urinate, his prostate pulsing out sporadic bursts of piss like wet machine gun fire. He finished, flushed the chain, and stumbled back to bed.

In moments, the rhythm of the snoring returned. The back door still squeaked gently as it swung on its hinges.

In the dark clearing, lit by moonlight and standing in the shadows of creeping oak trees, a darkened, agitated figure squawked an excited call into the silence, his typically bass-laden voice suddenly high pitched. "Whatcha get?"

"Jesus Daz, what the fuck happened to your voice?"

Darren frowned at his friend. "I'm excited."

"Like a little girl?"

"Fuck you Eddie."

Eddie laughed. Next to him, Malcolm, the third figure in the darkness—the tallest and stockiest of the three—silenced his laughing friend.

Malcolm kept a vigilant eye on their surroundings, watching for any trouble, listening for any sirens that would signal an end to their night. "Come on," he said hurriedly, hearing nothing but suspecting the worst. "Let's stash it; we'll sort it out in the morning."

They put the bags in the undergrowth, covering them with a layer of twigs and leaves. Even in the daylight no one would see the treasure that lurked underneath the blanket of foliage.

"Come on, let's split up, head home," Malcolm said. "Back here tomorrow morning, right?" He checked the faces in the darkness and acknowledged the nods of recognition. He waited for the others to leave, looked around one last time, and then followed them.

2

Sleep had glued his eyelashes together and when he reluctantly pried his eyes open, allowing a wash of bright light to penetrate the blackness that he had been so accustomed to for the last eight hours, it peeled apart Velcro. He groaned, and then saw his mother.

"Good morning Darren," she said.

Darren groaned again, but he felt a little more alert in her presence. She rarely ever ventured into his bedroom and when she did, it was never good news. Two weeks ago, she had entered his room to look for a cigarette and ended up leaving with his stash of porn magazines and a bag of weed. She told him that the magazines were degrading to women, that they gave his perverted little mind a skewed view of the world, then she sold them to the greasy perverts who were always hanging around the local liquor store. She never mentioned the weed, he knew she took it and, although she would deny it if he had the balls to ask her about it, he knew she had smoked it. She had probably shared it with Ian; her no-hoper prick of a boyfriend—the bald-headed dick-head who couldn't keep his eyes off the teenage girls in short skirts whenever he walked past the school; the depraved alcoholic who drank like a fish and stank like a rat.

"Morning," he replied. He knew she was up to something. She had been smoking crack or snorting speed again, he could see it in her eyes. They were red and wide open as if surprised. They darted around his room impatiently, absorbing everything in rapid gulps. "Everything okay?" he asked.

He watched as her jaw worked tirelessly, chewing the air she was breathing. She was gaunt, the skin on her face clung to her skull like paper. She hadn't always been like that, he remembered a different mother in his childhood, a mother that actually treated him like a son, a mother that cared for him and for herself. He didn't know exactly when she had transformed into the drug addicted, malnourished alcoholic freak that he knew now, didn't know when her kind hands and caring words had turned harsh and cold, but it was long enough ago for him to struggle to remember the woman she used to be.

He would have liked to blame Ian, but he was new. He doubted Ian would have stood a chance with a sober woman anyway. Ian wasn't his father; he had taken off when Darren was too young to remember and his mother hadn't held any grudges. They were both young, sixteen or seventeen, the same age as Darren was now, and what they had was fleeting, messy, and pointless. He only knew that much because she told him during an awkward conversation while she was high on stimulants and he was trying not to vomit.

There was a good chance that she had always been destined to turn out this way, a good chance that life had just caught up with her and dragged her down. She had always been predisposed to the darker side, she wasn't particularly bright, wasn't particularly suited to a life on the bread line, and she liked her booze and her drugs. It was inevitable. Darren was just thankful that she hadn't been this bad when he was a baby; God knows how he would have turned out if she was.

She had a troubled past, one that he didn't care to know about and one she didn't care to explain. There was a good chance that she hadn't changed; that she had merely reverted to whatever person she had been before she'd had him.

"I need some money," she told him, chewing her bottom lip with her yellowed, brittle teeth.

Darren sighed. For a moment, he thought his mother knew about the robbery. It was paranoia, brought on by his sudden awakening and her rare appearance, but she did have a knack for figuring out his wrongdoings. He didn't know whether that was the mother in her or the criminal in her.

"How much?"

Her eyes widened further at the possibility of getting what she wanted.

"Five. Ten. Twen—"

"I have a ten in my wallet," he interrupted, nodding to his pants on the floor.

"Any more?"

"No."

She grinned meekly and leant over to give him a kiss. She stank of body odor and stale cigarettes. She also smelled like Ian, a concoction of cheap aftershave and cheaper booze. Her dry, cracked lips brushed against his cheek and made him cringe. As she pulled away he tried to think of a time when her rare moments of affection *didn't* make him cringe. He couldn't.

She left the room in a hurry, not checking his pants. He frowned to himself, leaned over the edge of the bed and saw that she had already been through his wallet, taking what she needed. She probably only asked because he woke up while she was doing it, or because she hoped he had more to give her than what she had already taken. He shook his head and tried not to think about it. He had more important things on his mind. Last night had been a success and this morning he would reap the rewards.

* * *

Malcolm was staring at the ceiling when the alarm on his phone sounded. He snapped his hand down on the device, turning it off before the incessant tune had a chance to get louder. He sprang up on his elbows, turned to the window by the bed, and scowled at the smeared glass, through which he could see the dilapidated, imposing, brick-shit-house apartment building opposite.

The small block was wedged in the housing estate like a Meccano brick in a LEGO box. No one had any idea which architectural misfit had decided to dump it there and, it seemed, no one had paid any attention to it after it had been built. It couldn't have been more than a decade old and it was already crumbling like a freshly baked cookie.

The idiots on the top floor had been partying all night again, playing their music loud enough to keep the entire building, and the few dozen terraced houses that surrounded it, awake. The other residents hadn't complained, most of them had probably been partying with the careless and feckless people who owned the riotous apartment, and Malcolm couldn't say anything. He couldn't afford to draw any attention to himself or to his house, and not just because of what he got up to at night.

He had lived with his mother and father for most of his life, had suffered through their fighting. He had been there when his dad staggered back from the pub with a woman on his arm and then tried to invite her into the bed he shared with Malcolm's mum. Obviously, it didn't go too well; surprisingly, it was his dad who won that fight. He beat his mother while Malcolm and the woman from the pub watched; he was too young and shocked to intervene, she was too drunk. His mother slept on the floor that night, with his father in the bed, snoring his head off. The woman from the pub slept on the floor in Malcolm's room, he didn't invite her and he had no idea why she chose to stay, but he was happy to discover she was gone in the morning.

His mother took several more beatings after that, but she was on the winning side of a few herself. She drank as much as his dad and could be just as violent as him. There were several occasions where she had beaten his father with shoes, pool cues, and even a chair from the dining room; he had seen her throw plates, vases, and cartons of milk at him.

They were a reckless and violent couple, but they did show the odd moment of love, times when they would kiss or hug, or times when Malcolm had to listen to them do a lot more through the thin walls that linked his bedroom to theirs. But those moments were few and far between. They usually came when the drinking started, when the merriness was high and the depression and anger were still a few glasses away.

They had both been through a lot. Malcolm's dad was a second-generation immigrant from Nigeria, his father, Malcolm's grandfather, had moved to a house outside the city and suffered a decade of intolerance and violence due to the color of his skin. Malcolm's father had experienced it himself in his schooldays, but before long they moved to the city. There he met Malcolm's mother. She was as white and middle class as they came, and after a troubled youth being abused by peers for the color of his skin, Malcolm's father spent the next few years suffering abuse from his father because of the color of his *wife's* skin.

When Malcolm was twelve, his dad walked out. Malcolm blamed himself because he had been getting into a lot of trouble at school. His dad also blamed him. He called him a punk, a nuisance. Malcolm hated him at first, but he realized he would be better off without him and was happy to see the back of him.

His mother stayed for another six years, but in the end she went the way of his father. She walked out of the front door one day, never said where she was going, and she hadn't been back since. That was three months ago and he was confident he would never see her again. The house was still in their name but the rent was paid for by the unemployment checks. It was just a matter of time before they noticed that the woman claiming the checks didn't actually live in the house they were sent to. They wouldn't give the money to Malcolm; he was only seventeen, too young to qualify. He knew he could look after himself but they would either consider him too young and try to cart him off to a foster home, or would find him of age and let him rot on the streets.

He knew they would soon discover he was living there alone, but he had plans for when that moment came. He was stepping up his game. He was making sure that he had money. He was working, doing what his parents never did. What he was doing was illegal, but it was still work, and it would still put a roof over his head when the government decided to strip the existing one away.

* * *

"Get up!"

"Fuck you."

"Get. Up!"

"Fuck. You."

Eddie grinned as his mother walked out of his bedroom, cursing under her breath as she departed. He heard her talking to his father downstairs but he knew his old man wouldn't say anything to him. Neither of them would. He always had his own way and would continue getting his own way. They were too soft, maybe because he was an only child, maybe because their "*softly softly*" parenting approach—which hadn't worked through a mischievous childhood, and had failed miserably when that mischievous child turned into a criminal teen—didn't raise a child responsive to discipline.

He grinned, turned over, and closed his eyes.

He had a lot to thank his parents for. He was thankful that they were still together, unlike Mal's or Daz's, although he liked to fantasize about them breaking up, just to see which one would fight over him more and how much he could enjoy playing with their love. He was also thankful that they both worked and had enough money to own their four-bedroom house outright, although he liked to play down his parents' wealth and hated them for it whenever his peers mocked him and called him a rich boy. He wasn't rich; he was as street and as tough as they were. He got into fights, he took drugs, he robbed and stole and—

"Shit!" he rolled over, checked his phone, checked his watch and then sprang out of bed. His mother would get her wish after all, but not because he was going to join them on their regular trip to the counselor. He had tired of that bitch and her nagging, bullshit theories on why he didn't listen to authority. He was getting up because he had some loot to collect.

He dressed in a hurry, grinning like a kid at Christmas as he pictured returning to the spoils in the woods. His mother flashed him a smile when he went downstairs, he saw the flicker of delight in her eyes when she saw him awake and dressed and thought, just for a second, that he was obeying her. That flicker died a quick and painful death when he grimaced at her and headed out of the door without saying a word.

3

Darren grinned when he saw Eddie heading towards him; he squinted through the glaring sunshine, waited until his friend was just a few feet away and then asked, "D'you get ride from mommy and daddy?"

"Fuck you."

"You look sexy when you're angry."

Eddie sighed.

Daren continued, "I think it's the ginger hair that does it, it sets off your eyes and—"

"Fuck off!"

"Ah, did I upset you?" Darren put on a puppy-dog face and softened his voice. "I'm *sowwy.* Do you want me to kiss it better?"

"Wanker."

"Now, now children."

Eddie turned his snarling expression away from Darren when he heard Malcolm's voice. Malcolm was the unofficial leader of the three, the most respected one, the one the other two turned to when times were tough or things got complicated. They had all been friends since they were young. They went to the same nursery school and progressed through the same elementary school, middle school, and high school. Eddie's parents had wanted him to go to a private school when he turned thirteen, but he had convinced them otherwise. He didn't want to leave his friends behind, nor did he want to mix with blazer-wearing, purse carrying assholes as he told his mother and father.

"What're you two fighting about?" Malcolm asked.

"Daz is being a dick again."

Darren made a grumbling sound and waved his hand in a camp manner, "Ah, don't get your caviar in a twist."

"What the fuck? That doesn't even make sense."

"*That doesn't even make sense*," Darren mimicked.

"Grow up," Malcolm cut in, bringing a smile of satisfaction to Eddie's face. "So, you been to the stash yet?"

The others shook their heads and looked around suspiciously. The park was usually empty, but it was a hot day and the locals were out in full force, clad in T-shirts and shorts, soaking up as much sun as they could.

"Heard anything about . . ." Malcolm asked, trailing off as a boisterous family waddled a few feet behind them.

"It was on the news last night," Darren said.

"We're famous," Eddie bragged.

Malcolm nodded and absently stared at a middle-aged man struggling with a deck chair. He wore a pair of shorts and a T-shirt several sizes too small for his bulky frame; flab and coarse black hair poked out from all orifices of the tight ensemble. Malcolm couldn't see his face, couldn't see much beyond his bulky frame as he struggled to open the chair, but he imagined a grimacing red face, rife with frustrated beads of sweat and a mouth filled with grumbled obscenities. A chunky woman with fat thighs and an all-over yellow bathing suit rested on a chair alongside him, eyeing him curiously through a pair of large sunglasses. An army of kids ran around the pair of sunbathers, chasing each other, playing football and throwing tennis balls about. A dog mingled in with them, chasing the ball before getting bored and chasing the kids.

"Whole fucking town is out today," Malcolm muttered.

Eddie nodded, following his friend's eyes. "Should we leave it 'till they all piss off?"

Malcolm studied his friends and turned his attention back to the commotion around them. He watched as the fat man finally figured out how to work his deck chair, only to break the small wooden frame when he plonked his bulbous backside onto it. Malcolm could see his face now and it was even redder than he'd imagined. Beside him, the woman was trying to suppress a laugh, but failing miserably.

"No," he said, shaking his head, seeing that no one was paying any attention to them, that no one gave a shit what anyone else was doing. They were a small group of idle teenagers so they would be watched by suspicious and curious eyes, but no one would pay attention to where they went and no one would ask any questions if they disappeared into the woods. They'd assume they were up to no good, they always did, but they wouldn't do anything about it.

"Let's see what we've got, we can come back and pick it up later."

They had taken what they could, emptying drawers and dressers indiscriminately. They took what they thought looked expensive, what was small enough to carry but heavy or fragile enough to be worth something. They hadn't had much time to check the goods in the house and didn't have much light to do it by.

When they pored through the goods, with Darren keeping watch, they discovered that they had a collection of trash. Worthless junk, trinkets bought in overpriced gift shops in Paris, Rome, and an assortment of seaside destinations over the UK. They had snow globes, fancy key rings, lighters, and a mass of costume jewelry that would turn your skin green.

"I don't fucking believe it," Malcolm snapped, angrily tossing a small pewter globe into the undergrowth. "This is fucking worthless."

Eddie looked at his friend, returned to the loot and dug around some more. "This might—" he began, holding up what appeared to be a silver brooch.

"Trash," Malcolm cut in, snapping the object out of his friend's hand and bending it in half. "Fucking pewter. It's all trash." He dug around, took a handful of it and dropped it back in the bag. "I thought you said this guy was loaded."

"I *did*, he *is*," Eddie said, getting flustered, his eyes wide as they desperately scoured the bags. "I mean, I *thought* he was."

Malcolm shook his head, put a hand to his forehead and sat back. He had been through the other bags himself and hadn't found anything like what he had been expecting. He had hoped for expensive jewelry; watches, necklaces, earrings. He had hoped for a few antiques or a collection of gadgets.

"Nothing good there?" Darren shouted, trying to sneak a look in the bag while keeping an eye on the mass of people he could see through a gap in the trees.

"There's the cash we pocketed last night," Malcolm said. "Ninety and change."

"Nothing in that bag?" Darren asked, nodding to the one checked by Malcolm.

"A half decent watch, some DVDs, an old iPod, an older iPad." He shrugged. "Probably get another hundred for the lot. The rest is all trash."

"Two hundred." Darren said with an approving nod. "Not bad for a night's work."

Eddie seemed to brighten up. "I'm happy with that," he declared.

Malcolm looked at his friend's grin but struggled to reciprocate. Eddie's family were well off, they bought him things that Malcolm could only dream of owning, they spent hundreds on his birthday and at Christmas. He was only happy with the money because he didn't need more, he didn't really need *any;* Malcolm needed a lot more.

"It's cool, Mal," Darren said, scooting over to the stash. "That's like seventy each, not too shabby."

He nodded and watched his two friends as they checked the condition of the gadgets. "Yeah," he said. "I guess so."

4

"Put that back, now."

"And what the fuck are you gonna do about it if I don't?"

Eddie faced off against the shop assistant, thrusting out his chin and getting as close to the frumpy little man as he could. He could sense the fear in his eyes, he knew that despite his intimidating posture he was as petrified of delinquent teens as everyone else and they didn't get more delinquent than Eddie.

Eddie tossed the stolen bottle of wine from one hand to the other. It was a cheap mixer and tasted more like fermented nail polish than the Cherry Blossom the label professed, but it was alcoholic and would do the job as far as Eddie was concerned. He had picked it because it was the strongest thing on the shelves; they kept all the good stuff behind the counter where he couldn't reach.

"Put it back and I won't call the police," the shop assistant said, remaining on the safe side of the counter—as far away from the angry red-headed teenager as he could get without running out of the door.

Eddie laughed and shook his head. Malcolm had already walked out of the shop, taking his stolen wares with him and bolting down the road and into the nearby park, but Eddie was in a confrontational mood and he wasn't willing to back down. The shop was full of afternoon shoppers and most of them had stopped what they were doing to witness the spectacle. The large open doors that looked out onto the street were also filling with curious pedestrians who heard the commotion.

"Call the fucking pigs," Eddie said with sneer, his voice gravelly. "See if I give a fuck." He spat on the floor and grinned at the shop assistant.

He had been arrested several times in the last month alone. The police knew him and were always looking for excuses to put him in the cell for a night, but he knew they would let him go before long, probably with nothing more than a slap on the wrists. He was too young and they were too incompetent.

The shop assistant picked up his phone, his hand shaking. He was trying to play it cool in front of the two female staff that loitered behind him—looking lost and apprehensive—and in front of his many customers—a couple of which had surreptitiously pulled out smartphones and were filming the commotion—but he was terrified and it showed.

Eddie unscrewed the bottle cap and took a swig, knocking back half of the contents before dropping the bottle on the floor. It shattered at his feet, provoking a few gasps from his expectant audience. The assistant held the phone away from his ear and stared in disbelief at the juvenile delinquent.

"You can keep it," Eddie said with a satisfying belch and a smirk. "I'm outta here."

He walked casually out of the shop, picked up his pace when he was out of sight, and eventually kicked into a sprint.

* * *

"He's a fucking lunatic," Darren said between gasps of air, his hands on his thighs, his body bent double.

"Tell me about it," Malcolm agreed.

They had entered the shop together, had kept watch while each of them filled their pockets with small and potent bottles of booze. They had done it many times and had gotten away with it each time. The shop was big but near derelict. The cameras were duds, placed there as deterrents only, and the staff didn't give a shit. Now the cameras had been replaced, the staff had been warned to be on the lookout and the three teenage criminals had been spotted.

Darren and Malcolm did the sensible thing; they ran and offloaded their goods in the nearest trashcan. They didn't want to be arrested, didn't want to spend the night in a cell for the sake of a few bottles of booze. They needed to keep their profiles down, to limit their exposure to the police. They had only been burglarizing for a few months, but they had robbed a dozen houses in that time. If the police started sniffing around and found out, they would be locked up for a long time.

"He's got fucking issues," Darren said, straightening up, maintaining a pained expression.

Malcolm merely shrugged; he had been thinking the same thing. Eddie had always been the quiet one, the normal one, the one with a stable family and home life, even if he did manipulate that family, but recently something had clicked inside his mind and he had changed. He had become reckless and dangerous.

Malcolm and Darren liked to keep a low profile, they liked to involve themselves as little as they could with the people they stole from, it helped them to separate themselves from their crimes, to avoid sympathizing with their victims, but Eddie seemed to enjoy messing up the lives of others, he seemed to thrive on the infamy and the destruction that his crimes created.

Darren wiped a bead of sweat from his forehead and swallowed the dryness out of his mouth. "One of these days he's gonna lose his shit completely and—"

He stopped when Eddie, smiling and laughing to himself, came to an abrupt halt in front of them.

Darren didn't need to finish his sentence. Malcolm knew what he was going to say because he had been thinking along the same lines. *One of these days he's gonna lose his shit completely and hurt someone.* It seemed inevitable; if not, then he would certainly hurt himself. Malcolm just prayed that he'd be around to stop it.

5

Eddie seemed to have a limitless supply of weed. It was one of the main reasons that Darren and Malcolm stayed by his side despite his growing instability. That and the fact that they had *always* been by his side. They had been friends for a long time and it would take a lot—a lot more than impending insanity—to break them apart.

When the threat of arrest had died down, and the three had settled on a bench that was shaded by overhanging dense foliage in a secluded area of woodland, Eddie pulled out a couple of joints, lit one, and handed the other to Malcolm.

"What's next then?" he asked, taking a sharp breath and grimacing as the dense smoke hit his lungs.

Malcolm turned to his friend, watched his face turn a shade of red as he held in the smoke, before blowing it out in one long stream, the color fading from his face as the gray smoke drifted into the wind. "I don't know," he said with a casual shrug. He took a long drag from his own joint, held the smoke inside his lungs, and passed it to Darren.

"Another house?" Darren quizzed, staring at his friends' faces and slipping the joint between his dried lips.

Malcolm shook his head. "No more," he said, leaning back. "Not enough money. We need to aim higher."

"Bigger houses?" Darren offered.

Malcolm frowned at the suggestion.

Darren shrugged. "Worth a shot," he ventured. "They have money, they have phones, laptops, jewelry. None of this plastic trinket shit. Real worthwhile stuff."

"And worthwhile security protecting it," Malcolm reminded him. "The others have been easy. Old houses, shitty locks. No alarms."

"Ah, but they all have these crappy patio doors nowadays. My mate says he knows a way you can pull them outta their treads and slip the door straight off."

"And then what?" Malcolm quizzed. "We can't remove a fucking door without making a noise, and what if their alarm or security light is on? You don't think it'll detect us standing in the garden carrying a fucking door?"

Darren paused to mull it over, the joint hanging loosely between his lips. “Good point,” he said with a lethargic nod.

“I have an idea,” Eddie piped up, passing his joint to Malcolm who looked at his friend wearily, remembering that his last idea consisted of robbing the local drug lord, a man known to have an arsenal of illegal weapons and a conscience that didn’t object to using them. “My uncle says there’s this place outta town where the rich and famous go to get pampered and fucked up. Like one of them rehab centers you’re always hearing about in the news.”

“Is this the same uncle that said he was abducted by little green men in Adidas tracksuits?” Darren wondered.

Eddie looked coy. “He ain’t insane.”

“I beg to differ.”

“He’s just a little messed up, alright?”

Darren shrugged, suggesting he didn’t care either way.

“So,” Eddie continued with a furtive glance towards his friend. “It’s out in the middle of nowhere. A big fuck-off building, like an old manor house or some shit. Smack bang in some bum-fuck backwater with fuck-all around for miles but trees, rivers, and all that natural bullshit.”

“*Natural. Bullshit*?” Darren repeated slowly.

Eddie nodded vigorously, missing the mocking tone in his friend’s parroted voice.

“So what?” Malcolm wondered, drawing deeply on the joint and watching the ember flare madly. “You think we should turn this place over?”

Eddie nodded again, his wide eyes flicking between his two friends and the joint in Malcolm’s hand. “I don’t see why not. Think about it. No one knows about this place; I’ve certainly never heard of it—”

“Well,” Darren said loudly. “If *you’ve* never heard of it then it must—”

“Shut the fuck up,” Eddie snapped, sensing another joke at his expense.

Darren grumbled and fell silent.

"It's in the middle of nowhere," Eddie said. "They're keeping it secret for a reason, probably because they don't want the paparazzi snapping their *privileged guests*. If no one knows about it, they won't bother much with security and if it's full of rich and famous drunks and druggies, we could make a killing in there and they'd be none the wiser."

A silence fell over the three as they contemplated Eddie's words.

"What do you think?" Eddie asked eventually, his smile tearing his face into two happy slices.

Malcolm nodded, slowly took a long toke from the joint and then passed it back to Eddie. "Okay," he said, blowing a stream of smoke into his friend's face. "We'll check it out."

6

The bastards in the building across the street kept Malcolm awake again, he felt like he was losing his mind. He didn't sleep much and struggled to hold back his anger as he listened to them banging, shouting, laughing, and blasting music. Just when he thought he was drifting off to sleep, just when he thought his nightmare was over, a spark of anger would ignite at the back of his mind—how dare they? Have they no courtesy, no sense? Do they think they own the entire street? —and he was wide awake again.

He had nowhere important to go in the morning, he planned to pay a visit to the clinic, the "rehab center for the loaded" as Eddie phrased it, but there was no rush. Yet, when the music finally stopped, when the day broke and silence descended, he couldn't bring himself to go to sleep.

He was tired, his brain running on a slow gear, but he dragged himself up, showered, changed, and then texted Darren and Eddie, telling them to meet him around the corner in an hour. He had some business to attend to first.

He paused by his front door and felt his heart skip a beat. He could see the lazy figure of Bobby "Biffa" Turner loitering near the block of flats opposite; close enough to see, close enough to smell.

Bobby got his nickname from the waste removal company, the ones whose name was emblazoned on every dumpster in the area. He'd had the nickname for most of his adult life, ever since he matured from a problem child into a nuisance teenager. Bobby himself would have you believe that the nickname came from his stout build, the way his shoulders seemingly rose past his neck and gave his figure a square appearance, like he had spent his adolescence jammed in a vice, but the nickname was twofold; the second reason being that Bobby Turner stank like he'd been soaking his clothes in the local sewer.

Malcolm sneered inwardly and then deflated when Bobby turned around and peered at him, flashing him a black-toothed smile.

Malcolm hated Bobby, and not just because of the way he smelled. Bobby was a loudmouthed prick, a man who couldn't keep himself to himself. He liked to stick his nose in other peoples' business because he had none of his own. He was a penniless, jobless, friendless forty-something with no aspirations, no ambitions, and no experiences. He saw the world as a soap opera and didn't understand enough about social etiquette to know that no one liked him.

Malcolm hated him at the best of times, but now he was tired and his tiredness was making him bitter and cynical. He had never hated Bobby more, but he still had to maintain some level of pleasantness around him.

Malcolm stepped out of his house and locked the door behind him. "Hey Biffa, how's things?" he said, as amicably as he could.

"You know, same old, same old."

Malcolm nodded, thinking that *same old, same old* for Biffa meant peeping through windows to watch lonely women undress, queuing behind teenage girls just so he could get close enough to "accidentally" brush against their backsides, smoking fag-ends found on the street, and masturbating to lingerie catalogues until his cock grew callouses.

He took an instinctive step back when the smell of rotten garbage hit him. He tried not to twist up his face, tried not to grimace, but he couldn't stop himself. After an initial look of revulsion, which seemed to go unnoticed, he struggled his way towards a friendly smile.

"Say, Malcolm." Biffa took a few steps towards him and Malcolm knew what was coming: the town gossip needed new information. "I haven't seen your mother around for a while, she's okay, I hope?"

Malcolm looked back towards the house, "Fine. Mum's been a little sick, that's all."

Biffa nodded slowly, his eyes on the floor, his grubby hands inside his pockets.

Malcolm made a move to leave, but Biffa stopped him with more questions. "I haven't seen her leaving the house at all, not for a long time. She was quite active, your mum."

Malcolm nodded, hoping to think up a lie on the spot. He wanted to tell Biffa to get lost and mind his own business, but he needed people like him on his side. He didn't want the street to know he was living alone. Many of them didn't like him and would grass him up in a heartbeat, even the ones who liked him would mouth off just for something to do.

"She's got a new fella," he said. "She spends a lot of time away, usually leaves at night or gets back early in the morning." He knew that Biffa was rarely out in the small hours, he had a face fit for darkness but he liked to show it in the light.

"Oh, okay." He smiled and stepped back, allowing Malcolm to pass now that his inspection was over.

Malcolm smiled at him as he left but he grumbled under his breath as soon as the smelly gossiper was out of earshot. He hated keeping such a low profile around his own house, hated having to watch what he said or did around his neighbors. He knew that the sooner he moved out, the better. He would be away from the miscreants that populated the neighborhood, away from freaks like Biffa, and the assholes that kept him awake at night. He would get his own place; he would get enough money to give a landlord six months in advance and he'd be set. He just needed one big score and, if Eddie had his facts right, if his insane uncle was right, then the clinic could be just the ticket.

7

"How much was it?" Eddie's mother asked when he handed her back her credit card.

"*It*?"

"The album you said you were downloading."

"Ah," he waved a dismissive hand at her. "I didn't get it in the end."

She grinned and seemed relieved. She had given him the card last night; as usual she had a hard time refusing him anything. Money was still good, but it was getting tighter. They were trying to book a holiday, trying to cover the cost of the new computer that Eddie had bought a few weeks ago and trying to buy a new car. The album hadn't been much, but the thought that she'd saved just that little bit brought a smile to her face.

"I got some speakers instead," he told her.

The smile dripped from her face. She opened her mouth, looked momentarily angry and then closed it again. She composed herself before asking, "How much?"

"Three hundred," he said bluntly, watching as his mother visibly deflated. "I bought a new sub to go with them. Oh," he paused and scratched his chin, "make that four hundred. They had an offer on sound cards so I got a top-of-the-range one."

His mother sunk her head into her chest and stared absently at her card as her son grinned above her. A series of thoughts ran through her head, followed by an emotion that she rarely expressed in front of him.

"Is that okay?" Eddie asked.

She looked up at him and he saw something flare behind her eyes, he thought, for a moment, that he had pushed her too far.

"Yeah, that's fine," she said, tucking the card into her pocket. "Whatever you want."

He felt his phone buzz in his pocket and saw a message come through from Malcolm when he pulled it out. "Well, I gotta go," he told his despondent mother.

"When will you be back?" she asked as he walked towards the front door.

He turned, stared at her, shrugged, and then left without saying a word.

* * *

Darren stood and stared, he couldn't believe his eyes.

He didn't know where his mother was. He had been up for ten minutes or so and, after emptying his bladder in the upstairs toilet, he'd gone straight downstairs to make himself a drink. He liked to spend some time in front of the television when he woke, watching whatever mind-numbing entertainment he could find. He preferred not to be interrupted, so he should have been happy when he popped his head into the living room and saw that his mother wasn't there. But he wasn't happy, because Ian, her foul-breathed prick of a boyfriend, was there in her place.

He was slouched on the sofa, the top of his head facing Darren's disgusted stare. Ian had his hand stuffed down his tracksuit bottoms—a rank and aged pair of pants so thick with dirt and bacteria they had probably fused onto his hairy legs—and Darren could see the rapid movement of his clenched fist beneath the dirty material, as his wannabe stepfather pleasured himself to an early morning chat show, where a bubbly, middle-aged woman with rosy cheeks and an annoying voice was currently talking to other, equally annoying, women.

"You fucking disgust me," Darren said abruptly.

Ian stopped. He pulled his hand out of his pants and sat sharply upright. He looked at Darren in bewilderment at first, as if he had forgotten that he lived there, then his expression turned to anger. "What the fuck are you doing, you little pervert?" he spat.

"*I'm* the pervert?" Darren said, bemused. "I ain't the one wanking to *The View*. What the fuck is wrong with you? Is *Sesame Street* not on this morning?"

Ian stood up quickly and glared angrily at Darren. He was skinny with a body that seemed breakable, fragile, but what he lacked in muscle he made up for in stature and confidence. He thought he was a hard man, thought he could take on the world, and he didn't have any issues trying to do just that. He shuffled up to Darren, moved his face close enough for Darren to smell the stale booze and cigarettes on his breath and his clothes.

"Don't think I won't hit you jus' coz I'm fucking yer mother," he said softly.

Darren gave a twisted grimace and pulled away.

"You not like that, eh?" Ian said. He lifted his hand, extended a finger, and made to prod Darren on the shoulder. Darren edged quickly away.

"Don't touch me with that fucking hand," he said, staring at it like the diseased limb it was. "I know where it's been."

That was enough to burn Ian's short fuse, enough to fuel the fire behind his eyes. Darren saw him growl; saw the vein on his forehead throb and the expression in his eyes turn wild. He didn't see the punch until it was too late. Ian's fist caught him across the temple and sent him clattering into the doorway where he rebounded, his hand now on his head, in front of his attacker. Ian hit him again and again, until he was on the floor, holding up his hands to protect his face.

Ian left him there. When Darren finally removed his hands, he saw the world through a spinning, hazy vision; he saw that Ian was grinning at him. They locked stares for a moment and then Ian returned to the sofa, his hand back down his pants.

Darren lay on the floor until his cell phone alerted him to a new message. He cleaned himself up, showered, and then left, loitering near the living room first, contemplating storming inside and attacking Ian, but not finding the confidence to do it.

8

Malcolm stood before the desk with a smile on his face. All around him the scuttling, yapping noise of a dozen animals filled his ears; the scents of sawdust, food, and ammonia filled his nostrils and pleased his brain. There was something so strangely comforting about it, the nostalgia more than anything else. He enjoyed the smell of stale cigarettes because it reminded him of his early school days, sneaking around the back of the bike sheds to smoke a few with his friends; he enjoyed the smell of tomato soup because it reminded him of one of the few times his mother had been a mother to him, when they had spent most of the day brewing up a large batch, sipping mouthfuls and filling up so that when the soup was finally cooked, they didn't eat a drop; and he liked the smell of sawdust and the sound of scuttling because he loved the things that scuttled and the things that used sawdust as bedding: the mice, the hamsters, the gerbils, the guinea pigs, the rabbits. They didn't remind him of his childhood, he had never been allowed a pet, but they reminded him of the countless hours he had spent with animals to forget about his life, to forget about the misery that filled it.

"Hey Mal, what's up?"

Malcolm was grinning when Patchouli showed up, he grinned even more when he saw her. She was a good ten years older than him, but she had a soft, sweet smile and a young, beautiful face that belied her age. She could easily pass for seventeen or eighteen, the same age as Malcolm. She was a hippy, wore an armful of bangles and a neck full of pendants, amulets, and strange trinkets on leather bands. She always dressed in clothes that looked homemade and she always smelt of incense. Many times, he wondered if she smoked dope and if she would join him for a joint or two, but he had never had the confidence to ask.

"Hey Petti," he said softly. "Just dropping in to say, well, that I won't be dropping in today." He grinned, he always felt awkward around her, and not just because he was always trying to hide his true nature—trying to come across as someone prim and proper, someone law-abiding.

"Oh," she looked disappointed, he liked that. "Any reason why? If you don't mind me asking."

He shrugged, "I have a lot of studying to do, you know how it is."

She nodded, suggesting she did, though he certainly didn't know how it was. He had never studied. He had skated through school, winging it all the way, right up until his exams when, inevitably, he struggled to complete the work. He couldn't tell her the real reasons though, he couldn't tell her that he wouldn't be available to volunteer because he needed to have a look at a rehab clinic outside of town, and he definitely couldn't tell her why.

"I'll be in next week though," he said.

She smiled at him, a smile that, as always, came close to melting his heart.

He had been volunteering at the shelter for a few years. They took in abused, neglected, and abandoned animals. It was a small operation run by Petti's mother and father, two aging hippies who adored animals. It catered to all sorts, from mice and hamsters to cats and dogs.

He used to drop in as a kid, back when Petti was just a teenager. He went on his own and would often stare forlornly at the animals, hoping that he could adopt one of them himself. When he wasn't staring at them he was staring at Petti. She had matured since then and gotten better with age, but she had still been very pretty. He had also matured; he was nothing like the lost little kid who used to stroke the rabbits through the cages or feed treats to the dogs. Petti didn't recognize him, didn't know that the teenager who came in as often as he could to feed, clean, and care for the animals, was the same kid who had treated her parents' shelter like a second home.

He'd always had a thing for animals, and mostly preferred them to humans. They were innocent, helpless, and could be very loving. They had all the good traits of humankind and only a few of the bad. They didn't kill without purpose and didn't abuse. They weren't sociopathic, sadistic, or malicious. Humans used their sadism against animals; they tortured them, hurt them, and killed them for no purpose other than their own entertainment. In the wild a cat might toy with a mouse for sport, but a rabbit would never hurt anything; a dog would protect its owner to the death and greet everyone else as if they were the friendly, loving people they should be.

Humans are top of the food chain, the pinnacle of evolution, but only at the top, only with the greatest power, can the vilest atrocities be committed. Malcolm knew he wasn't the perfect human, far from it, he went into peoples' houses at night and stole from them, no doubt scarring them for life, but he felt like he had no other choice and was doing what he could to get by with the least amount of suffering to others.

Malcolm said his goodbyes to the animals and to Petti and he waited for Darren and Eddie on the corner, out of sight of the animal shelter. They didn't know he volunteered there and he didn't plan on telling them. He had a persona to maintain. He was the strong one, the one who didn't care about anyone or anything. That was the way he wanted it, the way it needed to be.

9

They took the bus out of the city and watched through the smeared windows as the assortment of derelict villages and towns merged into one drab, gray landscape. Malcolm and Darren stared absently out of the window, their minds elsewhere, but Eddie was more interested in what was inside the bus.

The bus was empty when they got on, choosing the seats at the back, but on the next stop they were joined by a pretty brunette. She was in her early twenties with dark Persian skin and thick black hair that she kept flicking over her ears. She gave the boys a friendly smile when she saw them staring.

"She's fucking gorgeous," Eddie noted when the woman sat down.

The others agreed, though they weren't keen on doing anything about it; Eddie seemed infatuated by her.

The fact that she had headphones in her ears and a magazine in her lap suggested that she didn't want to be disturbed, but Eddie had other ideas. "I saw the way she looked at me," he said, his eyes beaming lustfully.

Malcolm pulled his attention away from the window to glare at his friend. "*Really*?" he said with raised eyebrows.

"You saw it. She had that cheeky, flirty smile that they all have."

Darren turned to stare at Eddie, shaking his head in disbelief. "You've got some fucked-up shit going on inside that head of yours."

"What?" Eddie snapped. "You didn't see it?"

Darren and Malcolm shook their heads slowly. They had both seen her smile, but they hadn't seen what Eddie saw, or thought he saw.

"Then fuck you," Eddie said, turning back to the girl, staring at the back of her head, admiring the way the gloss of her lustrous hair reflected the sunshine that struggled through the grimy windows. "You don't know what you're talking about. I'm gonna go over there and talk to her."

"I don't think that's a good idea."

"Fuck you. It's a great idea."

Eddie stood up, steadied himself on the rail, patted down his jacket and then swaggered over.

"That kid has no shame," Darren said.

Malcolm nodded, hearing a touch of trepidation in Darren's voice and feeling the same way. Eddie hadn't always been like that. He used to be shy and distant.

"You think he was being serious?" Darren pushed.

They saw Eddie grin as he chatted to her. She turned her head towards him and they could see the meek and unimpressed smile on her face, a smile that suggested she wanted the crazy kid above her to get away as quickly as possible.

"About the way she looked at him?" Malcolm asked, watching his friend.

"Yeah."

"I hope not."

Darren nodded. He watched as Eddie's smile turned into a frown, watched as his confident stance shifted into an upright stance of intimidation. The woman turned away and plugged her headphones back in.

"Ah, shit," Darren said, just before Eddie kicked off.

"Fuck you, *bitch*," Eddie rasped, scowling at the woman who pretended she couldn't hear him. "I ain't into fucking dykes anyway!"

He turned around angrily, stormed back to his seat and slumped down next to his friends who both awaited an explanation.

"Lesbian," Eddie said.

Darren shook his head, "I thought you said—"

Eddie turned sharply towards him. "She was a fucking dyke, alright? She ain't into men. 'Nuff said."

Darren held up his hands and kept them there, until Eddie slouched back into his seat and turned his head back towards the front, his eyes still on the pretty girl with the Persian skin.

An awkward silence fell over them, interrupted by the sound of Darren clearing his throat and then saying, "She probably just doesn't like gingers."

* * *

The brunette got off before they did, leaving hastily without looking towards the back of the bus where Eddie's glare was waiting for her. They got off on the stop after her, the final stop the bus made. They clambered onto a smaller bus that looked like it had seen better days. It was rusted, full of graffiti, and impregnated with a musty smell. The seats were stained and ripped; two sets of them were missing all together, leaving small holes in the floor through to the tarmac below. They were the only people who got on, the driver, a man whose belly struggled to stay behind the wheel and whose eyebrows met in the middle, watched them suspiciously before the doors closed with a loud, reluctant creak and the bus began its journey, hobbling along the road with the comfort and guile of a one-legged ostrich.

After passing the remnants of a dilapidated council estate, the bus hit a series of bumpy country roads—poorly maintained, pockmarked tarmac that led a thin and winding stretch through fields thick with overgrown grass, trees, and the occasional solitary horse, their noses stuck through a fence watching despondently as the bus rolled past.

"Where the fuck are you taking us?" Darren wanted to know, his attention on Eddie.

"I told you, it's in the middle of nowhere. That's how they keep it so secret." He gave Darren an enigmatic smile.

"You just want to get us alone in the woods so you can rape us."

"Fuck you, Daz."

They remained the only ones on the bus, watched in the rear-view mirror by the fat, greasy bus driver who rarely carted anyone along this route. It was a strip of nowhere between two shit-hole towns. His regular customers were single mothers, carrying their screaming babies from town to town, and decrepit old people who never spoke or smiled and took forever to do everything.

He was suspicious of them. The ginger one looked insane, like he was high on drugs; the black one looked alert, ready for something; the other one seemed to be half asleep. They were up to something, he knew that, but ultimately he didn't care, as long as they didn't do it on his bus.

10

A cold wind cut through the wild grass, stirring waves in the fading yellow stalks. The three teenagers watched their loose coats and baggy pants blowing like parachutes behind them.

Eddie was grinning madly, Malcolm looked concerned, Darren was slowly shaking his head.

"Well, fuck me sideways," Darren said into the wind. "This is *literally* the middle of nowhere."

"I told you," Eddie announced, as if it was something to be proud of.

In the distance, beyond the grass and weeds, past the mown fields where a handful of cows—lifting their heads curiously to stare at the specks in the distance—calmly grazed, there was a wall of trees. They could see glimmers of light in the gaps between the trees, but most of it was thick and looked impenetrable from this distance, even the cows didn't seem to want to venture inside.

"I don't see a huge building," Malcolm said, taking the words out of Darren's mouth.

"It's through the trees," Eddie said, before adding, "I think."

"*You think*?" Darren said, turning his head sharply towards his friend. "*You think*? You've gotta be shitting me." He turned towards Malcolm, "Where did we find this idiot?"

"It's there, trust me."

"I told you," Darren said with a wry smile. "I. Don't. Trust. Gingers."

Eddie lowered his head, furrowed his brow, "You wanna watch your fucking mouth—"

"Come on," Malcolm cut in, stepping between them, sensing another bitch-fight that would end with Eddie furious and Darren hysterical. They had been friends for a long time and had been at each other's throats since day one; he had seen it all and heard it all before. Eddie may have been quieter when they first met, but he always gave as much as he got where Darren was concerned. It had been fun in the beginning, Malcolm would even join in, but it became tedious and he didn't like taking sides. Each one was as bad as the other. "Let's go."

They hopped over a small fence that separated the fields from the road. The grass was overgrown on both sides of the fence, it already enveloped the small, run-down bus shelter and had begun growing through the cracks of the road.

The grass came up to their shins, thin wispy blades that begged for sustenance and seemed to be growing out of dry and undernourished soil. There were several clumps of flattened grass where the debris of human life had been tossed in; rusted wheelless bicycles, shopping trolleys, bags of waste.

"Is that a fucking mattress?" Darren said, stopping. It was layered with various stains and had been worn by use and the environment; the springs were exposed around the edges, pointing their rusted edges menacingly towards the cold day. "Who dumps a fucking mattress in a field?" he asked, looking around at the vast emptiness as if to emphasize his point.

"Beats me," Malcolm said.

"They fucking carried it in this far as well," he noted, turning back to see that they had already travelled several feet from the roadside before stumbling on it. "Why not just dump it over the fence?"

"People are weird," Eddie said.

"I think it was your uncle," Darren said quickly, receiving an equally quick glare from his friend who had been expecting such a retort, was *always* expecting such a retort. "I think this is where he brings his girlfriends after treating them to some leftover, dumpster McDonald's and some homemade hooch from his filthy fucking bathtub."

Eddie didn't say anything but Darren could see a vein throbbing on his temple; it usually took a lot more than that to anger him. He smiled and continued. "I think—"

Eddie cut in, his words spoken through gritted teeth. "—I *think* you wanna shut your fucking mouth before I wipe that smile off your little fucking face."

Both Darren and Malcolm turned towards Eddie in surprise, sensing the venom in his words. "For fuck's sake Eddie," Malcolm said, rapping his friend roughly on the back. "He's just kidding."

Eddie seemed to soften at Malcolm's words, "I'm sick of his shit though," he said, the venom no longer there. "He's always at it."

"He's just kidding."

"Yeah," Darren agreed. "No need to go fucking psycho on me."

"I'm fed up of you taking the piss out of me all the time," Eddie said to his friend. "I'm only—"

Darren interjected quickly, "No need to go all fucking Hallmark on me either," he said. "Grow a pair of balls and shut the fuck up."

Eddie opened his mouth, let it hang open and then shut it again. Something glimmered behind his eyes but he shook it off.

"Come on then," he said, glancing at the mattress and then back to the field. "We need to keep going."

They stopped again when they reached the cows. They expected them to move, to filter away like pigeons as they approached, but the cows didn't shift an inch and didn't seem at all perturbed by the three cautiously advancing teenagers.

They stopped in front of one and maneuvered around it. Malcolm was the first to approach. As the others watched, he put his hand calmly on the cow's face, gently rubbed its forehead and its nose, spoke softly to it. It didn't seem affected either way and merely continued to munch grass as Malcolm stroked it.

"Look," Darren said softy. "It's the fucking cow whisperer."

Malcolm ignored him and continued stroking the cow. Eddie advanced to his side with a cheeky look in his eye. "You think we should push it over?"

"What?" Malcolm said.

"Topple him over," Eddie said gleefully. "Cow-pushing."

"Cow-pushing?"

"Yeah, it's a thing ain't it? You push them over and they can't get back up. Hilarious."

Eddie rested his hands on the cow's side and received a worried glance from the animal out of the corner of its eye. Malcolm watched in bemusement, his mouth hanging ajar. Just as Eddie looked like he was about to put some effort into his push, he stopped him.

"Leave him alone."

Eddie stepped back and relaxed his hands. "Why?"

"Because I fucking said so, that's why."

"But—"

"*But*, if you don't remove your hands I'll break them off, alright?"

Eddie began to object but quickly retreated.

"Yeah," Darren said, previously reluctant, but now happy to step in front of any strange animal if it meant a chance to mock

Eddie. "Poor fucker doesn't want some ginger dickhead trying to push him over." He stood beside Malcolm but kept his hands firmly in his pockets as he looked the cow over, tilting his head this way and that as the cow returned his curious stare.

"So," Darren said after a while, his hands still in his pockets. "This is where Big Macs come from then?"

Malcolm gave his friend a disapproving stare, "*Really*?"

Darren shrugged. He turned to Eddie who was standing a few yards away, looking sheepish. "Is this why your uncle comes out here, to *care* for the animals? I know he's been with a few fat cows in his time but—"

"Shut it," Malcolm said, shoving his friend and stepping away from the cow.

He looked towards the trees, they could see through them now. What had appeared as a deep forest was nothing more than a few trees deep. They were close together, separated by a muddy forest floor with a small stream flowing through it, but Malcolm could see a field on the other side and beyond that, on the tip of the horizon, he saw what looked to be the top of a large building.

"Is that it?" he asked.

Eddie rumbled up to his side and looked through the gap in the trees at the chimney poking up in the distance. He could see thick plumes of gray smoke spiraling outward. "Must be," he said with an assured nod, thankful that they were on the right track.

"All right." Malcolm moved forward, giving the apathetic animal one last glance, "let's get a move on."

11

The building rose out of the horizon, an ominous stony mirage. It was spectacular, an imposing edifice of intricate red brick that blocked out the afternoon sun and spilled an oily shadow onto the ground. It was three stories tall, with arched gothic windows on all stories, like bleak and generic gravestones. It stretched across the landscape, swallowing vast swathes of the surrounding green field.

A graveled path spiraled around the neatly manicured lawn with numerous flower beds, vegetables patches, and benches overlooking the open nothingness. The grounds were split and further down, past the lawns and flowers, the boys could see a tall chain-link fence with another garden within.

A few feet from the building a picket fence, scarred by weather and blackened by time, formed a neat border around the imposing structure, tall flowers grew behind it, clawing at the building and climbing as high as the third floor. It looked more like a prison than they had imagined, more like a building designed to punish than to help, and its sheer size could cater for a vast volume of prisoners.

"It certainly doesn't look like a place that rich celebs will pay a fortune for," Darren pointed out.

The others nodded.

"It might be better inside," Malcolm said.

"I would fucking hope so." Darren agreed. "What about that?"

Malcolm didn't need to follow his eyes to see what his friend was looking at; he already knew. The chain-link fence was easily seven- or eight-feet high. He hadn't been in prison, but he knew that the chain-link fence, set deep within the garden and surrounding the property, was designed to keep people from getting out.

"I have no idea."

They approached cautiously, felt the chill of the wind as it continued to cut through the surrounding fields. They scanned the windows, expecting to see people peering back at them and preparing to act accordingly, to play nonchalant or to hide, but there was no one there, or at least no one they could see. Darren thought he saw the curtains flutter in a window on the second floor, but it was gone before his eyes could establish it as anything more than a trick of light.

He felt a sense of dread creep through him and tried to reason with his mind. It gave him goose bumps, lifted an uneasy feeling on the surface of his skin, and penetrated every fiber of his being. He wrapped his arms instinctively around himself and pretended to brace against the cold (sighing the mandatory sigh of a shivering man) just in case anyone was watching. The others weren't watching him, they were too interested in scanning the building, in checking the windows as *he* had done, but something told him that someone *was* watching and, whoever that someone was, he thought it was wise not to let his fear show.

Eddie was the liveliest of the three, the one whose footsteps strode further ahead than the others, the one who looked upon the building with an almost joyful gaiety. This was a big deal to him. This was *his* choice, *his* job. Not only could he share the spoils, which promised to be big, but he could take the credit and gain the respect that he deserved. He was eager and desperate for this.

Malcolm kept his eyes on the windows, checking each of them in turn. As they walked closer—the building looming larger, the gardens close enough to smell—he felt the same unease as Darren felt, only for different reasons. There was no one in the windows, no one in the gardens. The image of a rehab center like this was of patients in dressing gowns smoking cigarettes, looking forlornly out of windows or wandering aimlessly around the garden, their trudging slipper-clad feet kicking the dew from the grass as they scowled and filled their lungs with tar, wishing for something just a little bit stronger. But there were no walkers in the garden, no forlorn watchmen in the windows. It was desolate, yet deep down Malcolm knew it wasn't a deserted or empty building. It had a certain life to it, not only was it clearly well maintained, but it oozed with recent activity. He hadn't seen it at first, but now they were closer he could see cups on a picnic bench that looked out over the garden. There were three cups in total and beside them, on the ground, someone had dropped a jacket; the stark white material glared at Malcolm.

Something didn't feel right, something *wasn't* right, but Eddie felt differently. While Malcolm and Darren held back, staggering their approach to further study and deliberate, Eddie raced up to the side of the building. He placed his hands to his head and then pressed himself against one of the windows.

The others watched and waited, slowing to a near halt, as Eddie studied the insides of the building. He could see the entrance from where he stared, the main doors were just around the corner, and the reception desk. He could also see a security point, a small enclosure in the corner with a few banks of monitors. A man in a blue uniform sat behind them, looking disinterestedly at the screens that Eddie couldn't see. The man looked like he was asleep.

Eddie saw a security camera near the front door, but he also saw that the front door was unguarded and likely unlocked, no doubt to allow the patients to come and go as they saw fit, he thought, so they could enjoy their expensive rehabilitation with as much freedom as they wanted.

He peeled away from the window and turned towards his two friends who had warily approached and were peering over his shoulder. They both pulled back when they saw his face.

"It's perfect!" he said.

Malcolm tried to hush his friend but Eddie shook it off. "The guard is fast asleep," he said. "He doesn't give a shit. Probably sick of looking after rich fuckers all day, probably never gets any action up here. Who the fuck would want to break in here?"

Darren raised his eyebrows.

"Well, yes, *us*," Eddie said with a nod and a glance back towards the window. "Coz we're smart." He paused, waited for Darren to jump in and then frowned when he didn't. He didn't register the unease on his friend's face, the way he had wrapped his arms tightly around his torso. "And I think tonight is the night."

"What?" Malcolm said.

"I don't know what's going on here," Eddie explained, "but no one is here and the guard is asleep. If he can afford to fall asleep, he must know that no one, not even the receptionist, is due back anytime soon to wake him up and give him a kick in the balls."

Malcolm wasn't keen on the idea of rushing into it, but he couldn't argue with Eddie's reasoning. "Still," he said with a gentle shake of his head. "It's too soon."

Eddie disagreed, shaking his head vigorously. "Look!" he gesticulated, pointing towards the window, watching and waiting as Malcolm peered inside. "There's no security, nothing stopping us from going in and taking what we want under the cover of darkness. With a few tools, we can get in through one of these windows. Hell, we can probably walk right through the front door."

Malcolm pulled back, examined the window. It was probably older than he was. It wouldn't take much effort to get it open.

Eddie seemed to get more exited as he thought he was winning his friend over. Darren remained at the back of the three, keeping his distance, staring upwards at the building. He thought he saw something moving again, another flicker in one of the top floor windows. This time it lingered and left more of an impression that it might have been human, then the curtain stilled. He felt the same chill run through his body and wrapped his arms tighter around himself.

"Come on," Eddie pleaded. "What do you say?"

"I say you're fucking crazy." Malcolm offered.

"Here, here," Darren voiced from the back, a little less enthusiastically as he would have liked.

"But . . . you're right," Malcolm said, bringing a smile to Eddie's face. He turned to Darren, "What do you say Daz, tonight?"

Darren tried to hide his apprehension with a smile. He tried to loosen up. "Sure," he said. "Why not."

12

The skies were already darkening when they returned home, but they didn't intend to hit the clinic until the early hours of the morning. They would take the last bus out there at ten, wait a few hours to make sure the place had locked down for the night, and then get moving. They didn't expect to find much money lying around, they weren't naive enough to think that rich people carried their millions with them, but they knew they would find some cash and, more importantly, a lot of jewelry. And this time it wouldn't be hordes of pewter or piss-poor nickel-plated trinkets.

Darren was rarely happy to be home, he had spent the last few years trying to get away from his house, but he felt relieved when he got home. He was cold and still felt a little creeped out. The rehab facility still had him on edge when he shut the front door and tracked across the hallway, and he felt worse when he peered into the living room and saw Ian and his mother spaced-out in front of the television.

The marks where Ian had hit him that morning were still sore. He felt wary being around him again, but a part of him that rarely surfaced, was comforted by his mother being there. Not because she was the protective sort of mother who would stand by him and stop the world from hurting him, but because he knew Ian wouldn't try anything when she was there. He wouldn't want to jeopardize his relationship, even if the house was just a place to empty his balls and fill his veins.

He shifted into the living room, made to sit down on the edge of the sofa and stopped when Ian glared at him.

"Where have you been sneaking off to?" he asked.

Darren frowned. He thought about telling his wannabe stepfather that he had no right to know what he did with his life, but he decided against it.

"You been up to no good again with those friends of yours?" he pushed.

Darren held his stare, he still didn't reply. His mother looked out of it as usual, she was watching the conversation with a simpleton smile on her face, a smile he could have mistaken for motherly warmth if he didn't know that the warmth was provided by a vial of tainted smack.

"I seen you, with that black kid and the little rich one," Ian sneered. He gave a disapproving shake of his head. "Those kids are bad apples, especially the black one, watch out for him."

Darren's mouth hung open in shock, he turned his appalled expression to his mother, who didn't seem to realize what was going on, and then back to Ian who was intent on continuing his lecture.

"They're all the same these blacks, it's part of their culture, part of—"

"You've gotta be fucking shitting me," Darren snapped. "How dare you—"

"Hey!" His mother said, suddenly waking up from her temporary coma to snap at her son. "Watch how you talk to your father."

"My father? My *father*?" He gave an abrupt laugh, saw the grin on Ian's face and then shook his head in disgust. "You're taking the fucking piss, aren't you?"

Ian was up in a flash, springing from the sofa in an ugly, pale blur before sticking his face in front of Darren's.

"Watch your fucking language," he said, thrusting a finger into Darren's chest. "That is, 'less you want another beating, eh?" he grinned, flashing his yellow and black teeth, the crooked smile of a lifetime addict and waster. Darren felt sick just looking at him, but he also felt angry. He was angry that this horrible, despicable excuse for a man was in his house, in his life. He was angry because of the beating he had given him in the morning, because of the way his finger pressed into his ribs. He was angry because of the way he described his friends, he didn't know them and he didn't have the right to talk about them like that.

He moved backwards and watched the smile spread over Ian's face as, for a moment, he thought he had won, thought that the teenager was backing away, but Darren wasn't backing away. Darren punched Ian as hard as he could, throwing his weight into the swing and wiping the smile off Ian's face. The punch connected with his jaw and Ian toppled backwards before Darren kicked him in the shins, a hard toe poke to his bony leg.

Ian fell to his knees and Darren jumped on him, tackling him to the ground and swinging punch after punch. He heard Ian saying something, he didn't know whether he was shouting abuse or offering submission, but he didn't care. He released all his pent-up anger—anger at his mother, his life, and himself—into Ian's face and body. He hit him until his hands hurt, until Ian's face was unrecognizable beneath the blood.

When he stopped, breathing heavily and grinning madly, he heard his mother's voice. She was standing above him, her hand in her mouth as she bit down on her own flesh. She was screaming softly, a low droning sound, and he realized that she had been screaming at him all along. He realized that the white noise he had heard in his head, the noise that had tried and failed to break through his rage, had been his mother. Tears rolled down her face as she stared at her lover on the floor.

Darren followed her eyes and looked at Ian, as if seeing him for the first time. He could make out the whites of his eyes through the smear of blood and the inflamed flesh. He was breathing slowly and softly, his mouth was filled with blood and he released small bubbles of crimson with every labored breath.

"Shit," Darren said, his smile fading. He looked at his fists like they weren't his own.

"You bastard!" his mother screamed above him, her eyes now flooded with tears as she looked directly at her son. "You *devil*! Look what you've done."

Darren scrambled to his feet and stood on shaking legs. He looked from Ian to his mother and back again. "I'm . . ." he wanted to say sorry, but he wasn't sorry. He had taken it too far, but he hadn't killed him. He had given Ian exactly what he deserved.

"Get out of my house!" his mother screamed at the top of her lungs. "I never want to see you again!"

He could see the anger flaring in her eyes through the worry that she still expressed for Ian, but he also saw fear in the way she seemed to edge further away from him.

"Look, mum—"

"*Get out!*"

He stared at her, listened as her heavy and rapid exhalations produced a whining sound which seemed to emit from the pit of her lungs.

"*Now*!"

"I have nowhere to go."

"I don't care," she said. "Just fuck off. I never want to see you again."

He saw the last morsel of maternal love leave her eyes, felt the last sorrow he would ever feel for her. He nodded and hung his head. "I'll go get my stuff," he said, before leaving his grieving mother to cry over her beaten lover.

13

On the way back to his house, Malcolm saw the perpetrators of the noise, the reasons for his sleepless nights. He had seen them before and had been forced to walk past them, ignoring them and pretending that he didn't despise them. They were outside the block of flats, drinking cans of lager, laughing and joking. Their voices echoed off the enclosed surroundings and seemed to filter directly into Malcolm's ears as he approached. He felt himself getting annoyed and losing his patience as he approached his front door and tried to block them out.

They can't do anything quietly, he thought bitterly to himself. *They think they own the neighborhood, they think—*

They shouted at him, interrupting his thoughts. He turned around, tried and failed to hide the resentment on his face.

"You, kid!"

Kid? He thought. He raised his eyebrows at their choice of words. *Who the fuck do they think they're talking to?*

"Get over here."

Malcolm stood still for a moment, pondering what they wanted. There were three of them. They were just a few years older than him but he didn't really know them, who they hung around with, what school they had gone to. All he knew was that they were loud, annoying, and—

"Are you deaf?"

That was all it took for Malcolm to move towards them. He instinctively clenched his fists, felt his blood boil. They were all waiting for him, one of them had been sitting on a wall drinking but as Malcolm approached he put his can down and jumped off. They must have seen the anger on Malcolm's face because as he drew nearer he saw their expressions change, saw the defensive postures they took as they felt the threat of violence in the air.

He stopped in front of them and looked at each of them in turn. He didn't say anything; no one said anything for a few moments.

"What's your name?" one of them asked.

Malcolm turned to him and stared at him, but he didn't reply.

"You live in that house all by yourself?" another asked.

"What's it to you?"

He had avoided conflict; he had avoided even getting to know his neighbors. He needed to stay on the down-low, but something inside him refused, something inside him was begging to tear these three idiots apart. He remembered all the nights he had stayed awake, remembered how frustrated and angry he had felt as he listened to their screeching, yelling, bitching—

"I'm just—"

"What?" Malcolm snapped before the guy could finish his sentence, firing spittle at them. "You're just what, eh? Just asking? Well, fuck you; it's none of your fucking business." He was yelling so hard he could feel his throat being stripped raw. They had backed off, they tried to maintain an air of bravado, but they had seen the anger in his eyes, they had felt the rage in his voice, and they were all worried.

Malcolm was breathing heavily. He bit his bottom lip, eyed each of them up and then, softly, said to the one in the middle: "Take your beer *and* your friends, and fuck off."

Malcolm watched as they returned his stare and then he turned to leave, staying aware just in case they tried to pounce on him. He looked back when he was at his door, they were all feigning confidence, but an awkward trepidation hovered over them.

Malcolm's hand shook as he stuck the key in the lock. He paused and tried to gather his thoughts. He had no idea what had come over him, he wasn't an angry guy, but everyone could be pushed to their limits and with the situation with the house and the noise and—

He shook it off. It wasn't worth thinking about. He was stressed, he let it get to him, that was all, there was no point in finding excuses. He had been an idiot, had blown his low profile and now the neighbors would want to restore some of their credibility. After a few beers and some more bravado, there was no telling what they would do but he was sure that things were going to get a lot worse for him.

14

Malcolm turned off the living room light and stuck his head out of the window. It was pitch black outside, the nearby streetlights were a constant source of amusement to the local kids who liked to smash them with stones and pellet guns. The council did their job and repaired them often, but they were losing patience and they hadn't fixed the latest batch for a couple of weeks.

The small cul-de-sac that separated Malcolm's house from the flat block was lit by a thin stream of silver light, projected from a small kitchen window on one of the ground floor flats. The light was enough to illuminate the three figures that loitered at the edge of the building.

One of them was smoking a cigarette, Malcolm could see his face light up with a sickly pallor when he toked on the small white stick. He was too far away and it was too dark to recognize him or his friends, but Malcolm knew they were the same three idiots he had encountered earlier in the day.

They seemed to be looking right at him, plotting their revenge, but he knew they couldn't see him, knew he was just letting his imagination run away with him. He let the curtain close, stood up straight, and stared at the blackened fabric.

They were certainly facing his house and they were certainly the types who would want to seek revenge. He had bruised their egos and they wanted to return the favor. He was outnumbered and, as they had time to stew and plot, there was a good chance they were carrying weapons. He didn't stand a chance.

They were probably waiting for the lights to go out, until they thought he was in bed, then they would break in and attack him while he slept like the cowardly pigs they were. He peeked back through the curtains and grimaced at the ghostly figures.

He wanted to unleash his anger on them, to go out there and give them what they deserved. But he managed to restrain himself, he didn't need the hassle, not tonight; not ever.

He checked the clock on his phone, dropped it back into his pocket and took a moment to breathe, closing his eyes despite the blackness around him. He nodded to himself, glanced one more time at the curtains, at the cowardly figures beyond, and then exited through the back door.

* * *

Eddie looked uneasy. He was standing outside his front door when his friends approached, shifting uncomfortably from foot to foot, his eyes darting around, up and down the street. His parents didn't object to Malcolm and Darren, his parents rarely objected to anything, but Eddie liked to keep his friends and his parents apart, they had never asked why and didn't care either way. They rarely went into his house and rarely encountered his parents.

"You okay?" Malcolm asked, noting the unease in his friend, the same unease he was feeling.

He nodded quickly and unconvincingly. "Yeah, just feel a bit . . . you know. *Excited,* I guess."

Darren gave his friend a quick glance, his eyebrows raised. Malcolm nodded.

The day was winding down. There were few cars on the roads, fewer people on the streets. They were the only ones at the bus stop and the only ones on the bus when a disconsolate and half-asleep driver picked them up.

They rode in silence, barely saying more than a few words to each other. They all had their own inner turmoil to deal with, their own thoughts to process. Eddie looked more excited about the impending robbery than the other two, he sat with an eager twitch in his hands, his foot tapping incessantly on the floor of the bus as the vehicle bounced and rocked over uneven roads.

"Where are you boys going this time of night?" the bus driver asked as they climbed off, an air of suspicion in his voice and his eyes.

Malcolm began to respond politely, not wanting to arouse suspicion. Eddie had insisted that the robbery wouldn't be on the news, that the clientele at the rehab center wouldn't want the world knowing what went on behind those doors, but Malcolm had his doubts and didn't want to test his luck with a potential witness.

"We're just—"

"None of your fucking business," Eddie jumped in, sticking his face in front of the driver. "You've done your job, now shut the fuck up and piss off."

He left the bus driver glowering at the back of Eddie's head as the doors staggered shut behind them.

"Really?" Darren asked when the bus pulled away, his attention on Eddie who still had an aura of excitation about him.

"What?" Eddie asked, shrugging his shoulders.

Darren merely shook his head.

"Come on," Malcolm said, moving into the wind which had remained fierce throughout the day.

The sparse littering of streetlights stopped providing them with any light by the time they entered the fields, and with nothing but the moonlight to aid them they struggled to see where they were going. The tall grass, blown chaotically in the wind, whipped at them as they clawed their way through.

As they neared the end of the field, the dense grass thinned out and they could see the lights from the top floor of the building beckoning them. They picked up their pace, Eddie nearly tripped over his own feet in his excitement.

The building looked different in the nighttime. It looked just as empty, just as desolate, and it felt just as odd, but now it didn't just loom from the horizon, it dominated it. It stood in front of them like a mighty wall, drawing their attentions away from the bland and black landscape that wrapped around it.

A scattering of lights were visible through the ground floor windows, rooms tucked away in the back or the corner of the building. They couldn't see much through the thick veils that covered the windows and allowed only for a glow of orange to emanate outwards; they didn't see any shadows of movement or any flickering curtains.

They all stopped in front of the building. Darren was the first to speak. "Now what?"

He turned, sensing Eddie's excitement. "Now," Eddie declared, his eyes almost glowing in the darkness. "We rob these fuckers blind."

15

They crept past the window that Eddie had pressed his face up against earlier in the day. There weren't any curtains up, but not a hint of light broke through the glass. The three boys watched their gray reflections in the window as they passed: Eddie looking eager and excited, Darren wary, Malcolm focused.

Darren felt like he was being watched, as if something threatening lurked behind the pale and worried image of his own reflection. He tried to shake it off, to shrug away the chill that crept through his body and cut deep into his bones—as strong as the wind that ruffled his clothes—but he struggled to find his composure.

He had never experienced this feeling before. He rarely thought twice before the burglaries in the past. If anything, Eddie had always been the nervous and fidgety one. When they were fourteen and they committed their first burglary, Eddie had been shaking like a leaf, they thought he was going to pass out or throw up and leave a trail of bile and undigested Pop Tarts behind him. But Eddie had hardened, it had been gradual at first, he stopped being nervous, stopped shying away from others when they insulted him. He had always retaliated when Darren mocked him, but never with strangers. Then something changed in him.

"He's lost his mind," Darren had joked at the time, the first time they watched Eddie throw himself at a kid in school who called him a ginger dickhead. But then, as the craziness continued, he believed it.

Now, as Eddie practically bolted around the side of the building, disappearing in his eagerness to get to the entrance, Darren found himself wondering if this was a step too far; if this time they had been the crazy ones for agreeing to go along with Eddie's plan.

He stuffed his hands in his pockets, gave the final window one last, shy and wary glance—his heart stopped and sank when he saw movement, before jumping back into his chest when he realized it was his own reflection—and then turned the corner. A vast field of black opened in front of him. He could see a gravel path leading to the entrance ahead and branching out before wrapping into a circle to form what he assumed was a car park, but he couldn't see any cars, or any signs declaring a purpose or name for the building.

The windows on the front of the building were bigger and the blinds were drawn, he couldn't see in, nor could he see his own reflection as he scurried past. Eddie was already at the door, standing back and arching his neck to look up at the looming facade.

He turned to his friends and gave them an exaggerated shrug.

"Now what?" Darren asked, part of him hoping the answer would be, "*now we turn around and go home.*"

Eddie shrugged, took a moment to ruminate on something and then stepped forward. The entrance was a large double door with one side blocked off and a smaller door etched into one of the panels. It had once been a glorious entranceway, there to impress the carriages that pulled up outside with privileged guests, but now it was clinical and felt more like the entrance to a prison rather than the stately home that it might have once been. Eddie put his hand on the handle, turned, and pushed. Even in the darkness, Darren and Malcolm could see the gleam on their friend's face as the door gave way and steadily creaked open.

Malcolm stepped forward, trying to sneak a peek over Eddie's shoulder; Darren reluctantly followed. Eddie threw a finger to his lips, gave his friends a wide-eyed stare, and then poked his head through the gap. A large unlit room greeted him. The inside of the building was a little brighter than the outside, the back of the room was lit by an ethereal glow, a scattering of light provided by a distant room or hallway that had crept under the crack in one of the doors. The front end was dotted with stars of red and green, little pulses of light from electronic equipment, most of which was behind a reception area. The reception area was empty and partitioned off by a sheet of Perspex. Opposite it, a smaller but equally reinforced area also offered an array of lights. This was where Eddie had seen the security guard sleeping earlier in the day and, as he strained his eyes to stare at the silhouette slouched before the array of monitors—all of them turned off, their standby lights aglow—he saw that the man was still immobile.

He frowned curiously at the slouched figure before ducking his head back out of the room and closing the door slightly to shield his voice from the inside.

"The coast is clear," he said.

"Really?" Darren hissed, bewildered.

Eddie nodded. "The security guard is still asleep."

"The same guard?"

Eddie nodded vigorously. "I think so."

"But it's dark in there," Malcolm noted. "If he's trying to sneak a few winks, why did he turn all the lights off? Hardly inconspicuous, is it?"

"Inconspicuous? Where the fuck did you learn that word?"

Malcolm frowned and stared at his redheaded friend.

Eddie shrugged. "Maybe he can't sleep with the light on, who knows; who *cares*? The point is, he's asleep and the door is open, so what the fuck are we waiting for?"

Malcolm turned to Darren, swapping a concerned stare. They were both thinking the same thing. They both felt the same pangs of dread and sensed that something was wrong, but what was the worst that could happen? Eddie was right, the doors were open and the guard was asleep. They could be in and out before anyone knew what had hit them.

"After you," Malcolm said, nodding to Eddie who was delighted to be given the lead.

16

Eddie was first, his feet stretching out and landing delicately on the hardwood floor inside the building. He made sure he had a firm footing, made sure his night vision had correctly adjusted and he made sure he knew which direction he was walking in, then he stepped inside. The others cautiously followed with Darren the last in, shutting the door gently behind him and cringing when he heard it squeak.

The wind had died down outside and they could hear the sounds of their own heavy breathing and their own pounding hearts as they ventured further inside the building. Eddie made a beeline for the light that bled through the door up ahead, a door that led to the hallway and the rest of the building, but he slowed his steps and held his breath as he passed the small security area.

A cutaway piece of Perspex looked out from the security office onto a thin passageway bordered by a metal railing. It was there so that the guard could check everyone that entered and exited the building, giving them the once-over before they moved onto the reception area on the other side. But the guard was fast asleep in his small alcove, his feet up on the desk, his shadowed face peering spookily at the three teenagers as they crept past.

Eddie paused at the end, just before leaving the inspection point. The railing on his left ended, curving into the ground. On his right was the entrance to the security room—made to be locked and secured at all times—and the door was wide open.

He felt Malcolm bump into him, felt his friend pinch his lower back and urge him forward, not wanting to speak or even whisper when they were so close to the sleeping guard, but Eddie didn't move. He contemplated ducking inside and shutting the door, he thought about making sure that the guard was asleep, or doing his best to make sure that the guard wouldn't wake up. He knew his friends would object, they wouldn't want anyone harmed, they never did, but if—

He stopped his pondering when a loud bang erupted inside the room. He felt his heart jump into his throat, his knees bend and his body crouch almost instinctively, preparing to duck into the fetal position. Then he felt the wind on his back and heard the high pitch whistling as it rushed through the room, in and out of the crevices.

The wind had picked up outside and had blown the door wide open, slamming it against its hinges. Darren hadn't shut the door properly; he had been too worried about the noise it made as it crept on its hinges that he hadn't clicked it into place.

They all stood still, rigid in fear. Their attentions immediately turned to the security guard, whose shadowed form they expected to stand up and snap on the lights. He didn't move, didn't seem affected by the sound of the wind as it cut through the building, or by the sound of the door as it slammed a staccato, nerve-jolting beat against the wall.

Eddie was about to exclaim his relief to his friends when he heard a noise from elsewhere in the building. This one came just as suddenly, but was far more worrying. The door at the end of the hallway suddenly sprang open, throwing a veil of bright, warm light onto the hardwood floor. The sea of orange was darkened by two looming shadows that paused at the doorway and then entered the room. They were talking to each other but their voices were incoherent, sounding rushed and jumbled.

They were footsteps away from turning the corner and seeing the three boys standing there. Eddie turned around, looked towards the door as it continued to rattle in the wind. It seemed like a mile away, he knew they would see him as he ran for it, but at least he would be outside, at least—

He felt two strong palms on his back as he was pushed into the security room. He stumbled inside, with Malcolm following close behind.

"*Hide*," Malcolm hissed, his voice hushed but sharp.

The room was small with a thin desk that wrapped around most of it. The security guard was at the top end, his feet up on the desk. Eddie, on his hands and knees, scurried under the part of the desk that sat underneath the window, out of sight from anyone who tried to creep by. Malcolm joined him, squeezing tightly beside him.

They both looked up forlornly as Darren's darkened figure approached. They could see the whites of his eyes and the terror inside them as he realized there was no room for him.

Darren thought he was going to be seen. He was sure he was going to give the game away. An avalanche of thoughts rushed through his mind.

Should I make a run for it?

Should I lie down on the floor and stay low?

He heard the voices increase, heard the speedy tones grow in volume and rapidity. It was like white noise, an encroaching, mumbled assortment of audio static and one that was accompanied by shuffling footsteps, unstable feet that scurried animal-like across the floor.

He could fit underneath the desk opposite, but then he would be visible through the window and the open door. If they turned on the main lights, which they probably would, it would just take a glance to spot him.

They're going to see me. They're going to see me.

The voices stopped. Darren silenced his thoughts; held his breath. There were no footsteps, no noise. He looked towards the doorway, angling his vision towards the back of the room where they were approaching from. He expected to see a ghostly figure staring at him, looming over him with a wicked smile. He saw only blackness and then, after hearing a faint *click*, he saw the back of room explode into light.

The voices started again. The footsteps continued their shuffling.

They were closing in on the room. He could hear them just a few feet away.

The security room was still dark. But they were turning lights on as they went and, as soon as the main light clicked on, they would see him crouching there.

He knew there was only one thing for it. He had only one reasonable option. He had to shuffle past the sleeping guard and hide underneath the desk that he was sleeping in front of. He wouldn't be seen through the window or the door and there would be enough room for him there. He could see the gray block of space beckoning him.

He scuttled forward, ducked to a crawl and stopped when he felt a wet and cold substance seep into his pants and soak into the palms of his hands. He grimaced, tried to shake it off. He told himself that the guard had probably spilt his tea or coffee when he had fallen asleep, but worried that it would be something far more disgusting.

He had seen tell-all documentaries about night workers like security guards. They were alone all night, bored out of their minds, and prone to depression and insomnia, the sort who relished the late hours and the solitude. They often drank themselves into a stupor and spent the night singing merrily or watching online pornography. He worried that this guard had done the same, that he had drunk himself into a drunken stupor, fallen asleep, and then pissed himself.

The thought made him sick, especially as he couldn't see the substance that coated his clothes and his skin. He didn't want to know what it was, not while it was dark and he couldn't do anything about it. He didn't make an effort to smell his clothes, didn't even allow himself to breathe through his nose. He tried to blank it out as he crawled through it and hid underneath the desk.

The three teenagers held their breaths when the lights snapped on in the main room. Malcolm and Eddie watched the reflections of the two men on the wall opposite as they strode past the checkpoint. One of them seemed to walk with a shuffling, staggering movement and both of them looked like they were wearing robes, something that was confirmed when the shuffling one paused in the center of the window and turned to look inwards. He was wearing a dressing gown on top of a pair of pajamas, they both saw it and they both thought it was strange, but they had more pressing worries to address. They thought he had seen them and were sure that their game was up just as quickly as it had started, but after getting a good look at the room and whatever was inside it that took his fancy, he continued onwards.

One of them spoke in a heavy whisper, a mumbling, bumbling, and cursing voice. The two teenagers listening intently under the desk picked up nothing coherent except a barrage of random curse words. The other one seemed silent, they heard him mumble at one point, a heavy and bass-filled affirmation, but he didn't make another sound.

The men in gowns shut the front door and the two teenagers heard them lock and bolt it. They knew there was little chance they would be able to escape through there The door was solid and without a key they wouldn't be able to get through, but they had no concerns about getting out, not yet anyway. They were still intent on finding out if there was anything worth their while inside.

The men in gowns shuffled and walked back to the end of the room, turning off the lights one by one before heading back into the hallway.

Eddie and Malcolm were relieved, a rush of adrenaline pulsed through their bodies, translating into soft laughs and wide grins. They were just short of giggling like school girls and high-fiving each other. It took them a few moments to realize that Darren wasn't joining in, took them some time to see that their friend, hiding underneath the desk and staring in horror at the slumped man above him, wasn't laughing or smiling.

Darren had thought he was going to get caught. He knew that if they turned the lights on, the security guard would open his eyes and see him. It didn't occur to him until it was too late, but Darren could see the guard's face, albeit dark, which meant the guard would be able to see his. When the lights had snapped on and his face had been illuminated, Darren realized that the guard wouldn't be able to see him, because he was never waking up.

The guard was in his late sixties, maybe younger, but his pallid expression belied his true age. His face was white and decaying into a subtle shade of blue. His eyes were wide, glassy and staring upwards, into the low ceiling of his office and the abyss beyond. A thin red line traced over his neck where his throat had been slit, the blood had congealed and clogged on his skin like tomato sauce around the lips of the bottle.

Darren felt his breath catch in his throat. He realized that the substance he had crawled through, the one that now coated his hands and his legs, wasn't coffee, tea, or even urine. It was blood. Cold, sticky, congealed blood. He felt sick, he didn't know if he wanted to pass out or throw up. He tried to do the latter, gagging a few times, but there was nothing inside his stomach; his body refused to let him release, to let him feel relief.

17

The three teenagers fell silent with only the sound of their heavy breathing penetrating the blackness. After the sudden display of light and the rapid descent back into darkness, their eyes were beginning to adjust again. They could see each other's faces. They could see the horrified expressions that were developing.

"Dead?" Malcolm asked after a while, feeling like something was stuck in his throat. "Are you sure?"

"What do you mean, *am I fucking sure*?" Darren rasped. "D'you think I don't know what a dead person looks like?"

Malcolm frowned at this friend, his expression hidden by the blanket of gray. "Have you seen many dead people before?"

Darren shifted uncomfortably. "Well, no, of course not."

"So—"

"He's dead, alright?"

Silence fell over them as they all contemplated their next move and shot curious glances at the dark form of the slouched guard above them. Eventually the silence was broken by Eddie who mumbled in frustration and crawled out from underneath the desk, before quickly getting to his feet.

"What are you doing?" Darren asked, remaining where he was, fearful to move an inch, scared to move past the dead man in case he reached out from beyond the grave.

"I tell you what I ain't doing," Eddie said, fumbling in his pockets. "I ain't sitting in the dark under a fucking desk like some numpty." He pulled out a Zippo lighter and flicked the top. With a trembling hand he took a few steps towards the guard, stretched out his arm, and then struck the lighter.

The spark ignited the room and they all caught a glimpse of that pallid, horrified expression, but the lighter didn't ignite and the image vanished as quickly as it appeared. They waited in the darkness with Eddie still holding the lighter in his outstretched arm.

"Did you see that?" Darren whispered.

Malcolm nodded, unwilling to open his mouth.

Eddie tried again. Another spark, another flash, and another sighting before the darkness returned as quickly as it had departed.

"I think I'm going to be sick," Darren said.

Malcolm didn't respond, but he knew where his friend was coming from.

Eddie struck the lighter again, this time the flame caught and the room stayed lit. They saw the guard in all his deathly glory; his lifeless face and the mass of blood that had coated his torso and dripped to the floor.

"Holy fucking shit," Malcolm hissed softly. He climbed out from underneath the desk, kept his distance from the guard as Eddie remained close, seemingly very interested in the rigid corpse.

"Who do you think did this?" Eddie wondered aloud.

Malcolm had no answer for that, he didn't know who had done it and didn't know who was capable of doing such a thing. It looked like the killer had snuck up behind the guard and slit his throat. There were no signs of a struggle, no signs that the guard had even seen his killer.

Eddie turned the flame towards Darren as he slowly and sluggishly emerged from underneath the desk, inches from the guard's limp and bloodstained legs.

"What the fuck happened to you?" Eddie asked, noting the blood covering Darren's legs and arms.

Darren allowed himself to acknowledge the blood and felt another wave of desperate nausea. The coppery scent was overwhelming, but the sickly smears of drying crimson that coated his clothes and his flesh was worse. He hated blood, he typically only hated it when it was his own and was proud of his indifference when it was someone else's—gory films or televised operations had no effect on him—but this was worse than his own, yet it clung to him as if it *wanted* to be a part of him.

When Darren looked up, through the flame and beyond the pale features of the guard, he saw that Eddie had a smirk on his face. That smirk angered his blood and activated a bitter part of him that ignited as fast as the flame had.

"You look worse than him," Eddie mocked.

"Fuck off you ginger asshole," Darren spat.

Eddie's eyes flared in retaliation. He didn't speak, didn't give any warning of his intentions before he launched himself at his friend, dropping the lighter in the process. The flame extinguished in the congealed blood, Darren's vision went to black seconds before he felt Eddie's hands on his neck, before he felt his friend's clammy fingers curling around his throat.

He tried to yell in retaliation but his words merely choked out of his lungs; he tried to stop Eddie, to claw at his hands and his fingers, but his friend was far stronger than he had anticipated.

"I'm fucking sick of you," Eddie yelled, spraying spittle at his friend. "I'm—"

He felt Malcolm's hand on his back, tugging him away. He forced himself further forward, shrugged off his friend's advances and kept his fingers around the neck of his other friend.

"Always with the fucking jokes, always—"

"Eddie, get the fuck off him!" Malcolm yelled, his voice low but getting louder.

"—Always taking the piss. Ever since we were kids—"

"Get off him!"

"I'll show you, you little fucking cunt, I'll—"

"Leave him!" Malcolm yelled at the top of his lungs and simultaneously whipped his fist across the back of Eddie's head. Eddie toppled sideways with his hands still on Darren's throat. He released him, allowing his friend to breathe, as he lost his balance and clattered to the floor, missing the edge of the desk by inches.

Darren fell to his knees and threw his hands to his throat, feeling the swelling as he tried to restore life to his body and his lungs. The anger had gone; he had felt it right until the point he realized that Eddie was seconds away from killing him.

Eddie mumbled on the floor; thrust himself up onto his elbows and then his backside. He stared at the other two figures in the darkness and gave them each a meek smile.

Malcolm was standing above them both, still breathing heavily, feeling an intense and shocked anger rushing through his body.

He opened his mouth to ask Eddie what had gotten into him, when the sound of rushing feet stopped him. All three heads turned towards the hallway at the back of the room, and then towards each other.

"Shit," Darren rasped through a dry and haggard throat. "Now look what you've done, you ginger—"

"*Shut up*!" Malcolm said quickly, keeping his voice to a stern whisper. He reached over and grabbed the back of Darren's collar with one hand and Eddie with the other. "Get the fuck up, we're going."

"Outside?" Eddie said, clambering to his feet.

Malcolm shook his head, turned towards the door and listened for the footsteps. They were coming down the same hallway they had come from before, he could see the bouncing shadows through the slit in the bottom of the floor. He looked towards the front door, it was locked and the men in gowns had the key. He knew they wouldn't be able to break through and wouldn't have anywhere to run if they were caught. He looked towards the other end of the room, to a door opposite the one where the footsteps were echoing from.

"Follow me." He was moving before he spoke. He was crouching, staying low, but moving quickly, at a half jog. He heard the whispers behind him, heard the muttered calls of resistance, but his friends were following him.

He felt exposed when he left the security area and scuttled across the main room. It was big and empty; a big black hole that could land them in a lot of trouble should the door open as they were crossing.

His heart pounded in his chest, his mind raced. He struggled to hear the sound of the footsteps over the rapid *thump-thump* of his own chest and the sound of his friends' footsteps behind him.

Darren was still struggling to breathe, to keep up with Eddie in front of him and Malcolm further ahead. They looked quicker, more agile. Darren was feeling faint and weak. His body was still suffering from the beating his step father had given him, and from his near-death experience at the hands of his supposed friend. He could only watch, feeling a great sense of abandonment and impending doom, as Eddie pushed further away. His lungs were on fire, he felt like his stomach was trying to leave via his throat. He could hear the footsteps behind him, could hear them slow down as they neared the door. His end was nigh, he was sure he was going to be caught; he was sure he would end up like the security guard, his throat smiling for eternity. As he struggled to keep up with his friends, he begged to any god that would listen that the people behind him would slow or trip.

Malcolm made it to the door. He breathed a heavy sigh of relief and then pushed it open, greeting more waves of blackness. He slipped inside the hallway, stood up straight and turned around just as Eddie ducked in behind him. He expected Darren to be right behind him; his heart hit the pit of this stomach when he saw that his friend was still in the middle of the room and had seemingly given up hope of making it to the other side.

The door on the opposite side of the hallway opened a crack, bathing the room in enough light for Malcolm to see Darren's face clearly. He had stopped completely, frozen rigidly like a rabbit caught in the headlights. Malcolm beckoned him forward, begged him to run towards the door. Darren gave him a meek shrug in reply and then turned towards his fate, just as the door opened all the way and the two figures appeared in the doorway.

Malcolm closed the door, leaving it open just a touch. He felt Eddie's hand on him, tugging him away, but he couldn't close it, he wouldn't leave Darren to whatever fate those sick murderers had planned for him.

He watched the two men in the doorway opposite. One of them was short, stubby, and seemed awkward on his feet; the other was tall and thin, looming a good two foot over the short one in front. They were both ugly, the tall one had a long and thin face with a protruding forehead, eyes that looked lost in his skull and lips that looked like the recipients of a botched botulism job. The short one had a rough, hardened face, dotted with scars and stubble.

Neither of them were looking into the room, neither of them saw Darren standing on the edge of the pool of florescent orange light that spilled out from the brightly lit hallway.

"Fuck you, fuckhead," the short one was shouting. Malcolm recognized him as the mumbling man he had heard before, his voice was louder, much more annoyed. "I got here first, fuck off before I twat you one."

The tall one replied with a disapproving, bass-filled grunt, a single note that expressed his annoyance and intent better than any sentence could. He put his hand on the short one's forehead, held him out at arm's length and then tried to bundle him out of the way in a patronizing manner. The short one didn't budge; he defiantly swiped the hand from his forehead and then launched himself at the skinny man. He tackled him hard around the waist and they both clattered out of view, leaving their impression on the door as it swung backwards and forwards, diminishing and expanding the pool of light in which Darren still stood, looking transfixed and waiting for his life to end.

Malcolm yanked open the door without thinking, he took a few big strides to get to the center of the room, to his baffled friend. He grabbed Darren by the arm and pulled him away, towards the door, towards the hallway, before throwing him inside and shutting the door behind them.

18

"What the fuck was all that about?" Eddie hissed venomously, directing his attention at Darren.

Malcolm turned around to hush his friends as he peeked through a gap in the door, keeping his attention on the room opposite. The tall man and the short man were still fighting. He could hear their grunts, the sounds of their bodies clattering into the floor and against the walls.

"Me?" Darren said in retaliation, finding his voice through his pained throat. "What about *you*?"

Eddie didn't answer. The two friends exchange a heated stare.

"You got what you deserved," Eddie said eventually.

Darren shook his head in disbelief. "You nearly killed me."

"You got what you deserved," Eddie repeated.

Darren laughed softly. He felt his anger return but he kept it at bay for his own safety and for Malcolm's. He had already risked both of their lives.

"It's always the fucking gingers."

"What did you say?"

"*Shh*!" Malcolm hissed. "They're coming back."

The short one emerged, looking beaten and worse for wear, but with a broad smile on his face that suggested he'd won. The tall one hadn't retreated completely; he lumbered a few feet behind, looking even worse. They pushed open the hallway door, snapped on the light, and lit up the main room.

Malcolm pulled the door closed, preparing to close it all the way. He stopped when something on the floor caught his eye. He felt his pounding heart sink to the bottom of his soul, felt a strain of disbelief on his nerves.

He looked at Darren, slumped down in the hallway to his left, covered in sickly swabs of someone else's blood; and then at the floor in the main room where Darren had stood. The floor was dotted with spots of blood, smears and smudges that had washed off Darren's feet and dripped off his clothes.

The bickering men were walking straight past them, further into the room. Malcolm followed their movement, tracing the path he had run, the path that Darren had run. There he saw them: stained crimson footprints, marking a path along the floor, right the middle of the room where Darren had paused, then to the door where they now stood.

"What is it?" Darren whispered, sensing the fear on his friend's face when he turned to look at him.

"Take your shoes off."

"What?"

Malcolm didn't need to explain. He simply pointed to the floor, to the prints that marked their entrance into the hallway.

"Holy fuck."

"*Take 'em off!*"

* * *

Darren's feet slapped loudly on the floor, clapping against the cold, hard wood with every stride. He received frustrated stares from Eddie and worried glances from Malcolm, but none of them said anything.

They stopped at the end of the hallway. A sound even more disturbing than the sound of Darren's feet screeched into their ears and turned their blood cold. It was a hot and cutting scream, of someone in unbearable torment, someone not long for this world.

Darren felt the cold seep through his naked toes, felt it crawl up the backs of his legs, up his spine, and into the deepest recesses of his mind. It was like nothing he had ever heard, like nothing he had ever felt.

"Holy fuck," he said slowly, feeling his jaw hang open of its own accord. He turned to Malcolm and saw the look of reciprocated horror on his friend's face. That made things worse. Malcolm was the cool one, the calm one, the one he looked up to, and the one whose sanity and reassurances he sought. There was nothing reassuring on his face now, and, as the scream ripped another hole in the silence, Malcom's sanity looked like it was trying to flee.

Eddie had turned white. The black hollows of his eyes looked stark against his pallid skin and his red hair. Darren saw the opportunity for a joke but his fear, and the continuing scream, stopped him.

When the inhuman screech died away, it left a resonance in the hallway, a feeling that clung to the walls and the air like a toxic plume.

Malcolm wanted to speak, to tell his friends that whatever was making the noises through the door ahead, was worse than what was behind them. He was going to tell them to go back the way they came, back into the clutches of Little and Large, the brawling idiots who were sure to be on their tail, but he knew they couldn't go back.

He moved towards the door and reached out, just as another scream rocked the hallway, this one was softer, heavier; the voice was fading, giving up. He closed his eyes, forced the mental images away and reached for the handle with a trembling arm, twitching an anxious tic when he felt the cold steel brush against his finger-tip.

"What the fuck are you doing?" Darren said, stepping forward. He pulled his friend away from the door, his hand pressed weakly into the soft flesh above his shoulder. "We can't go in there."

Malcolm looked at his friend and then back down the hallway. The door had been blown open a touch and a sliver of light shined through the gap.

"We can't go back there." Malcolm said.

Darren released his grip and turned towards the end of the hallway. He ran a hand through his hair, looked around with apprehension. "You're fucking kidding me," he said, shaking his head. "What the hell is going on here?"

"It's fucked up whatever it is," Eddie said.

"This doesn't look like no rehab place to me," Darren noted with a trembling voice.

Eddie shrugged and turned away.

"You think they're on drugs or some shit?" Darren asked.

Malcolm raised his eyebrows.

"Well, what else could it be?" Darren begged to know. "You think they're robbing the place?"

"Wearing dressing gowns and white robes?" Eddie wondered. "You think they're being robbed by the fucking sandman?"

"Well, what's your fucking answer then, smart-ass?" Darren snapped.

"I don't—"

"—Will you two shut the fuck up!" Malcolm said, stepping between them to silence them. "It doesn't matter what it is or who the fuck they are, what matters is that they just killed a security guard and they're probably gonna do the same to us."

His harshly whispered words shuddered the hallway into silence. Darren hung his head; Eddie shook his slowly

"Check your phones," he said.

"Why?" Eddie wanted to know. "We can't phone for help. We came to rob the place, they'll arrest us."

"I'd rather be arrested than dead," Malcolm said. He pulled out his phone, stared at the screen and shook his head. "No signal."

"Same here," Darren said, looking towards Eddie who didn't seem as deflated as the other two. "This literally is the middle of fucking nowhere you've brought us to."

Eddie shrugged.

"So, what do we do?" Darren asked eventually.

Malcolm didn't answer him. Instead he turned back to the door, composed himself again and pushed it open. As soon as he took a step inside, with Darren treading his naked feet behind and Eddie languishing further back, the screaming started again.

19

The corridor stretched out ahead of them with an ominous shine of buzzing lights. At the end of the corridor, before it branched off, the lights struggled to ignite, flickering with a sporadic laziness, illuminating, and shadowing the final stretch intermittently.

Malcolm was the first to enter, the first to feel the force of the screaming as it punctured his ears and reverberated through his skull; the first to smell and taste the stench of putrefaction that hung in the air like a morbid cloud. The hallway was lit, bright, and headache inducing, an overpowering light he had always associated with the sterile environment of hospitals, but this was far from sterile. The floor underfoot stuck to his shoes, as if he was walking on a thin layer of honey. He felt it resist against the soles of his trainers but he didn't want to look down. He didn't need to glance at his feet to know he was treading in congealed blood.

He turned around and prepared to warn his shoeless friend who was still coated with the blood of the security guard, but when Darren stepped into the corridor, the blood underfoot that seeped through the gaps in his toes was the last thing on his mind.

The scream was fading; a faint whisper of its former self, but it coincided with a loud bang, one that vibrated through to where the three teenagers stood. They all looked ahead, towards the source of the noise.

To their left and right were corridors that stretched into the blackness, ahead and to their right was a door, it was shut but they could see the light from inside and could see the shifting shadows that obscured it.

A sheet of smeared Plexiglass covered the wall to their right, just beyond the door. There was little crawl space below for the teenagers to slip by unnoticed, but the curtains had been drawn on the other side, exposing a slit of light in the center where the two sides of blue and white striped material struggled to meet.

The corridor ahead of them was flanked with doors, all leading to rooms with similar windows and equally gaudy curtains. From what they could see, despite the lights above and the noise in the room to their right, all the other rooms were empty.

"*Please, please, don't do this.*"

The teenagers exchanged glances when they heard the startled, strangled plea. It sounded harsh, tired; croaked out of lungs that had all but given up. Darren felt his heart quicken, felt a stab of fear rising inside of him. Something was telling him to run, to flee immediately. It didn't matter about his friends, didn't matter about the horrors behind him or the potential doom ahead, his body was working on a primal instinct and that instinct was begging him to run.

He restrained himself. His legs twitched violently, as if trying to break free from the rigid embrace they shared with the floor.

Malcolm was the first to move forward, heading for the room ahead, from which poured a melee of noise and fear. The other two eyed up the corridors to their right and left, preparing to flee.

He didn't know why he needed to see what was going on, he could make a good assumption that something terrible was happening to someone inside that room and he didn't need verification, but something moved him forward. He pinned himself up against the wall, keeping to the side of the door, out of view of the smeared glass. He could hear heavy breathing coming from two people inside the room, one was harsh, curdled, tired, and pained; the other was out of breath probably from exertion, but mostly sounding giddy. It sounded like the wheezing, excitable breath of a hyperactive child.

He heard mumbled voices and heard the excitable one talking, but he couldn't make anything out. The pained one replied, softly at first and then with a throat warbling scream, but his words were distorted and sounded like they were traveling through water.

He saw Darren gesturing to him out of the corner of his eye, but he ignored his friend's frantic waving. Malcolm lowered himself to his knees and scuttled under the glass panel in the door and along to the window. Behind him, Darren edged closer to the corridor on his right, it was dark down there, an ominous tunnel that led to an abyss, but it felt safer than where he was standing.

Eddie looked less worried and didn't seem to know what to do with himself as he watched Malcolm move to the window. He was intrigued, baffled, but something else lurked inside of him; it wasn't apprehension or curiosity, he didn't share either of his friends' prevailing emotions. His was something else, something that seemed to be gripping him and taking control. He looked down the corridor to his left and saw something shift in the darkness, a shadowed figure that cut a hole in the blackness and filled it with gray before shifting back into the nothingness again.

What the fuck was that?

He didn't know whether he should tell his friends, whether he should run away or whether he should follow the shape in the darkness.

He looked to Darren who looked like he was already preparing to run and leave his so-called friends in the lurch.

Fucking coward. He made him so angry, with his constant fucking jokes and now this. He was a liability, what the fuck were they doing still hanging around with him anyway?

Darren saw Eddie scowling at him and flashed him a curious stare, Eddie grimaced and turned away. He thought he saw something else in the corridor to his left, something bigger, faster. It moved through the darkness at the back of the corridor and into a segment of light further on, closer to Eddie. It stopped at the borderline between the blackness and the buzzing white of the fluorescent lights. It stayed there as if watching Eddie, waiting for him to make a move, and then it disappeared again.

Eddie wasn't sure what he was looking at. He wasn't entirely sure that what he had seen was real or just a trick of the light or his imagination. He dismissed it and turned back to Malcolm who was now crouching below the window.

Malcolm positioned himself underneath the gap in the curtains. He peered upwards, through the window and through the gap, but he saw only the reflection of the room opposite. He stood up slowly and moved his face closer to the glass until the room came into view.

He felt his breath catch in his throat, felt his heart stop and then start with a staccato flourish. "*Holy fuck*," he whispered.

The room was a blood bath, an abstract work of morbidity. The walls and ceiling, once a blank canvas of dull white, were splattered with viscous blood. The carpet had probably been cream or white and over the years it had turned gray, but in an instant it had been dyed red.

The walls had been decorated with the odd painting and framed picture, and everything had been whipped with slashes of stark blood, obscuring whatever reality existed within those innocent framed worlds. It looked like an office or a conference room, a quiet place designed for a limited number of people to sit and talk, but that veil of quietude had been torn.

A small square table took center stage in the room, surrounded by four chairs, three had been toppled and lay strewn across the floor. The fourth was occupied by a complacent looking man with a face like a rat. He was tall and skinny with a long, pointed expression that seemed to be melted on his head and an evil stare that was directed towards the other side of the room.

Malcolm followed his beady eyes; he felt his heart stop and start again in his chest, felt the hairs on the back of his arms rise. A stocky man with a bald head was being held up against the back wall by a man wearing a white dressing gown that had been stained red.

The attacker had his back to Malcolm but the victim was looking right at him, although Malcolm doubted he could see anything. His face was a bloodied pulp; he had been beaten beyond recognition. His eyes were swollen shut, his jaw and nose were broken and his skull looked like it had been fractured in several places. His rounded, bloodied face was shaped like a swollen football and it looked like it was about to burst.

The attacker was strangling him, but stopped when his victim lost consciousness. He lowered him to the floor, slapped him violently until he came around, and then continued to strangle him. He had been stabbed and slashed, beaten, and broken, but he was still hanging onto his life and his attacker was doing his best to make sure he did. He wanted to prolong his suffering for as long as possible.

Malcolm felt angry. He felt his blood boil, felt a desire to break down the door and help the helpless man, but at the same time he felt sick to his stomach because of what he was seeing. He tasted bile crawling up his throat, the bitterness on the back of his tongue.

Darren had edged into the corridor and his view of Malcolm was now obscured. Eddie glanced across at him, gave him a contemptuous glare and then began to edge closer to the room, keen to see what Malcolm was seeing, keen to see what had shocked his friend into silence, what had caused his eyes to open wide, his pupils to dilate, his skin to turn an angry red and then a sickly white.

As he peered through the window, struggling to blink, breathe, or comprehend, Malcolm felt like he was playing a graphic computer game or watching a violent film; he was looking through a lens, witnessing this carnage through the eyes of someone else. It didn't feel real, it *couldn't* be real. But it *was* real, and when the man in the chair turned around and saw Malcolm peering through the corner of the window, when his rat-like face lit up with an expression of sadistic glee, Malcolm realized just how real it was. He peeled his face away from the window and turned to Eddie, who was trying to peer over his shoulder and see what Malcolm had seen, and Darren, who was doing his best not to see anything.

They saw the fear spread over Malcolm's face, shared in his apprehension and terror and then, as he opened his mouth, they heard the door open and heard the screams from within, right before they heard their friend's warning:

"*Run*!"

20

Malcolm saw his friends quickly run off, one going down one corridor, the other going down another. He thought about following one of them, they needed to stay together, but before he could decide which, Rat Face and the one with the crimson dressing gown appeared in the doorway and blocked his view. He paused, stuck rigid for a moment, staring into two sets of eyes that seemed both dead to the world and alive with an evil he had never encountered before.

Rat Face looked at Malcolm with a hunger, he had watched his friend destroy someone, had sat back and been the spectator to the show of carnage, and now he wanted his turn. The door leading into the corridor threw open and Malcolm saw Little and Large burst into the corridor. For a moment, there were four of them and Malcolm was vastly outnumbered, but then the one in the crimson dressing gown turned around abruptly, grunted at them and thrust out his hands, pointing down to the two darkened corridors where Darren and Eddie had fled. They nodded in recognition, took a moment to decide who should go where, and then set off after the escaping teenagers.

Crimson turned back to Malcolm, moved a step closer, ahead of Rat Face and his bloodthirsty eyes.

Malcolm had only seen his back before, had only seen his bloodstained clothes and fierce hands as they gripped and squeezed the life out of the tortured man who had been left to die inside the room, but now he saw his face in all its sickly glory. He had prominent cheek bones that sat sharply on his face, arrowing down to a thin chin adorned with a collage of messy stubble. His forehead was square, thick, and stuck out from a hairline which seemed to shy away from the rest of his face.

He grinned at Malcolm, exposing a row of teeth that were yellowed and rotting between blood and chunks of flesh. His cheeks dimpled as he smiled, small contours of innocence typically reserved for mischievous youngsters.

"You want to play as well?" His voice sounded thirsty.

For a moment Malcolm couldn't turn away, like a passing motorist drawn to a car crash. He wasn't thinking, wasn't acting, wasn't preparing, his world had stopped, slipped into the abyss for several valuable moments. When the thoughts finally started again, kicking into action like the engine from an old motorbike, he turned on his heel and bolted down the corridor, going as fast as his legs would take him.

* * *

Darren ran on sweaty feet that slapped hard against the floor, echoing a noise around the dark hallways that would announce his impending arrival to everyone nearby. He needed to slow down, but he didn't know who was chasing him; he needed to stop and fight but he feared for his life.

He saw the hallways fill with light behind him, heard the clicks from the light switches and the static buzz from the fluorescence as they exploded into life and spilled their ghostly glow onto the sterile floors. The man chasing him was snapping on the lights as he went, as Darren looked back, struggling to keep his legs pumping, he saw that the darkness was vanishing and the light was advancing.

His heart fought to leave his chest and his limbs surged with a trembling rush of adrenaline; a shaky, powerful feeling that suggested they were capable of running faster and harder than they had ever run before, but equally capable of just giving up.

He heard laughter, a high-pitched cackle that cut through his bones and gripped tightly on his heart. It was an eager laugh, an excited laugh.

He sped past closed doors; past dark windows that looked into what he hoped were empty rooms. He turned corner after corner, shooting worried glances over his shoulder as he went. He had never been so scared for his life. He had never been so sure that his life was about to end.

With breathless spurts, his voice gasping out of tired lungs, he begged whatever god or cosmic force would listen, promised them that he would believe if they just let him live. He would stop robbing; he would stop being a mischievous little prick. He would even stop taking the piss out of Eddie. None of it was true, but it seemed that somebody or something was listening to him.

He could no longer see ahead of him; the light had stopped gaining on him and the corridor was now shrouded in an impenetrable blackness. He shot a worried glance over his shoulder and saw that the blackness extended down the full stretch of the corridor and around the corner of the next, whoever was chasing him had stopped.

He felt a stab of relief in his chest, felt a pressure lift off his mind, then he felt the full force of a wooden door as he ran straight into it.

Mullch. Mullch.

Arrrrrrhhhh.

The noise was the first thing that greeted him.

The door had been ajar and the force of his running was enough to propel him inside. It was as dark inside as it has been in the hallway and, beyond the merry assortment of stars that danced in the corner of his vision, he couldn't see anything.

But he could definitely hear something, and it didn't sound friendly.

Mulllch. Mulllch.

Arrrrrrrhhhh.

It was a sloppy, wet sound, like a dog chewing on something soft or the passionate kiss of two toothless seniors; followed by a heavy, wheezing, gurgling asthmatic breath. He jumped to his feet, hoping the noise was an amalgamation of his fear and the fall, but when he climbed to his feet, stared into the darkness, and tried to get a picture of where he was, he heard it again.

Mulllch. Mulllch.

Arrrrrrrhhhh.

It made the hairs on the back of his neck stand up and every muscle in his body froze.

It grew in frequency, each note different to the last, each lick or slurp heavier or softer.

Mulllch. Mulllch.

Mulllch. Mulllch.

Arrrrrrrhhhh.

It paused for a moment and when it did he thought he saw something light up in the middle of the room. It looked like an orb, like the spectral spots of light that ghost-hunting shows make such a fuss about, but it was gone as soon as it appeared and the noise continued.

Mulllch. Mulllch.

Arrrrrrrhhhh.

It was coming from in front of him; it definitely wasn't part of his imagination or his fear. He reached out his hand until he felt his fingers brush the light switch. He paused, held his breath, and asked himself if it was a good idea, if he really wanted to face what was in the room. He knew it couldn't be human, he also knew it couldn't be hostile; if it was, the light wouldn't make a difference, it would have heard him or felt him when he fell into the room.

He met the explosion of light with trepidation and felt a wave of dread and horror as soon as his eyes adjusted to what had been making the noise. He knew that what he saw would be the precursor to every nightmare for the rest of his life, if his life extended beyond the reaches of this small, dark and macabre room.

A man was sitting in a chair a few feet ahead of him. His hands were tied behind his back, his head, lolled to one side, was aimed at Darren. His throat had been slit but he was still alive, struggling to talk, to express himself in his final moments, as the blood seeped aggressively from a large opening in his neck.

He had been wearing white, but his clothes were now a collage of crimson, stained with his own dwindling life. His feet were untethered and splayed out uselessly at the bottom of the chair; his body was slouched and spent, his face was beaten, bruised, and bloodied beyond recognition. Darren couldn't tell if the man he was looking at was eighteen or fifty.

Mulllch. Mulllch.

After every struggled sentence that bled out of his throat, he paused for a long and deep breath that rattled in through the gap in his neck and bubbled the blood that seeped down his torso like spilled food from a messy meal.

Arrrrrrrhhhh.

As Darren stood there watching, he saw his eyes open wider, saw his bloodied expression change to tell Darren something that his broken voice couldn't express. He creased his forehead and moved his head backwards, the cut in his throat opening like the gleeful grin of a sadistic clown.

Darren felt his heart kick against his chest and his stomach fought to find a way out of his throat. He shook his head slowly and creased his face into something resembling sympathy. There was nothing he could do for the man; he knew that he couldn't help him no matter how much he pleaded.

"I'm sorry," Darren said softly, his words nothing more than a whisper.

The man realized that Darren wasn't reacting and began to kick his feet and gesture more frantically. His throat was opening and closing as he rocked his head back and forth, the wound gushing and seeping as it sealed and opened. Darren shook his head, squeezed his eyes shut, and repeated himself.

"I'm sorry."

He reached out and snapped off the light with the back of his hand. The room fell into an instant blackness, Darren breathed softly, happy that the image of the dying man was out of his head.

Arrrrrrhhhh.

In the darkness Darren listened to his breathing, the words had stopped, he couldn't even try to express himself anymore. He was dying, holding onto the final seconds of life. There was nothing Darren could do to help him and he knew that the sooner he lost his struggle, the better.

He took a step backwards, out of the room and back into the dark corridor that now seemed so welcoming. He stopped when his heels knocked against something.

He thrust out his hand to check where the door was, where the wall was. The door was wide open on one side with the wall on the other; he knew there shouldn't be anything behind him. He took another step backwards, lifting his feet high, and brought them down on top of the object he had bumped into.

He was standing on someone's foot.

He moved backwards with a timid step and bumped into something hot and heavy, something human.

The warbles continued from the throat of the dying man and Darren realized that he hadn't been trying to ask for help. He had been trying to warn Darren that his attacker was standing behind him.

Arrrrrrhhhh.

He turned towards the wall, began slapping it with his palms until he hit the switch and room burst into light. He turned around, ready to greet his foe and to make his escape.

A red headed beast with a bloodied mouth and a crooked smile stood in front of him. Darren could see his own reflection in his glistening eyes, the same reflective orbs he had seen dancing around in the darkness earlier. He could smell the rotting flesh and metallic blood on his clothes and on his breath.

"*Fuck.*"

21

Eddie got a good jump on his chaser, he was a fast runner and he never looked back. He kept his attention in front of him, kept his eyes on the empty corridors that flickered with occasional light from above. The hallways seemed endless, flanked by matching doors, and covered in darkness.

He had the feeling he was running in circles, doing laps around the building, and would end up back where he started. He didn't want that to happen, didn't want to bump into the psychopaths who had instigated all of that screaming. He bolted through one of the doors. It led to a cold, empty staircase.

He ran up the small flight of stairs, listening his footsteps echo loudly as they slapped against the hard flooring. He climbed two small flights and came to a doorway, inset with a square of glass which looked out onto another blackened hallway. He ignored it and climbed another two flights. There was a window at the top that looked out over the garden, bleached with moonlight and appearing ominous in the silent night. The window was too small to climb out of and there was nothing below but a sheer drop. He continued upwards, to what he assumed to be the third and top floor of the building.

A door greeted him at the top; it was light in the hallway beyond, a flickering, maddening light that refused to expose anything for long. He crept through the door, cringed when it squeaked on the hinges, and then paused, aiming an ear back to the staircase.

"Come out, come out, wherever you are."

The voice was raspy, harsh, and followed by the loud and abrupt sound of a slamming door. Eddie continued to listen; he heard heavy breathing, and then the sound of footsteps climbing the stairs. He hadn't been entirely sure that someone was following him, but now he was and now he knew that they were still on his tail, just a few dozen steps behind him.

He moved away from the door, allowed it to slam back into place, and ran as fast as he could down the hallway, back into the unknown.

* * *

Malcolm opened door after door and saw nothing but tiny rooms, cells with single beds, toilets, and the barest necessities. He continued on, knowing that with every step, with every door he opened onto nothing, his chasers were gaining on him. They were snapping on the lights as they followed, lighting the darkness just as he stepped into it.

He didn't know what he wanted to find. There would be no savior behind one of the open doors, no one willing to help him, and he certainly wasn't looking for anything valuable. On finding the dead security guard his objective had changed from wanting to find a good score, to wanting to make it out alive.

As he opened more doors and discovered more cells, he doubted he was inside a clinic. Eddie was wrong. This wasn't a plush place for the rich and famous to while away their days and forget about their hedonistic habits, this was something much more sinister, something much more clinical. It wasn't quite a prison, inmates wouldn't be allowed such an open environment, but it certainly wasn't a place of rehabilitation and healing.

He stopped when he opened the final door at the end of the corridor, the pounding feet of his chasers were just a few dozen steps behind him. The hallways were thin, short, and twisted, flanked by a sterile white wall on the left and rows of rooms on the right. They were checking the open doors, making sure he hadn't ducked inside, so he had bought himself some time, but, as he stared at the occupant of this room, he realized that whatever time he had bought, was currently being sold in the eyes of the smiling simpleton standing in front of him.

"Hello," the man said with a grin.

Malcolm took a step back. There was something mischievous and devious behind those eyes, something far from friendly. It was there, he saw it, but it passed in an instant and changed into something far more innocent, something stupid and naive. He was tall, a good foot and a half taller than Malcolm, and he had a hunched posture suggestive of years bent double, straining under low ceilings and arched over computer desks.

"What's your name?" Smiler asked.

Malcolm looked down the corridor, to the right where the footsteps continued, to the left where a nothingness of bright lights and seemingly endless corridors awaited him. He looked beyond Smiler, into the cell. It was much larger than the others and much less sterile. The walls were adorned with hand drawn pictures, colorful depictions of an array of characters, like a child's drawings of his family. He saw books stacked high on the floor, saw pens and papers resting on top of them.

"Will you be my friend?" Smiler asked.

Malcolm stepped away, looked forlornly into the hallways to his left. He could keep on running, but he didn't know what he was running into. He needed to hide, needed to get his bearings and figure out what to do next. He needed to find his friends and get out of this nuthouse.

"Yes, yes," Malcolm said with a quick nod. "You can be my friend if you help me."

"Help you?" Smiler frowned, setting deep furrows in his chubby face. He looked like a toddler trying to calculate an algebra equation. "How?"

Malcolm moved forward and put a reassuring hand on Smiler's elbow. "Hide me." He tried to move him, to usher him gently backwards, but he was built like a wall and wasn't moving unless he wanted to. Malcolm released his hand, took a step back. The pounding feet were closing in. They were just around the corner now, checking the last few doors that he had opened, all of which were tiny and dark rooms that wouldn't take more than few seconds to cover.

"Come on mate," Malcolm said, trying his best to fake a friendly smile. "Help me out."

Smiler grinned from ear to ear and moved to the side, gesturing for Malcolm to enter. Malcolm didn't need a second invitation; he ducked inside and immediately threw himself under the bed, dragging the duvet down over the side so that he was obscured from view.

He listened to the big man in the corridor. He expected him to enter the room, to help him, but he remained there as the pounding footsteps encroached and then stopped.

He heard his chasers talking to Smiler, grunting angrily. "Where is he?"

He didn't hear Smiler say anything but seconds later they were off again, bounding down the corridor. Malcolm breathed a sigh of relief, moved the duvet away, and rolled out. When he was about to stand up, to thank the big man for saving his life, he heard the cell door slam shut. He turned around to see that Smiler wasn't smiling anymore, and the darkness had returned to his eyes.

"Now, *friend*," he said, moving towards Malcolm. "I want to play a game."

* * *

Eddie felt like he was running around in circles, seeing the same nothings he had seen moments before. He had avoided the rooms, not wanting to run into more scenes of torture like the one they had encountered downstairs. He kept to the hallways that wrapped around the edges of the building.

He slowed his pace, hoping to catch his breath.

There were banks of windows on his left, looking out onto the garden below. The moon was thin, the light it provided was barely enough to capture the dust that hung in the corridors, billowing under the impact of Eddie's tired breath. He rested his hands on the window ledge and pressed his nose up against the glass.

In the distance, he could see the forest that they had cut through and parts of the field beyond, but he was only on the second floor, not high enough to see over the menacing foliage that cut a stark picture against the moonlit canvas. The windows opened at the top but the opening was small and had been barred on this side. Even if he could break or dislodge the bars, there was no way he could fit through. He didn't want to escape anyway; they had come this far and he wasn't going to let a few drug-fueled nutcases ruin his big score.

He sneered at his distorted reflection in the glass, peeling his face away from the window until he saw himself and not the world outside. He looked angry, and rightly so. He'd spent the last ten minutes running away from a minuscule drug addict with more money than sense, some murderous midget who probably thought he was better than everyone else just because he had money.

Fuck him, Eddie decided. It didn't matter what was going on inside the building, it didn't matter how many nutjobs were running around. He wasn't going to let them get to him, he was going to do what he came here to do and if they got in his way, then they would regret it.

He felt pumped up on his own rage, felt a torrent of adrenaline rushing through his body and kick-starting every nerve and every fiber of his being. That anger faded, changed into something else when he heard the pattering of hasty feet in the corridor behind him. He stopped in his tracks, silenced his own raging thoughts.

The midget with the snarling expression and cursive tongue was just around the corner and gaining fast. Eddie turned around and dove for the first door he saw. He found himself in a large room, the contents of which he couldn't make out. He heard the little man closing in so he didn't risk closing the door, didn't risk the squeal of hinges or the click of a lock. He hid next to the door, feeling the lip of the frame digging into his back as he turned his head and watched the corridor.

The little man bolted past him, Eddie heard his heavy breaths as he heaved and wheezed, heard his footsteps as they slapped the floor and echoed a thick vibration through the corridor. Eddie then heard the little man stop and he could feel his presence on the other side of the wall.

"I found you."

Eddie felt his heart stop at the little man's words. He heard retreating footsteps as his stubby little feet backtracked, back to the open doorway. The retreating steps quickened and then, in an instant, burst into a run as the little man headed straight through the open door.

He stopped when he ran past Eddie, skidding to his haunches, his knees bent and his legs apart. "I'm gonna fucking rip you open you little cunt!" he snarled aggressively. "Where are you?"

He moved towards the door, grabbed at it roughly and then slammed it back against the wall, grunting with pleasure and then sighing when he didn't feel the resistance of human flesh on the other side.

"Little fucking prick," he snarled.

He took a long step forward, then another, then he turned sharply, towards the back of the room, with Eddie in his periphery. Eddie didn't move, he knew the little man would detect movement; knew that darkness, silence, and complete stillness, for now, was his friend. Soon, when his eyes adjusted to the darkness like Eddie's had, he would spot him.

The little man took a few more steps into the room, a few more steps away from Eddie. "I know you're in here," he warned. "I can fucking smell you."

He scuttled towards the back of the room, leaving Eddie enough room to escape.

"Get out here, you little prick."

Eddie looked to the door; saw the escape route beckoning him.

"Come on you little fuckwit."

It was brighter inside the corridor and the light enticed him like the light at the end of a dark tunnel, but something else enticed him more.

"I'm gonna fuck you so bad you little cunt."

The little man's back was facing him, exposed in its vulnerability. Eddie peeled himself off the wall and moved towards it, one cautious step at a time; the little man was still searching the back of the room, still sweeping his head and his eyes across every nook and cranny.

"Come on, come out and play. I've got something to show you."

Eddie reached for a chair but stopped, noticing something on the table that glimmered and caught his eye. He reached for it and grinned, then he felt the cold touch of steel on his fingertips. It was a fountain pen, not a knife, but it was solid and sharp; it would do the job.

Just as Eddie picked up the pen and ran the mental images through his head, picturing what he would do to the creepy little man, the room burst into life. He looked up, shocked, and saw that the little man was standing by the other door, one hand on the light switch, the other holding a knife.

Eddie's smile dripped from his face; the little man beamed menacingly. Before Eddie could react, before he could decide what to do, the little man was charging at him, snarling like a hungry dog. He hit Eddie hard, knocking the wind out of him with one heavy tackle. The little man wrapped his arms around him and tried to stick the knife in his side, but Eddie swatted him away and heard the knife clatter to the floor, along with his own makeshift weapon.

Eddie rocked backwards for a few paces, kicking over chairs and nudging tables before he fell with the little man pinned on top of him. He felt his grubby hands on his face, felt his fingers poking into his flesh, nipping his cheeks, cutting his skin, and trying to claw out his eyes. Eddie tried to keep his grasping hand from doing any damage, but the little man had him and now he wasn't letting go.

He wriggled on top of him and seemed to be enjoying every gyration, like a randy dog dry humping him. Eddie felt sick under his sweaty, heated embrace. He could smell his sour breath washing over him, could almost taste the disease that oozed from his rotten mouth as he shouted and screamed in delight, spraying Eddie with showers of spittle.

Eddie managed to wriggle some movement and shot a knee upwards, catching the randy midget in the groin. He squirmed, yelped, and paused momentarily. That was all the invitation Eddie needed. He threw himself upwards, propelling every ounce of energy into the movement, and tossed the little man off him. He was fuming; his blood boiled through his body, his breaths came in short, heated rasps. His teeth were gritted and his eyes flared as he stared down at the little man, now on his back, looking up at Eddie with a sly expression on his ugly little face.

Eddie flung himself on top of him and wrapped his hands around his grubby throat. His flesh felt dirty and grimy under his fingers. He stared into his eyes as he squeezed. The little man tried to free Eddie's fingers, tried to pry them apart, but he had no chance. He tried to squirm, to wriggle and to kick, and he succeeded in inflicting pain with a few lucky blows, but Eddie ignored them. He concentrated on the bulging eyes, on the way his strangled breath and his fragile windpipe felt between his tightening fingers.

The little man turned blue, then purple. His eyes bulged like a cartoon character, flaring white orbs that popped out of his purple face and provided a stark picture of unreality. Eddie continued to squeeze even when the kicking and the squirming stopped, he continued when the eyes faded over and the flesh turned a shade of dark purple.

When he released his grip he felt the pain in his groin, his legs, and his back where the little man had connected with kicks and knees; he felt the stinging grazes on his hands and saw the streaks of blood where he had clawed, peeling off skin and opening wounds. He didn't mind, he stared at the empty eyes in front of him, ignoring the smell of defecation that began to fill the air as the body expelled its waste for the last time.

"Now who's the fuckwit?" he asked breathlessly, spitting every syllable. "Fucking dick."

22

Darren didn't see the punch, but he felt it. The fist crushed his nose and propelled his head backwards, the rough skin and pointed knuckles connected with his forehead and his eyes, injecting an intense and immediate agony inside his skull.

He toppled backwards, immediately losing his balance and falling on the floor, back where he had been when first stumbling into the room, before seeing the gurgling man in the chair; before seeing the man with the reflective eyes.

He had a split second to look up after the fall, a split second in which he saw his attacker loom over him, but his vision was blurry and his world was shaking. He didn't see the kick that connected with his ribs, or the ones that landed on his thighs, his groin, and then his head. He was barely conscious when the big man straddled him, laughing as he wrapped his legs around him and pressing his sweating, stinking body on top of him.

For a brief moment Darren worried that he was going to be raped, then he was worried that he was going to die, then his world turned black and his worry disappeared.

* * *

Smiler just stood there, as if waiting to see what Malcolm's next move was. Malcolm took a few steps back until he was pressed against the back wall, then he realized that backing himself into a corner probably wasn't such a good idea. The emptiness in Smiler's eyes sent shivers up his spine, he turned his head away sharply, aimed it directly at the stack of artwork on top of the books.

The freshly drawn creations depicted smiling humans, as did the ones he had seen on the walls, but none of these humans were alive and all of them were clearly suffering. They were mutilated, their bodies destroyed by unseen and unknown hands. Malcolm swallowed thickly and glanced at Smiler's hands which hung by his side, he was flexing his fingers, clenching and unclenching his fists as if in preparation.

Malcolm turned back to the artwork, to the walls. He hadn't seen it initially when looking in, but these figures, these smiling humans, were also suffering. They weren't portraits of happy families or loved ones, this was mutilation porn and, judging by the reams of them covering the walls, Smiler was a horny little bugger.

"They let me keep them," Smiler said, unprovoked.

Malcolm frowned at him, his eyebrows and expression asking the question.

"The nurses," Smiler explained, his eyes perusing the art. "They used to try and take them down. I didn't like that. I got angry."

"I can imagine," Malcolm said earnestly, hoping to do what he could to make sure that he didn't make the big man angry.

"So they let me keep them. I drew a lot, didn't I?"

"You did," Malcolm agreed.

"Do you like?"

Malcolm turned back to the art, taking his time to study them. They made him sick. Smiler used a lot of over-the-top bright colors, but he was a good artist with a sickening sense of the surreal and an equally disturbing knack for creating realistic faces and anatomy.

"Yes. They're very nice."

"Do you want to help me create some?" Smiler asked, a hint of childish excitement back in his voice.

Malcolm turned to the paper and the pens with relief. He wasn't much of an artist, but he was happy to do anything to keep the big man happy. "Okay, I don't see why—" He looked back at Smiler and swallowed his words. He had produced a flick knife and was pointing it at Malcolm.

"Shit." Malcolm rasped.

Smiler advanced. "You can be my muse."

* * *

He didn't know how long he had been out, if those images and those feelings were a dream from a micro-sleep, a nightmare from a deep sleep or the reality behind his closed eyes, but when Darren finally peeled open his eyes, he craved to return to the abyss. He was still in the same room, the dim light above and his distorted vision provided a fading, obscured view of the evil that stood in front of him, holding his hands to his hips and leering at him.

Darren twitched upon seeing him, an involuntary and primal reaction of disgust. He remembered the way he felt when he was on top of him. He could still smell his sickly scent that had, moments or hours earlier, been pressed against him. He fought to move, to retrieve his hands from behind his back, but they had been tied and they wouldn't budge. Every movement caused the rope to dig further into his skin.

"What do you want?" Darren managed to emit a sound that seemed to grate out of his chest before falling limply out of his lips. He coughed, cleared his throat and then repeated himself with equal timidity.

The man in front of him didn't say anything.

He was wearing pajamas, innocent and childish prints of cartoon characters that would have looked fitting on a five-year-old being read a bedtime story, not on a madman covered in blood and holding a beaten teenager hostage.

He snickered, an abrupt noise that began and ended in an instant. It was excitement, pure childish glee.

"What do you want?" Darren asked again.

The man in the cartoon pajamas didn't answer, he remained standing in front of him, leering over him. Darren couldn't see his face, it was too blurred, too hazy, but he knew that the man was smiling, knew that he probably wore a grin that stretched from ear to ear. He lifted his head to stare at him for a while, waiting for his vision to clear and the face to focus, but eventually his throbbing head tired and he lowered his chin to his chest.

He stared at his own torso and legs. Like the man before him, he hadn't been secured to the chair by the torso or legs, they were free to move, to twitch, and to squirm, only his hands had been tied, but he was too beaten and too unsure on his feet to think about fighting the restraints.

He moved his legs, stretched them outwards to test his strength and his reflexes. He withdrew them when he saw what lay just a few feet away. He had assumed that he was in a different chair, sitting alongside the man whose throat had been slit, the man who had gurgled and warbled a series of unheeded warnings, but that man was lying in a heap on the floor behind of the man in the cartoon pajamas.

Darren realized that he was sitting on the same chair, that the wet patch underneath his backside, a patch he had suspected was his own urine, spent through fear, agony, or unconsciousness, was actually blood. His vision was clearing, as if the realization was forcing his brain and his eyes to synchronize once again. He raised his head, ignored the pain in his neck and at the back of his skull.

He saw his attacker's face; saw the grin which did, as suspected, stretch from ear to ear. Darren realized that it was his turn. He was going to suffer the same fate as the lifeless, bloodless body that lay crumpled on the floor.

* * *

Malcolm waited for Smiler to attack before he made his move. He wasn't much of a fighter, he used his experience and intelligence to avoid fights, but he'd had a few scuffles and knew how to handle himself. Despite a few close shaves with weapons and one kid who attacked him with a baseball bat, no one had ever attacked him with a knife.

As well as being armed, Smiler was bigger than him and considerably stronger, but Malcolm didn't get disillusioned and didn't drop his guard. He waited until Smiler was within touching distance and then he diverted his attention just past his arm, towards the door. He allowed his face to look shocked, his expression to crease in confusion.

Smiler followed his gaze and turned around. He was big and armed, but he was simple and naive. When his head turned, Malcolm kicked out, connecting his knee with Smiler's groin, grimacing under the contact and the sound that his knee cap made as it crushed Smiler's genitalia up against his pelvis.

Smiler squealed and dropped the knife. He pressed his hands to his groin but he remained standing and Malcolm could see the mischief fading from his eyes, being replaced by anger.

Still gasping from the pain, emitting faint squeaking noises, he lashed out with the palm of his hand. Malcolm wasn't expecting it and the swipe caught him in the side of the face, slapping against his cheek and knocking him over. He collapsed against the toilet and felt his knee buckle.

"You shouldn't have done that," Smiler announced, cupping his testicles and advancing on Malcolm who was trying to rise to his feet.

Smiler reached down and grabbed Malcolm by the hair, lifting him up by the locks. Malcolm felt like the top of his head was peeling away; he yelped and thrashed, his wild punches made contact with flesh but it felt like he was hitting a brick wall.

As Smiler continued to hold him by the hair, Malcolm felt an intolerable anger rising in him. He felt the desire to rip out Smiler's throat and to vanquish that cheeky grin from his face forever. He let the anger boil so much that he couldn't hear Smiler's taunts, couldn't see him as he bent over and picked up the knife with his free hand. The anger was so high that he didn't even feel it when the knife pressed against his cheek and sliced open a small, warning wound.

He put all his might into one punch, catching Smiler on the wrist and forcing him to drop him, to release his grasp on his hair. He kicked him in the shins and then hit him once, twice, three times in the chest, still feeling the resistance but continuing until his hands ached, until he felt his knuckles displace and his fingers bleed. He pummeled the big man backwards. Smiler dropped the knife and sank to a stumbling, hunched fetal position as Malcolm continued to rain blows down on him.

He was nearly frothing at the mouth, muttering obscenities as his bleeding hands beat the life out of the big man. Smiler was groaning, nearly crying, but Malcolm continued.

Through the haze of his own rage, he saw that Smiler, crouched beneath him, was beaten. His face was battered and bruised, his mouth a mess of broken teeth and split gums. He turned away, picked up the knife, and then stood over Smiler.

Smiler looked up at Malcom with pleading eyes that bulged out of their sockets, already swelling beyond comprehension. He didn't say anything; even if he wanted to, he probably didn't possess the ability to. Malcolm aimed the knife at his throat; saw the fear and the helplessness in Smiler's eyes. He pressed the knife into Smiler's throat without breaking skin, testing his target, taking aim, then he pulled back and prepared to drive the knife deep into Smiler's throat.

He stopped midway. He was still frothing, still fuming; his body was still on fire and he still wanted Smiler dead, but something stopped him. Malcom locked eyes with Smiler, saw a look of pity and fear where there was evil before.

He shook his head and threw the knife angrily to the floor. He felt the rage subside, felt his vision dim, felt the redness fade. He put his hands to his head, pressed his temples as if squeezing away a migraine. He held them there, staring at Smiler through a gap in his fingers.

He wasn't a killer, no matter how messed up Smiler was, he didn't deserve to die. No one did. He knew that, yet he had been ready—

He shook his head again and released his hands with a guttural moan. He thrust his finger at Smiler, began to threaten him, to warn him not to move, not to leave his cell and not to follow him. But there was no need, he was barely conscious and certainly in no shape to follow him.

Malcolm picked up the knife, closed the blade into the handle, slipped it in his pocket, left the cell, and shut the door behind him.

* * *

"Please, don't do this."

Darren felt anger and fear well up inside of him. He wanted to scream, to fight, to break down and cry. In reality, he couldn't do any of those things and could only submit to the will of the psychopath in the cartoon pajamas.

"What is it you want?" he begged to know.

Cartoon Pajamas took his eyes off Darren, looked at the crumpled man on the floor and back again. He looked like he was ready to say something, but he stopped and aimed an ear towards the door.

Darren mistook the noise for the sound of his own pounding heart at first, but then he realized that the *thump-thump-thump*, that seemed to vibrate through the walls and floor, was actually the sound of hastily approaching footsteps. He thought of the man that had been chasing him, the one that had disappeared and left him to the fate of the psychopath currently standing idle in front of him, but it was two people who emerged in the open doorway, both looking flustered.

They were wearing white, one of them was covered from head to toe in blood, the other had a face like a drowned rat and didn't look too pleased.

"Where are they?" Rat Face asked.

Cartoon Pajamas looked annoyed. "Go away!" he snapped. "This one is mine."

"Where's the other one?" he persisted. "The black one."

Darren felt his heart jump, they were talking about Malcolm. He feared for his friend's safety at first, then he realized that if they were still looking for him that meant that Malcolm had escaped. The thought made him smile, a smile that was noticed by the two men in the doorway.

Rat Face stepped forward. "What the fuck are you smiling at?"

Darren didn't reply, his smile didn't fade.

"You got a problem? You think this is funny?"

Darren felt like saying he didn't even know what *this* was, so there was little chance he would ever find it funny, but he didn't say a word. Cartoon Pajamas looked annoyed at the intrusion and stepped in front of Rat Face, he held up his hand, stopping him from going any further.

"He's laughing at me," Rat Face accused, throwing his evil stare at Darren over Cartoon Pajamas's shoulder.

"He's mine."

"But—"

"Mine!"

The sound of the venomous voice shifted the smile from Darren's face. The man in the doorway took a step back. "Come on," he said to his friend. "Let's go." He moved into the corridor, his steps trailing off loudly and slowly, but Rat Face remained, facing off against his new-found nemesis.

Darren bit his lip and waited for the fists to fly.

23

Eddie kicked the body in front of him and delighted in the dull thump that his foot made against flesh. He picked up the knife that the little man had been carrying. It was a boot knife with a sturdy black handle and a dull black blade. Its edges were worn and stained with dried and crusted blood. He turned it over in his hands, wondered if he was holding the knife that had killed the security guard.

He saw movement in the corner of his eye and looked up towards the doorway, anticipating another encounter and another fight. The room in which he stood was brightly lit by a light that emitted a constant buzzing noise, sounding like tinnitus in Eddie's ear; the hallway outside was pitch black; no light escaped the room because something was standing in its way.

It moved as soon as Eddie caught it in his gaze, too quick for him to realize who or what it was. It bolted down the corridor, out of sight, allowing the light to spill out from the room and splash into the corridor.

Eddie edged forward, creeping slowly towards the door with the knife gripped tightly in his hands. He stopped inches before the threshold and held his ear to the open door. He heard nothing but the incessant hum of the light above, a buzzing that seemed to grow in volume the longer he listened to it.

He took another step, composed himself and dipped his head forward, turning to look out of the door and down the corridor where the shape had vanished. It was dark down there, lit only by the secondhand light from the room in which he stood, but he could see something shifting around in the blackness, something that seemed to swim inside the darkness.

"You want a fucking go as well?" Eddie asked, stepping out of the room and holding his head and his chin high. "Did you see what I did to your friend?"

The shape didn't move, it seemed to stare at Eddie, testing him and trying to intimidate him.

"Come on!" Eddie punched his chest with his free hand, keeping the knife hidden behind the wrist of his other hand. "Let's see what you've got."

The figure moved again, turning out of sight.

Eddie gritted his teeth and allowed the knife to be exposed. "Fucking prick." He walked quickly forward, darting into the darkness in search of his next target.

* * *

A wailing sound stopped Malcolm in his tracks. It was dark in the corridor, it felt cold and hollow. The sound was a cross between a laugh and a cry; a horrifying, warbling screech that traveled through the cold corridor, echoed off the walls, and dissipated into the darkness.

He felt a tide of goosebumps rise on his flesh, felt his muscles freeze under the rigid embrace of fear.

The noise sounded again, echoing louder than before. It sounded closer, stronger.

A small window, the glass thick and unbreakable, allowed for a square of moonlight to break into the corridor and aid Malcolm's vision. He could see the outline of a pair of double doors further ahead, but there were no other escape routes and the noise that filtered down the corridor, creeping towards him like a threatening rush of wind, seemed to be getting closer.

A light snapped on somewhere along the labyrinth of corridors, Malcolm saw the orange splash spill into the hallway, filling it with a warm glow. He looked to the door and wondered if he should go through, and then back to the end of the corridor, now partially lit from elsewhere.

He heard heavy and quick footsteps that echoed thickly through the hallway. The noise continued, it sounded eager, desperate, and it wasn't too far away.

Thud. Thud. Thud.

He shot a glance over his shoulder. He knew he could go back the way he came, but he didn't want to run into Smiler again. There was a good chance the big idiot had gone to find his friends, a good chance they were questioning him right now. Malcolm didn't want to stumble upon them.

Thud. Thud. Thud.

The feet echoed loudly. The laughter increased. Malcolm could almost sense the change in the atmosphere; a feeling that his air, his space, was now being shared with someone else. Whoever it was, Malcolm pondered, they sounded big, heavy; they sounded desperate and out of their fucking mind.

He didn't want to face them. He had been lucky with Smiler; he wasn't confident he could get lucky again.

He forced his limbs into action and threw them forward one quick step at a time. He made it to the door just as the echoes of footsteps reached their peak. Whoever it was, they were just around the corner, seconds from seeing him.

He closed his eyes, prayed for the best and then opened the door and entered. When he opened his eyes, he didn't see another Smiler, didn't see another huge idiot waiting for him with a simpleton smile and nefarious intentions.

What he saw was much worse than that.

* * *

There was a tense face-off when Darren's two captors locked stares and tried to intimidate each other, a moment where nothing and everything was said in the blink of an eye. Darren watched indifferently, hoping for fists to fly, hoping for violence, but not sure that it would matter to him either way.

Rat Face looked the angrier, the aggressive one who was quick to attack, quick to fly off the handle, but Cartoon Pajamas had a dark side, an ominous air about him that suggested he could do a lot more damage.

Darren eyed them up like a spectator would watch two boxers at a weigh-in. He was petrified, facing his own mortality and possible hours of torture, yet he couldn't help but be an interested spectator to what was going on in front of him.

As he anticipated, Rat Face threw the first punch. In one hot and intense moment, the scene exploded from one of restrained rage and intimidation, to one of full blown violence.

Darren watched, winced, and wished; hoping that, somehow, they would both perish.

* * *

Malcolm noticed the smell before anything else, it was hard to miss. It hit him when he opened the door and strangled the breath out of his lungs when he slipped into the room. It was the stench of blood, decay, and human waste; it was the stench of death.

The room had once been a recreational room, big enough for a couple of dozen people to gather and sit on the mismatched sofas and chairs and watch television, listen to the radio or play board games. The room was probably full of people on any given day, relaxing, conversing, and killing time. It was full of people today as well, and these ones had an eternity to kill.

Two lay slumped over the table. They had been sitting down playing cards when their throats had been slit. Another lay on the floor, it looked like she had put up a struggle and been beaten for her troubles. Her skull was caved in, her hair, coated in dried blood, lay at all angles around her sunken head like some thick, scarlet spider.

Three people lay strewn on the floor, involved in a brutal and bloody fight they had lost. Their blood lay in cursive splashes across the floor and the furniture, one of them had been garroted, their internal organs scattered over their body; another's face had been mutilated beyond recognition and Malcolm thought he saw their lips and sections of their cheek lying a few feet away.

He raised a fist to his mouth to stifle a wave of vomit that threatened to unleash itself.

In the corner a black leather sofa and a tattered gray sofa sat around an old television set that had seen better days. The television was on, but it emitted no sound and offered nothing more than a constant wave of static which swam over the washed-out screen in hypnotizing, pixelated waves. A woman sat on the leather sofa with her eyes on the screen, seemingly fascinated by the constant wash of black and white. She was as white as a ghost; whatever life had once been inside her was now long gone.

Malcolm paused when he heard a noise on the other side of the door. The footsteps had slowed, the laughing had stopped, the source of both was now standing on the other side of the door.

He held his breath, prayed that his heart would stop beating in case the madman heard the heavy, chaotic thumps as it strained to free itself from his chest.

He thought he heard breathing, the madman's face close to the door, perhaps trying to pick up the sound of Malcolm's beating heart.

His body was screaming at him to run, to step over the mess of blood on the floor, to weave through the corpses and to pick up one of the chairs. It didn't matter if he made a noise, didn't matter if the person on the other side of the door could hear, because he had already heard, he already knew that Malcolm was in there. Malcolm forced himself to move, to use the chair as a weapon against whatever came through the door, but something held him back, something stopped him.

When the laughter sounded again, this time inches away from him, he felt his whole body spasm as every muscle contracted in shock like a myoclonic jerk.

Footsteps followed the laughter and this time the footsteps were moving away from him.

Malcolm breathed a little easier when they faded. Then he heard a voice inside the room—a grating, gravely whisper—and his fear returned.

"*Who are you*?"

24

He followed the voice down a flickering hallway, where the remnants of light spat staccato bursts, lighting temporary halos on the floor that Eddie passed through. He didn't see its shape. He didn't see its face. It seemed to be in tune with the darkness, walking through only when it was pitch black, as if it knew when the lights would flicker.

It turned another corner, passed through a door at the back of the room and entered a small staircase. Eddie followed it all the way, his footsteps steady, not wanting to race and attack in case that was just what it was waiting for.

The staircase was cold but it was brighter there. The stairs didn't go down, just up on a spiraling, narrow path. Small bulbs, encased in cylindrical plastic fixtures and rooted to the ceiling, lit the gray walls and strangely moist concrete steps.

He gripped the knife harder, ascended the first flight of stairs and then stopped. His feet made heavy echoes with every footfall, and the stairs seemed to go on and on, right to the upper echelons of the building, probably into an attic space. Yet he couldn't hear the footsteps of the man who had gone before him, nor had he heard them when he entered, when the thing that he chased should have been beginning its ascent.

He strained to hear anything in the silence. He didn't hear footsteps, but he did hear breathing. It was weak, as weak as the lights that illuminated him from above, but it was audible. It was a slow breath, one that wheezed on its culmination; a high-pitched, extended whistle that faded before the next exhalation began.

He took two more steps, strained his head to see upwards, towards the next flight that awaited him around the corner. He couldn't see anyone there, but the noise continued.

An inhalation. A whistle. An exhalation.

He reached the landing, turned towards the next flight and strained to see higher. There were at least two more flights. He didn't know where they were taking him, but he was confident of facing whatever awaited him. He gripped the railing and pulled his hand away in surprise when he touched ice cold metal.

The noise continued. The struggling breath sucked, squeezed, and released before repeating.

Eddie climbed upwards, taking each step one at a time, keeping the knife tight in his fist, so tight that it turned his flesh white.

He climbed the steps slowly, made it to the next landing and then stopped, holding the knife out before him, ready to attack.

A figure sat slumped in the corner, slouched in the shadows provided by the base of the bannister. It continued to breathe; its lungs continued to fight through the motion, continued to whistle as it inhaled.

"You!" Eddie said. "What are you?"

It said something that he couldn't understand. Its voice was weak and fading by the second.

"Why have you been running from me, what are you hiding?"

It grated and hissed a few words, its voice strangled.

"Are you hiding here, waiting for me?" Eddie wanted to know.

It said something in reply but none of the words made it through to him.

"What are you?" he asked.

Eddie leant forward for a closer look. It was a man, probably in his thirties. He was injured and he looked tired. No doubt from the running, Eddie reasoned. He saw a darkness in his eyes, an evil that lurked behind the white and speckled red. He was grinning sadistically, his lips curled into a sinister smile. He was mocking him, laughing at him.

"What's so fucking funny?" Eddie said.

"You," he said with a short laugh, his voice now steady and able. "Standing there with the knife, all paranoid and shit. You look a right fucking picture."

"What do you mean?"

"You fit the profile," he explained, dragging himself to his feet, sniggering as Eddie took a step backwards.

"Profile? What profile?" Eddie asked.

He laughed, a deep laugh that stirred up something hateful in Eddie.

"The sad, little paranoid ginger boy with no friends and—"

"I *have* friends."

"Really?" he moved towards him, he looked unsteady on his feet but his eyes and his face suggested he knew what he was doing. He was grinning, leering. "Where are they?"

Eddie didn't reply. He looked around as if to search for his lost friends.

"Exactly." He laughed. He reached out with a trembling hand, tried to rest to on Eddie's shoulder, but he batted it away. "They left you. They don't like you. No one likes a ginger."

Eddie's eyes flared. He stepped forward and shoved him back with all his strength. He toppled over and fell backwards onto the railing, the back of his skull clattering the cold, metal banister before bouncing to the floor. He didn't move and there was a good chance the impact had killed him, but Eddie didn't contemplate that possibility, nor did he care. He was fuming, his eyes seeing only what his anger wanted them to see. He jumped on him, pinned his body to the floor. He then drove the knife into his chest.

Eddie relished in the sound it made as it cut through skin, crushed bone, and penetrated muscle and organs. He pulled it out, wiped a tear of perspiration from his forehead and a spot of spittle from his mouth.

Then he stabbed him again, and again. He didn't stop until his anger was satisfied, by which time a pool of blood had formed underneath the body and was dripping down the cold staircase, turning it from a drab gray into a deep red.

* * *

Malcolm didn't know where the voice was coming from, but his attentions turned to the ravaged corpses. To each of the mutilated men and women that lay scattered around the room like the off-cuts at an abattoir. None of them were capable of talking; none of them were capable of breathing. They were all dead and judging by the smell, they had been dead for hours.

He looked at the woman in the corner, the one sitting in front of television. She was staring at him when he turned to her, her eyes wide open and waiting for him. He was sure she hadn't been looking at him before.

He thought about asking a question, asking if she had spoken to him, but he was still convinced she was dead.

Then she spoke again. He saw her lips move softly, saw the thin slits of near-purple open and close to repeat her barely audible words.

"*Who are you?*"

"I—I." He hesitated and shook his head, not believing what he was seeing.

Her head moved, a low and painful twitch. She seemed to smile, as if enjoying the horror on his face. "You look like you've seen a ghost," she said, cracking a pained smile.

Malcolm nodded. She was wearing a blue tabard. Her name on a small plate stitched in the upper right corner above her breast, which seemed to fold over her body as she leaned forward in the chair. She looked like she was preparing to whisper something to him despite him being on the other side of the room. She said something, but she lost her voice halfway through and he didn't hear anything. He edged forward, careful where he trod.

She didn't look a day over thirty, although it was hard to tell through her pallid skin, blue lips, and the gaunt look of death that had been etched across her face. She was smiling, it was a strange smile, a smile of agony, of acceptance; a smile from someone who has been through hell and has nothing left to fear.

She spoke again but he still didn't hear. She leaned back; her movements were so slow and painful that he thought the movement would finish her off. He moved to within two feet of her and stopped, he didn't want to go any further.

"Can I help you?" he asked, already knowing the answer and praying that she did too.

She shook her head, a movement that seemed to take the better part of a minute.

"*What are you doing here*?" she croaked, straining to look him in the eye, the curious smile still on her face.

"I came here to rob the place," he told her.

She laughed and then silenced herself quickly, grimacing and sucking in a fast breath.

"*How's that going for you*?"

"Not very well."

She nodded.

"What is this place?" he asked, glancing around, noting something disturbing lying by her feet. He had seen it before and couldn't quite believe it then. Now he was close enough to see it in detail and he knew that the image and this conversation would be forever burned into his memory.

She looked into his eyes, allowed the smile to slowly fade from her face.

"*You . . . don't know*?" she spoke slower, softer than before.

He crept forward, still keen to keep his distance. He didn't want to go near her, didn't want to edge too close to what lay at her feet. He shook his head.

"Psy . . . chia . . . tric Hos . . . pit . . . al," she staggered.

He nodded, half to himself. He had already guessed as much—the patients, the staff, the clothes, the rooms. It certainly looked nothing like the plush drug rehabilitation center they had been expecting.

"But, what's going on? Who did all this?" he looked around, gesturing to the mess of dead bodies. "Are these all staff?"

She shook her head slowly. *"Not . . . all. Most."*

"Have they gone nuts . . ." he paused and corrected himself. "Why are they doing this? What's wrong with them?"

"Not their fault . . . he did this." She coughed, a feeble, weak, wet cough. *"We never . . . had . . . a chance."*

"Who's he?" Malcolm asked. "Who did this?"

She looked into his eyes again. The smile had now completely gone from her face and was replaced with a look of contentment, a look of nothingness. He waited for her to answer, waited to hear her staggered voice again.

She didn't say anything.

He thought about checking her pulse, seeing if she was dead or if he could help her, but he knew in his heart that even if she wasn't dead, there was nothing he could do to help her.

He gave her corpse a sympathetic, pitying look and then he turned away, hoping to erase her image from his mind, to forget about the softly spoken woman with the gaping wound in her stomach. He wanted to forget because he knew why they had mutilated her that way, he knew why they had hacked open her abdomen and dug out the insides, and he knew that the fleshy, bloody mass that lay on the floor at her feet, wasn't one of her organs or part of her flesh, it was something that had been part of her for several months, something that would have been part of the rest of her life but now wouldn't see the light of day.

He struggled to fight his emotions, to hide his heartbreak and anger. He didn't know what would possess someone to do something so vile, but he knew that he wanted them to suffer as much as they had made her suffer.

25

Darren cringed when the first punch was thrown, when the sound of fist meeting flesh and bone sucked a hole in the air and sent a shockwave through the room.

The man in the cartoon pajamas rocked backwards, raising his hands to his face. He held his balance and stopped himself from falling over, but he was disoriented. Rat Face moved forward after throwing the punch, after breaking the silent staring contest that had seemed to go on forever. When Cartoon Pajamas stumbled under the impact of his knuckles, the rat-faced man hit him with a succession of quick jabs and then put all of his effort—twisting his body and throwing his back—into a right hook.

Through hazy vision and a struggling disbelief that the fight had started and he was already on the losing side, Cartoon Pajamas managed to anticipate the slow and heavy punch enough to duck out of the way. The fist glanced him on the nose, the knuckles grazing the fleshy nib, but the full force of the punch missed him. The wild punch caused Rat Face to lose his balance, to stumble forward, following through on his own attack, at which point Cartoon Pajamas sensed his opportunity and tackled his adversary to the ground.

They hit with force, Rat Face's upper back hit the floor first and took the strain of two brawling bodies against one hard floor.

He grunted, lost his breath, his voice, and his advantage in one fell swoop. Cartoon Pajamas kneed, punched, grappled, clawed, and kicked like an angry dog, staying tight on top of his foe and doing his best to keep his aggressor's limbs from returning any of attacks.

Darren grimaced, hearing the punches and the kicks, almost feeling the sharp knee that Cartoon Pajamas drove into Rat Face's groin, an attack that caused him to emit a high pitched squeal.

"I'm gonna fucking kill you!" Cartoon Pajamas said, frothing at the mouth, struggling to control his stamina as his movements slowed and softened. Rat Face took everything that was thrown at him and looked like he had taken all he could take. He was protecting his face with his arms and his hands but his rodent-features had still suffered several blows and severe swelling, with cuts on his lips, his nose, and across his cheek.

"He's mine!" Cartoon Pajamas hissed breathlessly. "I told you to—"

He stopped. He was in the process of throwing a punch towards his adversary's protected face, when he heard a noise that attracted his attention. He paused, his hand hovering in the air.

Rat Face slowly peeled his hands from his face, looked first to the fist above him and then toward the doorway.

Darren hadn't heard it at first; he had been too caught up in the fight, in the sights of violence and the huffing, puffing, squealing, humping sounds that accompanied it. He heard it now though. He heard the footsteps, heavy, bouncing footsteps, as if someone was running, taking great leaping strides. He also heard the laughing; a stuttering, bone chilling laugh, not quite despair, not quite happiness, something much more sinister and much more complex.

The noise increased. With every footfall that echoed thickly through the corridor and into the room, the laughing grew in volume and intensity.

Darren wondered who else was going to join the violence, who else was willing to fight so they could torture and kill him. He didn't like the look of Rat Face, didn't like that fact that he was so quick to anger and seemed to take an instant and deep dislike to him; he also didn't like what Cartoon Pajamas had done to the last guy who had been in the chair where he now found himself, nor did he like the sinister look in his eyes, but, as he listened to the quickening footsteps and the loud, sickening laughter getting closer and closer, he expected that he would like the new guy even less.

"It's him," Rat Face said, sounding scared, his voice breaking. A small bubble of blood ballooned when he spoke and popped when he closed his mouth.

Cartoon Pajamas nodded and looked around, horrified.

"We've disobeyed him," Rat Face said. "He's set his fucking lap dog on us, he's going to—"

"Fuck off!" Cartoon Pajamas said, finishing the punch he had been threatening for the last few seconds. He stood up quickly, looked from Rat Face to the door and then back again.

Darren also turned to look at the door, just as a behemoth of a man skidded to a halt in the doorway. He looked just an inch or two shy of seven-feet tall. He had a tire of fat wrapped around his waist, his cheeks filled like the pouches of a hungry hamster—but that fat concealed a lot of muscle and he was as broad and as strong as he was tall. He had a short crop of hair that had been gelled to a point at the front, and a simple but bright smile that spoke of gleefulness, idiocy, and outright insanity.

He was wearing a white coat, the sort worn by doctors, but underneath he seemed to be wearing striped pajamas.

"I'm sorry," Cartoon Pajamas said, stepping slowly away from the big man in the doorway. "What are you—"

"He isn't yours," the newcomer said. His voice wasn't the booming, powerful voice that Darren had expected; it was soft, timid, almost a squeak, and it culminated with a giggle.

Darren wondered just what the hell was going on, who the man in the doorway was and why the others seemed so afraid of him when he looked like he wouldn't hurt a fly.

"I'm just having a little—" Cartoon Pajamas tried to speak, to defend himself and his actions, but the big idiot in the doorway interrupted him again.

"This is wrong. The doctor told you to leave him alone."

"I know but—"

"The doctor said to leave him alone," he repeated, his voice still timid, still weak and pitiful, yet Carton Pajamas seemed to be scared of it. He looked like he was trembling and Darren noticed him glancing around, looking for an escape route or a weapon. Rat Face was still on the floor in a daze. He made no attempt to get up, perhaps thinking that if he lay still and silent, he wouldn't be seen.

Cartoon Pajamas charged at the big man. The action was quick and unexpected. He didn't make a noise as he ran, didn't announce his intentions with a war cry or even an alteration in his breath, he just sprang from his standing position, head down, and charged straight at the behemoth in the doorway. He had a knife in his hand, Darren hadn't seen him pick it up, hadn't seen him retrieve it. He held it forward like a phalanx, hoping to puncture his foe, but the small knife looked feeble against such a mountain of a man.

The big man knocked the knife away with a brush of his hand, swatting a fly. He took the tackle without a change in his expression. His torso sucked inwards under the impact and he moved backwards an inch or two as Cartoon Pajamas pushed with all his might to clear some room and to give himself the same advantage he had enjoyed over Rat Face. But he was tired and he was much weaker than the big man.

The behemoth put his hands on Cartoon Pajamas' neck and pushed down. He fell straight to the floor, face-first. Darren heard the crunch as teeth chipped and bone broke, he heard the groan, and watched as Cartoon Pajamas tried to lift his face from the floor, right before the behemoth planted a firm foot on the back of his head and held him there, keeping his face against the cold, hard floor.

Darren watched the big man's face and never saw his expression change. He was looking at Rat Face now, who was still trying to look inconspicuous on the floor. He studied him as he forced his weight onto his foot, crushing Cartoon Pajamas' skull between the heel of his boot and the hard floor.

Darren sucked in a lungful of air, felt every last hint of warmth leave his body and the hairs on the back of his neck stand on end. Cartoon Pajamas stopped squirming, stopped moaning; a pool of blood began to spread out from around his head. Darren felt sick, he turned his head away; there was already one dead man in the room, already one sickening image he didn't want to see.

He watched the behemoth walk calmly over to Rat Face. Rat Face immediately realized he had been seen and that his poor attempt at playing injured hadn't worked. He tried to reason with the behemoth, as Cartoon Pajamas had done, but he wasn't interested. He picked Rat Face up by the hair, as if plucking up a kitten by the scruff of the neck. He planted him on the ground and wrapped an arm around his neck and face. Rat Face continued to moan, to beg for his life, but the behemoth wasn't listening and, in one quick movement that ushered a sickening echo and made Darren gag, he snapped Rat Face's neck.

* * *

Malcolm inched the door open and poked his head through the gap. He was angry at what the inmates had done to the pregnant woman, angry at what they had done to so many others inside the hospital; he wanted to make them pay, but storming outside and running into one of them wouldn't be a wise decision. He knew that the best hope he had was to make it out of the hospital alive, then he could call the police and let them deal with the mess. There was a chance that people were still alive inside the building, if he could make it out and call for help, then he could save their lives.

There was a phone inside the room, an ancient device stuck to the wall. He had tried to phone for help, praying that he could get through to someone, but the line was dead. He wasn't surprised and doubted he had been the first one to try. The inmates had probably cut the phone early on, when the mayhem and the murdering started. He had checked his own phone again, a desperate and pointless act. He still hadn't been able to get a signal.

He held his breath as he looked up and down the corridors. He half expected the laughing man with the loud footsteps to be waiting for him; waiting to do to him what he had probably done to so many others, but there was no one there. He released his breath slowly and stepped outside, careful to shut the door behind him.

As much as he needed to escape and find help, he knew that he couldn't do it alone. He needed to find his friends, make sure they were okay. The three of them had been together all of their lives, they fought and they bickered, especially Eddie and Darren, but they were like brothers and they had been that way for as long as they could remember. That friendship, that kinship, that *closeness*, was what told Malcolm that something wasn't right. He had a feeling that they were in trouble. He didn't believe in telepathy or a sixth sense, but he had known Eddie and Darren a long time, long enough to know how they would be reacting right now; that knowledge and that experience was what told him that one of them was in trouble and needed his help.

* * *

Darren knew that his end was near. The man with the unchanging expression, timid voice, and gigantic frame, didn't mess around. He had killed two people and he hadn't broken a sweat doing it. The man had mentioned a doctor, but the way he spoke, in an almost robotic way, and the way the others acted around him, told Darren that he was the one to fear, he was the one in control.

Whether the doctor was real, an aspect of his delusion, or simply him talking in third-person Darren didn't know, nor did he care. The only thing that concerned him was that several vicious, blood-thirsty psychopaths had just fought over who would have the pleasure of killing him, and that pleasure had seemingly fallen to the biggest, strongest, and sickest of them all.

Darren dropped his head into his chest and waited for his life to end. He thought about everything that he was giving up. He thought about his mother, he thought about Ian, he thought about the fact that he didn't have a job, hadn't achieved anything at school, and didn't even have a home to go back to. That made him feel better about losing it all, but then he thought about his future. He was still young; he still had so many opportunities ahead of him, so many different paths that his life could take. He could be anything he wanted to be, if only he *wanted* to be anything.

In his final moments, he hated himself for wasting his life. He hated himself for living a life of crime, a life of delinquency, drugs, and burglary. He had been throwing away his youth and this is where it had led him: being murdered in a dark room in a psychotic clinic by some psychopathic idiot.

He also thought about his friends. He thought about Malcolm and wondered if he had made it out alive, if he would be able to make it somewhere safe and call for help. It would be too late for Darren by then, but at least his corpse wouldn't be left to rot in this building. He also thought about Eddie, the hyperactive, aggressive liability whose idea it was to go to the clinic. He cursed under his breath, "*Fucking ginger idiot.*"

Then he felt big, strong hands around his back. He cringed and twitched when those hands, hands that had just killed two people, touched him. He squeezed his eyes shut even tighter and waited.

He felt the ties being released from his hand, felt a soft and reassuring hand tap his shoulder. He sensed the big man by his side, and walking away. Darren opened his eyes and saw the behemoth's broad back in the doorway, before he turned down the corridor and disappeared.

Confused, Darren looked himself up and down, making sure that he was alive and that he hadn't been brutally murdered.

"What the fuck?"

The other bodies were still strewn around him, the room was covered in blood and the scent of death, but Darren was alive and unharmed. The big man, the psychopathic giant, had saved his life.

He heard giggling in the hallway, growing fainter and fainter as its source moved away. The giggling then broke back into a hysterical laughter, a succession of footsteps followed, echoing faintly through the corridors and then, moments later, the noises faded completely. The behemoth was out of sight and out of earshot. And for whatever reason, Darren was still alive.

26

Eddie wiped the knife on the seat of his pants, wiping a smear of blood on the tattered denim. He stared at the handle, at the bright-eyed reflection that beamed back at him through a crimson stain. He had done well. Not only was he still alive, but he had taken a couple of the psychopaths out. He doubted that Darren would have acted the same way, doubted that his dimwitted friend would even still be alive. Not only was Darren a weak link, Eddie mused to himself, but he was a liability.

He stood at the top of the staircase, looking up and down, his eyes skimming over the dead body at his feet. The thought occurred to him that he should find his friends, but it didn't stay with him for long. Malcolm was tougher than Darren, but even he would struggle to stay alive in these conditions. He also thought about his phone, wondering if he could find a signal. He was nearer the top of the building now and might have better luck, but he quickly dismissed that thought as well. He had a job to do and he wasn't leaving until he did it. He was also just beginning to enjoy himself.

Eddie looked at the corpse and the knife again. He gave himself an agreeable nod. He was the toughest, the hardest, the most resilient of the friends. They had mocked him in the past because of his upbringing, said he was a privileged softie, but now he had showed them. It was just a shame that they wouldn't be alive to see the day when he became a hero. Although, he thought with a smile, there was still a good chance that Malcolm had used his initiative to escape and a good chance that Darren had avoided capture by hiding in a cupboard, pissing himself, crying for his mummy, and waiting for someone to rescue him.

Eddie took a step towards the flight of stairs and something out of the corner of his eye stopped him. He thought it a trick of periphery at first, but when he pulled his gaze to the staircase, he saw a figure dart out of the light and into the shadows.

"*You*!" he spat. "Stay there. Stop fucking running!"

He moved towards the stairs, back the way he came. He stumbled over the dead body, regained his balance, kicked the corpse angrily for getting in his way and then bolted down the stairs, taking them two at a time. He couldn't see the figure down the next flight, but he knew where it had gone, he knew there was only one route it could take. He cleared the stairs with one leap, feeling his knees and his shins judder painfully on landing, before bolting through the door at the bottom and stumbling into the hallway.

He didn't stop to concentrate on where he was or on what might be around him. The figure had darted around a corner again and he was intent on following it. He followed it down a dark corridor, lit by a buzzing light in the distance. He followed it under that light, through it and back into the black. He slowed his pace and kept the knife ready in his hand as he tracked through the darkness.

He heard laughing. A strange mocking laugh. He knew it was the thing he was chasing; he knew it was mocking his inability to catch it. He ground his teeth, cursed under his breath. The laughter increased, the thing wasn't running away from him, it was running toward him.

He stood still. A light flicked on in the distance, he heard it buzz, pop into life, and saw the splash of light. His darkness became brighter.

He heard fast and heavy footsteps pounding the floor, shaking the walls. The laughter was increasing, growing in volume. It annoyed him. He knew it was mocking him, knew it was trying to make him mad, but he didn't know why it seemed to be coming straight for him.

Another light snapped on, this one just around the corner. The hallway was lit now and Eddie could see a shadow at the end, cutting through the orange light and nearly blocking it out.

The laughter increased again, the footsteps continued. Then the man, the *thing*, emerged. It wasn't a shadow this time, it was fully illuminated and it was massive. Much bigger than Eddie had anticipated, much bigger than he was.

The Thing stopped when it saw Eddie. It had a curious face, a smiling yet thoughtful expression. Eddie hid the knife behind his back, wanting to retain the element of surprise. He doubted the flimsy knife would do anything to the big man but that wouldn't stop him from trying.

Eddie was the first to move and, when he did so, he was surprised to see that The Thing took a cautious step backwards, back around the corner. Eddie held up his hand and put on his soft, manipulative voice, one better suited for a child or an animal, which this thing seemed to be a cross between.

"Stay there," Eddie said softly. "I just want to know . . . Who are you?"

The Thing looked back down the corridor from which it came, then behind Eddie, into the darkness. Its eyes also moved to Eddie's arm, it knew he was carrying a knife, knew what his intentions were, yet it made no move to stop him, made no effort to run or to talk. Eddie advanced closer and closer, when he was just a couple of feet away he asked, "What are you doing here?"

The Thing took another step back, but Eddie jumped at it, exposing the knife and launching himself in one quick and deadly movement. With his free hand, he grabbed The Thing by its bulky shoulder and then, with his other hand, he brought the knife over in one big swing, aiming high, for its throat.

Eddie was grinning, practically salivating at the thought of bringing The Thing down, but that grin shifted when it grabbed his wrist and squeezed. Eddie yelped. He dropped the knife and watched it bounce to the floor.

He thought he was finished, he knew he was powerless to stop The Thing from doing what he wanted to do to him, but he intended to fight him to the death regardless of how quick that death would be.

To his surprise, he simply moved him out of the way, pressing him up against the wall. Eddie looked into his eyes as he did so, studied his smiling expression which hadn't changed throughout. Once he had pushed him there, The Thing turned back to the corridor and ran like a gleeful child, taking big strides and giggling to himself.

"What the fuck?" Eddie said.

Eddie moved to pick up the knife, then he saw the shape again. He paused and studied it. He realized he was no longer interested in chasing it, was no longer interested in what it was. It certainly wasn't the thing he had encountered on the stairs or the thing he had just bumped into. Whatever it was, it was quick, fleeting, and very interested in him. Eddie was just as interested in it, and in where it was taking him. It wasn't out to get him, it wasn't trying to kill him or drive him insane, it was trying to show him the way, Eddie realized. It had taken him to one that had lurked on the staircase, taken him to The Thing that had just escaped his clutches. This thing, this *shadow*, whatever it was, knew that Eddie was there to save the day, to be the hero, and it wanted to help him accomplish that task by showing him the evil that lurked within the building.

He picked up the knife, gave the shadow a nod and a smile and then took off after it. It turned the corridor just as he reached it, but he didn't slow his pace.

27

The body had been dead for hours. The eyes were glassy, staring at the wall opposite and the abyss beyond. Her eyes bulged out of her head; parts of her hair had been glued to her forehead with perspiration, some of it stuck to her neck, glued to the thick red welt that wrapped around her throat like a crimson necklace.

Malcolm crouched down for a better look. She looked like a patient. She was wearing a dressing gown with a black nightdress on underneath. The dress rode up her pale legs, exposing wisps of pubic hair. Her legs were open and splayed apart, but he didn't think she had been sexually assaulted. She had been killed, pinned against the wall, and strangled, but there was no motivation other than murder.

It didn't feel right to just leave her there, her half naked body on show, but he didn't know what else to do. He wasn't religious, he didn't think that praying could help her now and he didn't believe that any eternal part of her had moved on, but it still didn't feel right to just leave her like that.

He covered her up, straightened out her dress to cover as much of her exposed flesh as he could and wrapped her dressing gown around her to cover the rest. He didn't know if she had been as crazy as the other patients, there was a chance that she had even played a part in the grisly murders back in the television room, but in death, in the peaceful, empty oblivion of eternity, she looked innocent.

He found more death in the room opposite. It was a small kitchen, a cramped space with a series of cupboards running along the top, and a microwave, toaster, and coffee machine placed on a length of counter that ran underneath. The worktop and the cabinets were a sickly brown, an horrible color scheme that probably hadn't been changed for at least three decades and had never been in fashion. The chipped brown paint and stained countertop had now been decorated with splashes of red, and great streaks of blood that injected color onto the bland surfaces.

The coffee machine had been ripped from the wall and the toaster lay on its side. A cutlery drawer had been yanked open, and its contents were spilled all over the floor. Some of the knives from the drawer had clearly been used to murder the man that lay slumped up against the counter. His body was in a similar position to the woman, but he hadn't been strangled, he had been stabbed. The knives were still wedged in his chest, his stomach and in the side of his neck. There were other wounds around his body; the knives that had made them now lay in his lap or on the floor. He looked like a human pin cushion. Someone had taken the time—probably when he was dead or dying and in no fit state to retaliate—to stab him with a dozen different knives.

Malcolm imagined their gleeful face as they took knife after knife from the drawer to plunge into the dying man, grinning at the glistening silver weapons like a child on Halloween, indulging in as many sugary delights as they could get their hands on.

The dead man was sitting in a pool of his own blood and that blood had seeped outwards, inches away from Malcolm's feet. It had coated the cutlery on the floor; only a few pieces had avoided the crimson wash. Malcolm thought about taking one, adding to the one that he already carried, a backup in case he lost it, in case it was taken from him, but he doubted he could bring himself to use either of them anyway. The image of the dead man sickened him, the puncture wounds where the knife had entered made a deep part of him cringe and shiver. He couldn't imagine doing that to someone, couldn't imagine creating those wounds or turning something living and breathing; into the pale, bloodied mess that he saw before him.

He left the bloodbath in the kitchen, tried not to look at the dead woman in the corridor and continued onward. The lights were on, but the hospital was still. He heard the occasional noise, sudden abrupt bangs and creaks, but he didn't know if he was listening to distant footsteps, fighting or the groans of an old building. He tried not to think about it too much, tried not to let his imagination wander. He concentrated on the job at hand, on making it through the corridors, discovering what was going on and where his friends were hiding, whilst trying to stay out of sight of the psychopathic patients that roamed the halls. He had seen some of them dead already, but he knew that there were enough of them alive to give him problems; he just hoped that some of the staff were also alive. He wanted answers, he wanted an explanation, and he wanted an escape route.

* * *

Darren walked steadily, taking care with each step and trying to listen out as he did so. His blood was racing through his body and he felt dizzy and unstable. He had been able to hear The Behemoth's heavy, slapping footsteps, but as he left the room where he had nearly breathed his last breath, he couldn't hear beyond the dizzying sound of his own blood rushing inside his ears.

He didn't hear the approaching footsteps around the corner, didn't notice that someone was right in front of him until he turned the corner and they ran into him.

The impact knocked out what little air was left inside his lungs, accelerated his already pounding pulse and worsened his aching head. His world turned black, hazy, and then red and he thought he was going to lose consciousness again. He hit the ground hard, his back buckled under the impact, his elbows crunched, and his skull just missed a violent connection with the floor. He skidded several feet backwards, until he was pressed up against the wall, staring into the well-lit ceiling as his attacker rushed him.

His attacker had managed to remain upright through the impact and was quick to rebound, jumping on Darren and pinning him to the floor within seconds. He dug a knee into his groin and struck a fist against his ribs, making sure he remained on the floor, letting him know who was boss.

Darren managed to catch sight of his attacker's face and he thought he saw Eddie. He didn't believe what he was seeing at first and struggled to maintain his vision as the blows continued to rain down, but he knew that hair, he recognized those angry eyes and that snarling mouth.

"Stop!" he yelled, but Eddie wasn't listening and Darren was forced to cover his face to protect himself.

"Eddie! It's me—" His words were cut short as Eddie grabbed him by the throat and squeezed. Darren pulled his hands away from his face and used them to claw at Eddie's hand, to try to pry his fingers away, but his grip was firm. He looked into Eddie's eyes, wondered why he wasn't stopping, why he hadn't recognized him. Eddie wasn't even looking at him; his eyes were fixed on his own hands, on strangling the life out of Darren and on—

Darren's eyes bulged when he saw the knife in Eddie's free hand. He felt his body tense, felt every muscle awaken as his body prepared every reserve of energy it could find. Eddie was holding the knife above Darren's squirming body, aiming for his chest.

"*Eddie*!" He tried to yell, but his voice struggled to splutter out of his throat, along with his breath. He tried to wriggle free, to buck and to kick his friend off him, he even landed a few knees on Eddie's back, but Eddie didn't move. His eyes were set on Darren's throat and chest; his goal was clear and a few bumps and scrapes weren't going to stop him from achieving it.

Darren tried to punch Eddie's hand away, but as soon as he moved his hands from his throat, from attempting to pry away Eddie's crushing fingers from his larynx, Eddie squeezed tighter and Darren moved one step closer to the abyss. He kicked harder, squirmed more, but his efforts seemed futile and he could only watch, staring into his friend's eyes, and hope that he would realize and stop.

* * *

Malcolm watched the man scuttle along the floor like a rabid, vociferous feline. He was on his hands and knees, his clothes torn to asunder around him; his flesh looking like it had been picked apart by hungry vultures. Malcolm couldn't see his face. He couldn't see beyond his arched back—pointing in a painful arc towards the stuttering fluorescence above—or the back of his head, his long hair parted down the middle and seeped with blood and sweat.

He had followed him down the corridor after watching him slowly making his way out of a nearby cell. He hadn't seen Malcolm and seemed oblivious to everything around him as he slowly dragged his way down the corridor, a trail of blood following him like the sticky remains of a snail.

The man mumbled as he crawled. "Silly fucking tosser. Thinks he could get the better of me. Ha! Prick."

Malcolm was mildly amused by the madman on his hands and knees and walked slowly behind him, his curiosity getting the better of him. He didn't want to turn back and go the other way, nor did he want to enter one of the cells that flanked the corridor. He could have easily stepped over the crawling man and walked away. He was in no fit state to run after him. But Malcolm was intrigued, and a little disturbed, by the scurrying gremlin in front of him.

"I showed him. Fucking cunt. Gave him a piece of my mind."

Malcolm knew who he was referring to. After the man in front of him had crawled out of the cell, Malcolm had poked his head inside, carefully to peek around the corner to make sure that whoever was inside wouldn't see him. The man inside the room wouldn't have seen him if he had been standing in the doorway doing a jig. He was dead. His body had been ripped apart. His flesh had been peeled off his skin and thrown around the room; his face looked like it had been half-eaten by a dog that had sickened itself on the taste of flesh.

Malcolm had grown indifferent to the slaughter. Nothing he saw shocked him after what he had seen in the television room, nothing could haunt his nightmares like that image would. It sickened him, the scent of fresh death and the sight of torn flesh disturbed him, but he blocked it out. To save his sanity.

Taking one step at a time, he kept pace with the mumbling man. He was living his last, the trail of blood behind him was getting thicker, his breath was getting heavier and his words more incoherent. Malcolm felt an urge to help him, an altruistic urge that resided deep down and indicated that the thing in front of him was still human and still needed saving. He did his best to ignore that urge, concentrating on the atrocities back in the cell, on the massacre in the television room, and on telling himself that the thing in front of him wasn't human. The thing in front of him wasn't even an animal; animals killed for food and necessity, this man, this *thing*, killed for pleasure. He killed because something in his mind told him it was fun.

Malcolm had once dealt with a rabid dog at the animal shelter. It had bitten its owner and mutilated their cat before making light work of a couple of hamsters and then going for their child, scarring it for life. It would have killed the toddler if a brave and horrified neighbor hadn't tackled it to the ground. The dog had been in the family for years; it was as much a part of the family as the child that it attacked. Then, one day, seemingly without reason, something inside its brain snapped and it went on a rampage. They still loved it, still thought of it as one of their children, and so they took it to the shelter, begging that something be done to rehabilitate it, to look after it. "He's a good dog really," the tearful owner had insisted. "Please don't put him down." The owner, had managed to get it inside a carrier, suffering a number of wounds in the process, and, as it sat in the waiting room, frothing at the mouth and trying to tear its way out of the kennel, the owner tried to convince Malcolm that it was a loving animal.

Malcolm had sympathized. He listened to the stories of when the dog was younger, when he was a sweet, caring, if a little hyperactive beast. But he had seen the dog, he had seen its handiwork, and he knew that there was no good in that animal. It was pure evil; whatever good had once been there was gone and wasn't coming back. He gave the woman his promise that the dog would be re-homed, then he phoned the authorities, told them what the owner hadn't, and they put the dog down.

He felt terrible for it. He didn't sleep properly for weeks, but he knew he had done the right thing. He had seen inside the dog's soul and he hadn't glimpsed even the remotest glimmer of goodness.

"Fuck. Prick. Wanker. Ha! He got it."

Malcolm felt the same way about the man at his feet. He hadn't seen into his eyes, and he doubted he had a soul to look into, but he knew that this man, this cursing, bleeding mess, didn't deserve to live. There was no good in him, nothing but violence, hatred, and evil.

That was the real reason he stayed in step with the scurrying, hemorrhaging beast; he wanted to make sure that he died.

* * *

Darren wasn't sure if Eddie was going to strangle him or stab him through the heart, he seemed to want to do both. The knife was still above his chest and Eddie's eyes were still staring gleefully at it, as if imagining the moment it went through his heart and savoring every thought of it, but at the same time, Darren's lungs hadn't had their vital dose of oxygen for a few dozen seconds. No matter how hard he tried to pry Eddie's hand away from his throat, he was successful only in feeling a small relief from his crushing fingers. His breath wasn't getting through either way.

He was feeling lightheaded and weak, he knew he didn't have long left. He had no other choice. He freed his hands; they instinctively tried to move back to his own throat when Eddie's grip tightened, but he kept them away. Eddie realized what was going to happen and he used that moment to end his dream and to satisfy his blood lust. He lifted the knife up and then thrust it downwards, aiming for Darren's heart.

Darren threw his right hand in the way. The blade dug into the flesh and sliced straight through. It stopped when the handle of the knife connected with knuckle.

Darren screamed. The blade was poking a few inches through his flesh; blood was dripping down his wrist, onto his neck, and onto his chin. Eddie released his grip on Darren's throat and Darren bucked out, successfully this time. He used his anger and his pain, used all the adrenaline that coursed through him, to knock his friend off the top of him. Eddie toppled over and Darren scrambled to his knees. The anger and the insanity had been banished from his friend's eyes, but Darren now felt that anger and madness running through him. He ripped the knife out of his hand, screaming as the white-hot pain screeched through him. He was huffing and panting, frothing at the mouth and grinding his teeth. He rolled onto his friend, spraying him with spittle as he breathed through his open mouth.

"Bastard!" he screeched. "Fucking bastard!" he waved his hand around, splashing Eddie with his blood. He held the knife to Eddie's throat; it trembled unsteadily in his weaker left hand. He pressed it there until he felt the flesh tear, until he exposed a small cut and a small trickle of Eddie's blood.

"Darren! Darren, it's me!" Eddie said, staring up at his friend.

Darren pressed the knife tighter. "*Really*?" he spat. "Are you fucking shitting me?"

"I'm sorry," Eddie pleaded. "I'm so sorry. I didn't know it was you."

Darren frowned, but felt some of his anger subside. The pain was still horrendous, the blood still poured freely, but he felt his heartbeat steady, felt his breathing slow.

"What the fuck?" he spat.

"I'm so sorry," Eddie said. "I didn't know it was you. I thought . . ." He trailed off, looking pleadingly into Darren's eyes, the knife still pressed to his throat.

Darren stared at his friend for a few moments. He looked into his desperate eyes and remembered how they had been just seconds earlier, how they had seemed in a world of their own as they stared blankly back at him; prepared to kill him.

"Honestly," Eddie said, his voice breaking.

Darren's breath was steady, the adrenaline was taking care of the pain, but it was still agonizing. He saw something in Eddie's eyes that he didn't like, but he was his friend, had *always* been his friend; he knew that he wouldn't try to kill him intentionally. They had their arguments, which had increased recently, but although Eddie had threatened to kill him many times, he knew he wouldn't actually go through with it.

He released the pressure on the knife, pulled it away from his friend's throat, and rolled off the top of him. He pressed himself up against the wall, holding his bleeding hand in his lap and watching as Eddie climbed to his feet, brushed himself down and then looked at Darren with an apprehensive smile on his lips. He looked at the knife still held in Darren's left hand, at the blood gushing from his right hand.

"Sorry about that," Eddie said.

Darren glowered at his friend. There was something disingenuous and rotten about his apology. He had just stabbed him, tried to kill him. Sorry hardly seemed good enough and the way he had said it, the expression he had on his face, wasn't even a good enough apology for standing on someone's toes.

"It's okay," Darren said, despite himself.

28

Malcolm carefully stepped over the body in front of him, turning to give him one last look, one last check.

The cursing animal had made it to the end of the corridor, a trail of his blood forming an expanding line, like a clogged artery, from the cell door to where he now lay; his face pressed against the floor, his arms and legs splayed out. He was still cursing to his last breath, right before his face lowered to the floor.

Malcolm crouched down, bent over, aiming an ear towards him.

He was still breathing, struggling to talk, mumbling like a drunk about to enter the abyss of unconsciousness. His words were unclear, indecipherable; Malcolm doubted that even *he* knew what he was saying.

Malcolm pressed his face closer when the breathing slowed and the words softened even more. He moved until he was an inch away from the top of his head, until he could smell the blood on his face and the musty stench that seeped from his unwashed hair.

"You!" His voice was louder than before, but still soft, still staggered. He looked shocked and Malcolm knew why. He could see it in his eyes. The man currently staring up at him thought he was staring into the eyes of his victim, the one he had butchered, the one who had injured him, and the one whose corpse and bodily fluids now decorated one of the clinic's many rooms.

The man moved, a slight but unmistakable shift. Malcolm sighed but did not move.

"But . . . I . . . killed . . . you," the man hissed.

Malcolm frowned. He began to move his head away, to give up on watching him die, when the man's head suddenly snapped upwards. The back of his skull clattered with Malcolm's mouth and knocked him backwards, he rocked on his haunches, scuttled backwards, throwing a hand to his face. The dying man's head had knocked against his two front teeth; he had felt them against the hairy flesh and now he could taste the dying man on his lips and on his tongue.

He was looking at Malcolm now, his neck arched backwards, the rest of his body seemingly already dead, incapable of movement. His glassy green eyes locked onto Malcolm's and his expression, initially filled with wry vengeance, changed into a look of bemusement.

"*Who . . . the . . . fuck . . . are . . . you*?" he staggered, each word carried on a single breath, each breath a countdown to his last.

Malcolm didn't answer; he just stared at him, keeping his hand pressed to his mouth, stuffing the flesh of his palm between his lips, hoping to erase the taste of the dying man.

The man stared for a moment longer, then his bemusement turned blank, his neck muscles capitulated and his face fell. He was finally dead. Malcolm shook his head, checked his hand for any signs of blood, any cuts on his gums or his lips, and then stood up straight.

He looked down the stretch of corridor, lined with the smudged trail of blood that he had watched being created; he looked to the cell, where the fight that ended this man's life had taken place. He pictured the atrocities there, the horrors inside; none of that made him sick to his stomach, but now, with the taste of this despicable, dead thing in his mouth, he felt like he had been poisoned.

* * *

Darren slowly removed his jacket and his shirt, making sure to keep his friend in his sights and the knife in his hand. The shirt was thin, flimsy. He handed it to Eddie.

"Rip that for me," he instructed.

Eddie stared at the shirt and then at his friend. He nodded and tore the shirt in half. Darren held out his injured hand, still breathing heavily from the pain. Without a word and while Darren held the knife in his free hand, Eddie wrapped the torn shirt tightly around the wound, making a knot at the end. Darren's hand was padded and he wouldn't be able to move his fingers, but it would help stop the bleeding.

He sat against the wall, staring at his bandaged hand.

"So, where did you end up?" Darren said after a while, when the pain had subdued and his breathing and his heart rate had returned to normal, or as normal as they were going to get. "What have you been doing?"

Eddie looked suspiciously at Darren. "What do you mean?" he asked.

"Did you find anything, a way out, some information on where the fuck we are?"

"Ah," Eddie nodded. "No," he said, bringing a look of bemusement to Darren's face.

"I don't think this is a rehab clinic." Darren looked up and down the corridor, wary of another run-in with one of the psychopaths that seemingly wandered freely. "What exactly did your uncle say about this place?"

"You calling my uncle a liar?" Eddie snapped.

"What? No, I never—"

"You better watch your fucking mouth Daz," Eddie said. "He's family. Watch who you're offending."

"I didn't—"

"What was that?" Eddie's attention was suddenly diverted. He looked over Darren's shoulder, down the corridor. Darren turned sharply, the knife held tightly in his hand, ready for use if he encountered more crazies who wanted to toy with him. He couldn't see anything, the light at the end was flickering, as it seemed were most of the lights in the building, but there was no one underneath it.

"You see that?" Eddie asked, looking alert, his attention still on the end of the corridor.

Darren turned to his friend and then back to the corridor. There was nothing there, he was certain of it.

"What?" Darren asked, his eyes still staring down the corridor. "You're seeing things." He stared for a moment longer, almost expecting something to materialize. When he finally turned back to his friend, he was surprised to see that Eddie had been gazing at the back of his head and was now gazing into his eyes.

Darren jumped and then tried to laugh it off. "What the fuck? You scared me. Giving me the evil fucking eye in a place like this, stop that shit, you'll creep me out."

Eddie didn't look away, didn't even blink. He continued to stare. Darren felt uncomfortable under his gaze. His eyes looked soulless, empty, and annoyed all at the same time. Eventually Darren looked away, turning his head and feeling uneasy, knowing that Eddie was still watching.

He turned back after a moment and found that Eddie had shifted closer; Darren could feel his breath on his face. He still wasn't blinking. He wasn't allowing a glimmer of emotion to cross his face.

"You better watch your mouth," Eddie warned, holding Darren's stare. "I ain't gonna put up with that shit anymore."

"What *shit*? What are you talking about?"

Eddie didn't answer. He moved his face away from Darren's and looked over his shoulder again, just for a moment, before swapping his intimidating stare for a faux grin. "Come on then," he said, stretching his grin wider, a little too wide for Darren's liking, it couldn't have looked more disingenuous. "We better start looking for Mal."

Darren stared at his friend for a moment, knowing that he was holding the knife tighter in his fist, keeping it closer to his body. "Okay."

"You lead the way," Eddie said, gesturing down the hall.

Darren shook his head, stepped against the wall, his eyes not leaving his friend. "No. After you."

Eddie shrugged and started down the corridor, Darren watched the back of his head for moment, wandering what was going on inside that brain, and then he followed, making sure his knife was pointed towards his friend.

* * *

Malcolm felt sick. The longer the taste stayed in his mouth and the more he thought about it, the sicker he felt.

The corridor led into a large room. At one end of the room a series of large windows looked out onto the back of the building; only one of the many lights in the room had been turned on, but the moonlight took over where the lights left off. At the other end of the room was a small enclosed area, like a ticket-seller's booth in the subway. At the front of this booth was a sheet of reinforced glass with a cutaway at the bottom, at the side was a heavy door that swung loosely on its hinges.

Malcolm didn't stick around to study the room, but he could see drawers and shelves of medications, most of which had been knocked on the floor, some of which had made it outside and littered the floor like some psychotropic collage. There was a large television and several chairs in the main area, along with a radio and a couple of tables; Malcolm was happy to see that this room wasn't filled with bodies.

He barged through the doors that flanked the outside of the room, searching for a bathroom, for some water to wash out of the taste of death form his mouth. His hand covered his mouth and his breathing was heavy and fast as he tried not to vomit, but when he opened the first door and was hit by a stench of putrefaction and a sight of pure evil, he nearly lost the contents of his stomach.

He gagged a few times and managed to shut the door as his stomach threatened to explode. He didn't count the bodies inside, but he knew they were all dead; living people didn't look or smell like that.

He opened the next door cautiously, and was relieved to see his reflection staring back at him from a small mirror above a bathroom sink. He turned on the tap and ducked his head underneath, opening his mouth and rinsing it out with the gushing cold water, allowing it to run all over his face. It took away the smell, took away the taste, and took away the images of the dead man in the corridor.

He turned the light on when he had finished. He looked at his breathless, red-faced reflection in the mirror. His pupils were dilated, wide-open to the horrors he had witnessed and prepared to witness more. His eyes were streaked with red and his face looked gaunt, he looked like he had been starving himself for days. He was about to look away, to continue his trek through this insane nightmare, when he caught something moving out of the corner of the mirror.

He stopped his shifting eyes, felt his heart and his breath follow suit. He could see the open door behind him, looking out into the large room; the scattered pillboxes on the floor, the edge of the reinforced pharmaceutical room, a solitary chair that sat back from the others.

He was stuck in a dimly lit, psychotic purgatory; it was late, dark, and he was tired, he knew his eyes could be playing tricks on him and he hoped that they were, but his instincts—the way his heart beat so fast and heavy and the way his palms flushed with a film of sweat—told him differently.

He saw it again. A shadow that scampered across the floor, it was quick, but slow enough for him to make out the shape, slow enough for him to know that the shadow was human. He continued to watch, hoping that whoever it was, they were friendly or, if they weren't, that they didn't know he was in the bathroom. He knew his hopes were futile, he hadn't exactly been sneaking around, he had been noisy; banging the doors open and closed, rushing to the sink, opening the tap.

He thought back to the room next door, to the collage of carnage that decorated the walls, the floor, the ceiling, and even the lightbulb. It was a crimson room, a coppery-scented boudoir that no self-respecting punter or prostitute would ever enter. Whoever had killed those people, whoever had herded them inside, or led them in one by one and then butchered them, was probably still alive and probably still—

He saw more than a shadow this time. A man was standing in the doorway to the bathroom, his figure fully illuminated, his face perfectly clear under the blinding light from above. He looked like he'd been bathing in blood, from the slick crimson on his forehead to his large red hands. The knife he held in his right hand was also dripping with it.

Malcolm didn't turn around; he continued to stare through the mirror, as if pretending to the beast behind him that he hadn't seen him, but Malcolm *had* seen him and the man standing behind him knew that.

The doorway was blocked, there was no escape route, nowhere for him to run, nowhere for him to hide. Malcolm closed his eyes momentarily, an expression of exasperation and dwindling hope. He didn't see the man behind him smile, didn't see his bloody mouth open, exposing bright white teeth that stood out like gleaming stars against the crimson night of his bloodied face.

29

Malcolm heard movement behind him; he sensed the air shift as the bloodied beast loomed over him. He could smell him now, an overpowering stench of must and death. Malcolm grimaced, flinched, and then opened his eyes.

The man wasn't looming over him preparing to slit his throat, nor was he standing in the doorway. Malcolm couldn't see him anywhere. His mind had been playing tricks on him; his fear creating images and scenarios in his head.

He froze, his eyes the only part of his body that moved as they covered every inch of the mirror looking for the crimson monster that had lurked behind him. The door was open, pushed up against the wall, so he couldn't be hiding behind there and there were few other places to hide inside the small bathroom. There were two cubicles against the far wall, but they were both shut and both out of the way, if he was in there hiding, waiting to jump out, he wasn't the brightest of mass murderers.

Malcolm knew he was hiding in the main room and that knowledge should have given him the advantage, he knew where his adversary was so he could act accordingly, but it didn't help him at all. There was only one escape route and only one option, he had to venture into the lion's den; the monster knew that and he was waiting for him.

He reached into his pocket, his eyes still on the mirror, and pulled out the flick knife he had taken from Smiler. He kept it hidden in his palm, just in case the beast was watching. He kept his finger pressed over the release-catch of the weapon. The knife felt reassuring in his palm, he'd felt naked before, heading into a fight with the armed butcher, but the knife evened the score, if only slightly.

He held the knife tighter in his hand, careful not to press the switch, not wanting to open in into his own flesh. He looked at his own reflection, psyched himself up with a few mouthed words, and then slowly turned around, his eyes on the door and the bright lights of the main room.

He saw the man standing beside him when he turned around. His mind didn't register straight away—his concentration was on the door, his focus on how he would approach his entry—and when it did it was too late. The bloodied beast had been standing next to him the whole time. He had watched, grinned a mocking grin as Malcolm scoured the reflection for him, not noticing he was standing right beside him.

He felt a hand wrap around his face, a viscous coating of blood on his lips and his cheek. He breathed in the metallic scent of blood as the hand tightly squeezed his jaw and his cheeks. He felt another hand rise to his throat, felt a wet, sticky blade press against it as the first hand ripped his head backwards to expose the vulnerable flesh.

Malcolm kept the knife steady by his side, more out of surprise than patience. He was still gathering his senses when he felt a hot breath on his ear, it crawled over his skin like a leech, tickling the stubble on his cheek and making his entire body quiver.

The voice that spewed forth from the sickly breath was as thick as curdled cream and just as unpleasant. It oozed with malignancy and vulgarity and it made Malcolm's blood run cold.

"And where the fuck do you think you're going?"

* * *

Eddie knew what Darren was thinking; he could read his blank expression like a large print book. He wasn't an idiot, but clearly Darren thought he was.

This is your fault, Darren was thinking. *In between fucking you and your mother, your uncle started spouting bullshit and you were dumb enough to fucking listen.*

My uncle may be a mad bastard and he may have been talking out of his ass about this place, Eddie thought, *but you believed me just like I believed him.*

Eddie nodded and grinned a wide and knowing grin at Darren.

"Are you okay?" Darren asked.

Eddie continued to grin. Darren shook his head and then dragged his eyes away from his friend. "So, now what?" he asked.

They were back near the front entrance, at the point where the three of them had split up. Darren was standing in the spot where Malcolm had stood, trying his best not to look through the window into the room where the staff member had been tortured. He had listened to his screams and they would haunt him for the rest of his life, along with the images of the man in the chair and the gurgling sound his dying lungs made; the last thing he needed was another horrific image to add to his collection of nightmares.

“It’s not his fault,” Eddie said. “You shouldn’t blame him.”

Darren raised his eyebrows. “What the fuck are you talking about?”

“He didn’t know.”

Darren felt his hand instinctively grip the knife tighter, his free hand, wrapped heavily in the makeshift bandaged, also tensed. “Are you talking about Malcolm?”

“You shouldn’t talk about him like that.”

Darren slowly shook his head.

“He was only trying to do us a favor.”

“Mate? What. The. Fuck?” Darren said. “Have you lost your fucking mind?”

Eddie’s face changed, from a smile to a snarl. He thrust his hand out towards Darren who returned the gesture by raising his weapon, preparing to defend himself, preparing to stab his friend if he needed to.

“You take that back!” Eddie spat.

“What the fuck is—”

“Take it back!”

Darren held up his hands, “Okay, okay, just chill.”

Eddie still looked annoyed, like he was moments away from fighting. Darren was ready for him, but he was injured, tired, and mentally drained, he didn’t need another fight, especially with his friend, even if that friend had lost the plot.

Eddie withdrew his menacing expression and lowered his arm by his side. He looked down the hallway, his eyes wide and alert, as if seeing something at the end, nestled in the darkness.

“You okay, mate?” Darren asked, following his gaze and seeing nothing.

Eventually Eddie nodded. “I’m fine.”

“It’s just you”

“I said, I’m fine.”

Darren met his friend's gaze again. He didn't see the Eddie that he had grown up with, didn't see the laughing, joking idiot that had been a part of his life for so long; he saw the crazy, unstable Eddie that had quickly developed over the last few months, the Eddie that snapped so readily when Darren made a joke, the Eddie that launched into a verbal assault against the woman on the bus, and the Eddie that had nearly killed him. He said he hadn't known it was Darren when he tackled him and Darren had believed him, but he was starting to doubt that belief, starting to wonder if he had believed him because he *wanted* to believe him. He didn't want to be alone in this place. He didn't want to face the fears and the horrors that waited around every corner, but a part of him knew that although Eddie could keep him company, he had the potential to be worse than anything that waited around any corner.

* * *

Malcolm felt the blood on his ear, he felt it drip to his neck and stick to his clothes as the beast pushed up against him and forced him out of the bathroom.

"I have some people I think you'd like to meet," he said, almost giddily.

Malcolm squirmed. He tried to break free from his grasp, but he was bigger than him and towered over him, his body almost enveloping him, sucking him into its bloody embrace. He edged him forward and when Malcolm resisted by digging his heels into the floor, he merely lifted him up and carried him.

He stopped outside the door to the room of carnage, lifted a foot, and kicked it open. Malcolm twisted his face in revulsion when the smell and the sights hit him again. He felt vomit rise from his stomach and into his throat and he was sure he was going to gag again, an action that would no doubt force his throat onto the blade.

He held it back, swallowing the acidic bile with a grimace.

"Don't they look comfortable?" The beast asked, his heated breath cutting through Malcolm's spine. "Resting peacefully in eternity."

"Are you fucking kidding me?" Malcolm spat, disgusted. The bodies had been massacred beyond belief and he knew that if their souls had existed and had escaped, they wouldn't be resting peacefully. They would still be suffering, still remembering, still trembling with fear as they looked at their butchered vessels and remembered the torture they had endured.

"You don't like?"

"Fuck you!"

Malcolm kicked back with his heel, catching the beast on the shin. He felt him recoil. He kicked again, harder this time, but the beast anticipated it and moved his leg out of the way. He released Malcolm from his grasp and for a split-second Malcolm found himself able to breathe, he found himself free of the sticky, bloodied embrace of the madman, but then he felt something heavy on the back of his head. He didn't feel any pain as he fell—face first into the blood and the decaying bodies—but when the viscous crimson carnage sucked him in, he felt the lightning strike through his skull. There was a split second of agony before his world turned black.

* * *

Eddie didn't tell Darren about the thing that he was following, Darren didn't see it, he wasn't paying enough attention. That was Darren's problem, he wasn't observant enough, he didn't understand the situation like Eddie did, didn't understand that he had to be vigilant and alert at all times. Eddie kept his eyes ahead, his attention on the threats that lurked around every corner, but every time he looked at Darren, to check if he was doing the same, he discovered that his friend was staring at him.

They had ventured away from the torture room in the hope they would bump into Malcolm. They were walking slowly, Eddie ahead of Darren, and they had barely gone a few feet before Eddie snapped.

"Why are you fucking staring at me?" he roared, standing still. He saw Darren flinch, saw him take a step back. He was armed, but Eddie didn't mind, he knew he could overpower his feeble friend in a heartbeat.

"I wasn't," Darren said.

Eddie stared at him. He saw the fear in his eyes and in his rigid body language. He heard it in his words. He looked down at Darren's hand, at the blood that had seeped through the thick material. Then he looked at the knife, gripped so tightly in Darren's fist that he knuckles had turned white.

"You have issues," Darren said.

"What did you say?" Eddie said, raising his eyes to meet his friend.

Darren furrowed his brow deeply and then slowly shook his head, "I didn't—"

"How about I show you some real issues, eh? How would you like that?"

Darren took a step back; Eddie took a step forward.

Eddie began to push him again, "How about I—" he paused when he heard voices down the corridor.

"What's the matter?" Darren asked, watching as his friend alerted himself to the noise.

"*Shh*!" Eddie threw a finger to his lips.

He heard talking, two voices, maybe more. They were hushed and seemed to be coming from further down the corridor, from one of the many rooms that flanked it. He couldn't hear what they were saying but he picked up a few words here and there.

He turned to Darren and grinned when he saw the fear in his friend's eyes. He looked like he was ready to wet his pants. "So, macho one minute and now this, eh? You're pathetic, you know that?"

Darren's mouth opened but he didn't reply.

"Come on," Eddie whispered, nodding down the corridor. "We need to move quick. If they attack us, be prepared to use that thing or to give it to me." He gestured to the knife.

Darren swallowed hard, nodded, and then followed Eddie down the corridor. Eddie followed the shifting shadow that had, once again, darted into the darkness.

* * *

Malcolm peeled his eyes open. An intense pain raced through his head, intensified when a stream of light cut through the gap in his pupils and set his skull on fire. He tried his best to ignore it, to focus through the haze of his eyes as they slowly opened and exposed the red-tinted room around him.

He didn't know how long he had been out but he was alive and, from what he could tell, his arms and legs hadn't been tied. He could hear a commotion above him, a white noise that filtered through to him like distant waves lapping a shore. He tried to concentrate on it, tried to understand what was happening, but he couldn't focus on it.

He closed his eyes, squeezed them shut, and prayed the pain away.

It subsided somewhat and he opened his eyes again. The noise above him had stopped. The commotion had ceased and his attacker was silent. Malcolm pictured him looming over him with a grin on his bloodied face, drops of crimson dripping from his curled lips. He found an urge to live, an urge to fight. The bastard above him had murdered a handful of people for no reason other than the desire to see them suffer, to watch the light of life fade from their eyes. Malcolm knew that if he didn't fight through the pain, if he didn't stand up and face the beast above him, he was going to be next.

He opened his eyes fully and waited a few moments for the haze to clear. He was lying in a pool of blood. Now that he could see it, he could also feel it on his skin, sticking to him. He felt his stomach lurch but he tried not to think about it.

He tilted his head, moving ever so slowly, not wanting his attacker to know that he was awake and ready to fight. He felt a glimmer of hope when he saw that his attacker was standing a few feet away with his broad back turned. He wasn't looking at him and didn't seem at all interested in him. That was just what Malcolm needed.

He scoured the floor, trying to see past the blood and the piles of bodies. He saw that the knife was lying within arm's reach, right where he had dropped it.

He felt a surge of adrenaline flush his body when his fingers curled around the handle of the knife. He grinned through the pain, clenched his teeth, and hissed his breaths out of his lungs. He looked up to see that the big man still had his back to him, he hadn't anticipated that Malcolm would fight, hadn't anticipated that he wasn't dealing with a feeble kid who would let him do what he wanted.

It angered him that the man had such a disregard for human life and it angered him more that he had nearly been his next victim. He held onto that anger, used it to fire his brain and his body into action as he clambered, as silently as he could, to his feet. He was covered in blood now, but he didn't linger on that, didn't let it get to him. Instead he thought about avenging the people whose blood now covered him like some crimson camouflage. They had died at the hands of this sociopathic monster, and now Malcolm would deliver them justice and he would deliver it in the very room where the beast had senselessly butchered them.

He hauled himself upright, his breath coming in gasps; the big man still wasn't paying any attention to him, his back was still turned. Malcolm stood behind the bloodied giant, staring at the back of his head.

He had something pressed to his ear; it looked like a radio or a walkie-talkie. Malcolm's eyes were smeared with blood; a drop had stuck to his eyelashes and hovered over his right eye like a veil, shrouding everything in a deathly red hue.

He lifted the knife, aimed, inhaled a deep breath and then threw himself at the big man. He plunged the knife into the center of his back. The blade sunk into his flesh, slicing easily through the mass of muscle and fat and then puncturing his heart and his lungs. Malcolm pulled it out with a satisfying gasp, nearly losing his balance in the process. The beast staggered forward but Malcolm followed, stabbing him again and again, until blood gushed out of the wounds, mixing with the blood already coating the floor and the walls.

The radio fell out of his grasp and hit the floor, shattering on impact. It had been fizzing, buzzing with words or music, but they stopped as soon as it clattered into the bloody floor.

Malcolm reached for the beast again, prepared to attack him for the dozenth time, but the big man toppled over something on the floor and fell. Malcolm nearly followed him, but he stopped short of tumbling over the large corpse on the ground. He watched the big man as he squirmed and groaned, he thought about jumping on him, delivering a few more blows, but he knew it wasn't necessary. He watched as he slowly turned over and he prepared himself to look into the face of a dying murderer, to stare into his twisted eyes. But it wasn't the same man. His face wasn't as strong or as bloodied. It was chubby and somewhat innocent. It was smiling slightly, despite what had happened; a smile of an innocent idiot.

Malcolm's jaw hung open, he looked to the knife and then back to the body.

"I don't—" he said, staggering his words before allowing them to trail off.

The man he had stabbed was staring at him and Malcolm hoped that his thin blue lips would give him the answer he wanted.

He returned the stare, waiting, but eventually he realized that those glassy eyes weren't looking into his eyes, they weren't seeing him or anything else. He was already dead.

He looked at the knife again and dropped it, watching it fall to the floor.

How long had he been out? Had he imagined the man with the bloodied face, had he—

He stopped his rapid thoughts, felt a freeze grab his heart and rush through his body. He took a step backwards, his eyes on the body on the floor, the body that the dead man had tripped over. It was the body of the butcher, the man who had knocked Malcolm unconscious. He was dead; it looked like his neck had been broken. He had been taken by surprise, attacked from behind, and then—

Malcolm looked at both of the dead men.

"Shit," he whispered softly, realizing he had just murdered a man who had saved his life.

30

Eddie was the first past the door, he turned around and waited for Darren to pass but Darren paused. The two voices inside the room didn't sound angry or menacing, they weren't filled with bile, rage and insanity; they sounded normal, scared. They were doing their best to keep their voices low and Darren was sure he even heard one of them telling the other to be quiet.

He turned to Eddie, wondering if he had heard it as well, but Eddie's expression hadn't changed. He glared at Darren for a moment and the gestured for him to hurry up; Darren shook his head and nodded to the door, trying to get his point across.

Eddie raised his eyebrows, an expression of impatience. When Darren still didn't follow him, he openly asked, "What the fuck are you waiting for?"

Darren felt his heart sink. He heard the voices in the room fall silent, heard one of them shush the other. He deflated and turned to the door, ready to open it and embrace who was on the other side—they needed as many allies as they could get and he was confident that the two men on the other side of the door were good guys—but the voice on the other side stopped him.

"Back off, we're armed!" It was filled with faux bravado; Darren could hear the fear in every word. They suspected that Darren and Eddie were about to launch into an attack, they had probably already fought off a few madmen in the last few hours and, as far as they were concerned, the angry voices outside the door were just another pair of blood-thirsty psychopaths.

"Leave," another voice ordered. "Or you'll regret it." The second voice was just as scared as the first, but he hid the fear better.

Darren took a step forward, "Come on," he motioned to Eddie, brushing past him. He didn't want to enter, didn't need to talk to the two men inside. He knew they were good guys, but he also knew they were scared and, if they were armed, he knew there was a good chance they would lash out at whoever walked through the door, be they friend or foe.

Eddie didn't budge; he was still looking ahead, at and around the door. Darren tugged on his jumper, urging him away, but Eddie moved a step closer to the door. He seemed transfixed by it; a smile curled the corners of his lips but the rest of his features were set in deep concentration.

"Eddie, come on."

Eddie took another step forward, then the trance broke, he averted his eyes, turned his grin to Darren. "We need to do this," he said with a sinister smile.

"*This*?"

Eddie simply nodded. He turned back to the door and then pushed it open. Inside it was dark, lit only by the moonlight that streamed in through a small barred window and by a lamp that sat on a desk against the back wall. Two men had been standing near the doorway, they immediately jumped back when Eddie entered and moved further away when he strode into the room.

Darren reluctantly walked by his friend's side. He could see that the men were innocent, could see that they were terrified. He could also see that they weren't armed and even if they were, he doubted they would be capable of using a weapon.

Eddie stopped in the center of the room and the two men stopped backing away, trying to regain some composure, to fix a stance of intimidation.

Darren looked from their horrified expressions to the one of glee on his friend's face. "Now what?" he asked Eddie.

He didn't like the look he received in reply.

* * *

Malcolm rushed back into the bathroom, slapping on the light and practically throwing himself at the sink. He twisted the tap until his hand hurt and stuck his face close to the sink, allowing the ice-cold water to quickly fill his hands before splashing it on his face.

He watched the blood mingle with the water, watched as the watery concoction dripped onto the cold porcelain bowl like wet paint onto a blank canvas. He thought about the beast, the man that had dragged him into the room of death. He thought about how close he had been to joining the bodies on the floor; thought about the man who had saved his life and how he hadn't exactly returned the favor.

The *drip-drip-drip* of the blood, diluted to a tame pink, steadied, and slowed.

He didn't know why the man had saved his life, but he didn't think it was intentional. The hospital was rife with murder and madness, patients butchering staff—and each other—without a second thought. The man he had killed wasn't the one that had dragged him to that room, but he was still a murderer and there was a good chance that if he knew Malcolm was alive, he would have chosen him as his next victim.

That made him feel better, but he was still sick to his stomach. No matter which way he looked at it, no matter how he tried to justify it, he had taken someone's life.

He straightened up and stared at his gaunt and blood-smeared expression in the mirror. He looked into his own empty eyes, into the worry, regret, and fear that resided there. He looked away when he sensed movement beside him. At first he thought someone was sneaking up on him and he was surprised by his initial reaction: it wasn't one of rigid fear or worry, instead he turned around, feeling a surge of anger, and prepared to launch himself at his attacker.

A small mouse looked up at him from underneath one of the cubicles, its whiskers twitching the air, its pinpoint eyes glistening in the darkness. It looked up at Malcolm who stood just a foot or two away. Malcolm wasn't struck rigid by fear, but the mouse was.

The bitterness and aggression on his face shifted, replaced by a smile.

"Hello little dude," he said softly.

He watched as the rodent took a cautious step forward, its face close to the ground, looking for a scent of food, a morsel of something satisfying in the cold, empty hospital.

Malcolm squatted down, pursed his lips and made a clicking sound with his tongue before slowly reaching out a hand.

The mouse looked at the extended appendage and studied its approach.

"It's okay, I ain't gonna hurt you," Malcolm said. He extended a finger and then watched as the mouse quickly darted past it, under his legs, and through the door.

It was hiding in the main room, pushed up against a corner. Malcolm heard it emitting a strange noise, a murmuring sound that he took to be panic, hunger, or desperation. He creased his face, feeling pity for the small animal as it pinned itself up against the wall and hoped that it hadn't been seen.

Malcolm dug around in his pockets until he found the remnants of a cereal bar. He walked steadily over to the rodent, keeping low and unassuming, and held out the honey-coated crumbs, hoping it would venture forward and take it out of his hand. The noise had increased, the rodent now extremely worried with the human so near. Malcolm put the crumbs down on the floor and began to retreat, but he stopped himself. He gave the rodent another glance, one of bemusement this time. He had dealt with hamsters, rats, and mice before and had never heard any of them make a sound. One of them, a pet mouse, often sat in his hand, trembling and defecating in fear and uncertainty, but it never made a sound.

Once he realized that the noise wasn't coming from the rodent, *couldn't* be coming from the rodent, he realized that it wasn't even coming from this side of the room. He straightened up, looked around and then saw the source of the noise. Nestled in an alcove in the far corner, obscured from the entrance and the bathroom door, a grief-stricken man sat hunched in the fetal position, his teeth nervously and mercilessly chomping on his fingernails and the nibs of his fingers; his sunken eyes staring straight at Malcolm.

* * *

They were in a standoff, four people waiting to tear each other apart. Darren was the only one with a knife and he wasn't moving, he didn't look like he was prepared to use it. He was a wimp, just like Eddie had always suspected. Eddie turned to his friend to urge him into action, or at least to ask for backup as Eddie prepared to fight; he saw desperation in Darren's eyes and knew that he wasn't going to fight. He watched as Darren lifted his hand slowly, all eyes in the room on the knife that he held loosely in his palm.

"I can't do it," Eddie heard Darren say. "They need to die, we need to kill them before they kill us, but I'm not man enough to do it."

Eddie had known all along; it didn't come as a surprise. He waited for Darren to drop the knife, for the sound of the metal to ring out as it clattered against the floor. The other two crept out from their hiding positions, ready to fight now that the weapon had been taken out of the equation, but Eddie quickly picked it up.

He glared at them with a glint in his eye. "I ain't a soft fuck like him," he announced, tossing the knife from one hand to the other, seeing the realization dawn on the two madmen.

He attacked them before they could attack him. He moved quickly, he had to; Darren wasn't prepared to back him up and, although he had the knife, he was outnumbered and disadvantaged.

He grabbed the closest one by the throat and squeezed tightly. He didn't do anything to defend himself, didn't try to throw a punch or a kick. He seemed to succumb to his fate, his eyes wide and pleading, as Eddie drove the blade into his stomach. He struck half a dozen times in quick succession before he let go, watching as the madman slumped against the wall, his hands clutching at his stomach, his legs unstable.

The second man came at him, showing some fight, but Eddie was too quick for him. He jabbed him with his left hand, caught him on the nose and caused him to stumble backwards, nearly toppling over his dying friend who was on his knees, breathing his last breaths. After staggering him with another quick jab, Eddie lashed out with the knife, driving it across his throat in an arcing motion. He felt the resistance rattle through the handle as the blade met with flesh and tore an opening; he heard the satisfying rip, felt the spray of blood as vital arteries opened and the madman fell to his knees, inches away from his friend, clutching at the mass of blood that rushed from his throat like a crimson tide.

"What the fuck?"

Eddie turned around and saw Darren staring at him, shock and awe in his eyes.

"That was amazing," Darren said, still standing rigid, seemingly too in awe of his friend's talents to do anything. "You saved my life."

Edie nodded proudly. He studied his friend, studied the awe in his face and his words. He hated him and if he wanted he could slaughter him in heartbeat, just like he had with the two men that were breathing their last at his feet, but something told him he needed to keep Darren alive, and it wasn't just because he was a kiss-ass.

* * *

As Malcolm edged towards the exit, he saw that the man in the corner was just a kid. He had a young face, no doubt helped by his gaunt features and gangly frame, but he looked to be the same age as Malcolm and his friends, if not younger. He was in his pajamas and a loose dressing gown, the uniform of the psychotic, at least as far as this building was concerned. But Malcolm didn't think he was psychotic, he looked like he could be a patient, but not one with an appetite for murder.

He also looked innocent. Malcolm knew not to trust appearances, madness and murder hides behind all facades, but there was no deception behind his face, no evil lurking in his eyes. He looked lost, petrified. When Malcolm stared at him, the youngster even averted his eyes.

"Hello, there," Malcolm said eventually, deciding not to walk away. Something told him to stay, to try to talk to the kid, to get answers or to help him.

The kid didn't answer but he did look at him.

"What's your name?" Malcolm asked.

The murmuring had stopped; the boy wasn't making a sound now.

"What are you doing here?" Malcolm asked.

The boy's eyes moved behind Malcolm and gave him a fright, and for a moment he thought that somebody was behind him, another murderous psychopath, but when he turned he didn't see anyone standing there. He only saw the mouse, who had ventured towards the crumbs from the cereal bar and was munching them hungrily while keeping his eyes and ears pointed towards Malcolm.

Malcolm asked, "You like the mouse?"

The boy nodded, peeling his hands away from his face as he did so. He saw his lips move, perhaps to answer his question, but only a murmur escaped.

"Is he your friend?" Malcolm had moved slowly towards him and was now just a few feet away. The boy didn't seem to mind and was swapping his glances between Malcolm and the mouse, Malcolm saw a smile creased his eyes and crack his dried lips when he watched the mouse.

The youngster nodded, enthusiasm in his eyes.

"What's his name?"

The boy turned to Malcolm and looked confused for a moment. Malcolm stopped moving, sensing he might have crossed the line, even though he didn't know where or what the line was.

"—e—e—e doesn't have—a—name." He stuttered slowly, his lips peeling apart with great difficultly.

Malcolm nodded slowly and moved forwards another couple of steps, until he was within touching distance. He could smell the boy now, a strong scent of body odor mixed with the rancid stench of stale urine. He squatted down, like he had done with the mouse, until he was eye level with him. The boy seemed more alert and open. He was smiling gently now, his eyes on Malcolm who was returning the smile.

"And what about you?" Malcolm asked. "Do you have a name?"

The youngster nodded slowly and then paused, as if remembering. "Neil," he said eventually.

"Nice to meet you Neil," Malcolm said. "So, what are you doing here?"

Neil looked back to the mouse and seemed disappointed and slightly alarmed when he noticed that the little rodent had scurried away. "I followed him," he explained.

"Do you always follow him?"

Neil nodded.

"Fascinating creatures, aren't they?"

Again, Neil nodded, before adding, "I like the way they eat. And move."

"Cute, eh?"

"I like that they don't change. Life changes. I change. I don't like that. The mouse doesn't change."

Malcolm nodded, not wanting to delve any deeper into what Neil was talking about. Clearly the kid had issues, otherwise he wouldn't be in the hospital in the first place, but now wasn't the time to bring those issues to light.

"Do you like all animals?" Malcolm asked.

Neil nodded again, with more enthusiasm this time. Malcolm could see a light behind his eyes, but not the psychopathic light he had seen in the killers, this was the light of innocence, of an enthusiastic child talking about his hobbies or his friends. He saw intelligence and pain, he had never been a firm believer that you could tell anything about a person from their eyes or their expression, but something about the kid in front of him—something that resided deep within his smile and his eyes—told him that he was dealing with someone complex, someone deep, someone intelligent and someone who had suffered a lot.

"I like the way they eat and move." Neil repeated. "Simple but funny."

"I like that too," Malcolm agreed. He paused and looked around, his eyes lingered on the slaughter room before he dragged them back to Neil. "D'you know what's happening here, Neil?"

Neil held his stare and then looked away. Malcolm thought he saw a timid nod.

"A lot of people are getting hurt," Malcolm said. "You don't have anything to do with that though, do you?"

Neil returned his stare and shook his head vigorously, Malcolm didn't need clarification, he didn't think that Neil was capable of lying to him.

"I tried to hide," Neil said softly. "They left me alone. But then . . ." he trailed off, his eyes tracing over where the mouse had been.

"But then you followed that little fella, right?"

Neil nodded.

"Do you know what's happening here?" Malcolm asked again.

Neil met his eyes for a moment and then turned away.

"Please Neil," Malcolm begged. "If you know something, you need to tell me. I want to help you and your little friend, but I can't if I don't know what's going on."

"You're not one of them, are you?"

"Malcolm shook his head. "I'm a . . ." he paused. "A *visitor* here," he said, knowing Neil wouldn't question him.

"So, do you know something?" Malcolm asked.

Neil raised his head again and stared deeply into Malcolm's eyes. Malcolm thought he saw a wry smile, a glimmer of something previously unseen, but it didn't linger. Neil nodded. "Yes."

31

Darren kept his distance, walking a few feet behind Eddie. Eddie was honored, but also a little disgusted, that his friend would revere him so much. They had known each other for a long time, he thought, it was about time that Darren finally showed him some respect.

Eddie had the knife now, still fresh with the blood of the two madmen that had tried to kill him. He had the upper hand in every way. He had worried that Darren might try to attack him, he clearly saw him as a threat and, when Darren had the knife, there was a chance he might have tried to take him out, but now he had lost his chance. It thrilled Eddie to know that at any moment he could kill his friend, but he wasn't going to. He was going to be the bigger man and give him a chance to redeem himself, to prove that he wasn't a worthless piece of shit who was afraid of his own shadow.

Eddie walked tall and proud through the corridors, on the lookout for any more threats while his weedy friend cowered behind him. He saw Darren try to hide a few times, saw him look like he was preparing to run away, probably to cower in a corner somewhere like the feeble prick he was, but Eddie kept his eye on him, showing him the knife in his hand and the intent in his eyes.

* * *

"I'm new," Neil explained. He wasn't comfortable looking Malcolm in the eye and preferred to avert his stare when he spoke, like a timid child being addressed by a stern adult. "They transferred me here a few weeks ago because . . ." he trailed off.

"What you're in here for isn't important to me," Malcolm explained.

"I didn't do anything bad," Neil said, quickly meeting Malcolm's stare. "Honestly I didn't, I'm a good kid, they all say that. I'm not violent, I'm not—"

"I believe you," Malcolm said, fearing he was losing him. "So, what happened? Were the others always this violent?"

Neil shook his head and looked thoughtful for a moment. "There were others who were just like me. Quiet. Soft. There were violent ones, too, men that screamed and banged all night long, but most of them were okay." He tightened up his posture, hugged his knees closer to his chest, Malcolm thought he saw him shiver.

"So what happened?"

He shook his head.

"You don't know?"

Neil shook his head again; he seemed reluctant to talk, reluctant to even contemplate what had happened.

"You must know something. How did this all start?"

Neil lifted his eyes, meeting Malcolm's questioning gaze and then down the hallway, into a stretch of flickering light, at the end of which was a pair of double doors.

"What's down there?" Malcolm asked.

"The security room," Neil told him. "That's where they watch the cameras." He looked up and Malcolm followed his gaze. Black fixtures the size of tennis balls were embedded at the top of the walls. Malcolm had seen them in many of the rooms and assumed they were lights, but, now that he thought about it, he hadn't seen any of them illuminated.

"Those are cameras?" he asked.

Neil nodded. "They attacked the security room first. That way no one could see what happened elsewhere . . ." he slowed his speech and then tucked his head into his knees when he had finished. "I saw it though." His words muffled as they filtered through his clothing. "I saw it all."

Malcolm nodded, he turned to the cameras and then back to Neil. The youngster look petrified and was visibly shaking.

"You don't know what started this?" he asked.

Neil didn't reply but Malcolm heard a strangled tear escape, then, after a few moments, he heard the murmuring restart as Neil began to rock—mumbling away his troubles, keeping his mind occupied and the memories at bay.

Malcolm rested a hand on his knee and then quickly retracted it when Neil flinched. He stood and looked down at him. "I'm going to go check something out," he said. "Will you be okay if I leave you here?"

Neil didn't reply, he continued to rock, to murmur.

"I'll be back," Malcolm assured him.

Still Neil didn't reply, but Malcolm couldn't afford to stay with him. He had to find his friends, to find answers, to find an escape route; he reasoned that the security room, and the monitors installed there, was probably the best place to start.

* * *

Eddie was becoming familiar with the smell of death, a sickly-sweet stench that invaded his sinuses and threatened to remain there forever, and he recognized it as soon as he entered the large room. The room was well lit, unlike the others, and looked fairly clean. A few bottles of pills had been scattered on the floor but there was nothing too messy, nothing too out of place. Then he saw the open door, saw and smelled the blood that had been painted over the walls and floors.

"Holy fucking shit," he whispered.

Darren was a few paces behind him and nearly fainted when he glimpsed the carnage. He backed away from the room while Eddie remained, standing in the doorway and grinning as he listened to his friend retching.

It was pungent, worse than the others had been, but it was the sheer volume of blood and guts that set this room apart from the others. Eddie was drawn in, unable to take his eyes from it. He was strong, unlike his friend. He didn't have a weak stomach and didn't feel nauseous at the smell; he enjoyed it, it excited a part of him that rarely had a chance to shine.

"Grow a pair of fucking balls," he called over his shoulder. "It's just a bit of blood." Except that it was more than just a bit of blood, and he knew it.

He looked around, took in the bodies that had been scattered over the floor like offal at a slaughterhouse. He ran over their faces, some rapidly decomposing, some mutilated beyond recognition, others face down in a pool of blood. He stopped when he studied the face closest to the door, he recognized him as the man he had bumped into in the hallway, The Thing, the bounding beast that had had a chance to kill him, but had merely pranced on by as if Eddie wasn't there.

Someone had caught up with him and judging by the wounds in his back, someone had taken advantage of him, stabbing him as he pranced on by, just as Eddie wished he had done.

Eddie felt a presence behind him and he turned, ready to congratulate Darren on finally having the balls to see this once-in-a-lifetime spectacle, but Darren wasn't standing behind him, the shadow he had chased through half of the hospital was.

Eddie stared at it, looking into where he thought its eyes should be. He didn't speak, didn't ask it any questions. He didn't lunge at it, threaten to stab it, or tackle it to the ground. He didn't want to grab it anymore, didn't need to know who or what it was, he knew what it was there for and he knew what he had to do.

When it moved away from the door, Eddie followed it.

32

The shadow led Eddie to the corner of the room, past Darren—bent-double by the entrance, a stringy line of vomit-tainted saliva stretching from his mouth to the floor—and past the open door to the bathroom. It led him to a small alcove and to the smaller boy who was waiting there, mumbling softly to himself with his head buried in his knees like some feeble-minded dimwit who had given up on life despite having never really gotten his start.

It loomed over the boy, as if the walls themselves were reaching out to grab him, and then it dispersed and the boy looked up at Eddie.

"What do you want?" he asked.

"I'll ask the fucking questions," Eddie said. "Who the fuck are you, and what the hell went on back there?" He hooked a thumb over his shoulder to indicate the room of death, the boy looked towards it but didn't seem interested. There was no emotion on his face, though he seemed very interested in Eddie.

"I—I don't know what you're talking about," he stuttered in reply.

"Bullshit." Eddie pointed the knife at the youngster and warned him, "Start talking or things'll get messy."

The kid looked at the knife and nodded slowly. "Okay," he said. "I did it."

"You killed all of those people?"

The youngster nodded and looked away shyly. Eddie had a hard time believing that someone so feeble could have butchered so many people, but it didn't surprise him.

He turned around and saw that Darren was still struggling to hold down his dinner. He was still hovering outside the room of death, still retching and trying to get away from the smell and the memory, both of which threatened to linger for an eternity. Eddie turned his attention back to the kid in front of him; he was looking at him, ready to meet his gaze. Eddie stared into his eyes for a moment, the kid was trying to look soft and naive, trying to feign a childish innocence, but Eddie could see it now; he could see the evil, the blackness in his soul. He had seen the same in the man on the staircase and he had seen the same in the two men that had threatened to kill him and Darren. He knew that no matter how weak and pathetic this kid looked, he was capable of horrific things and he needed to stop him.

* * *

The double doors led into a short corridor, flanked by two large wards. At the end of the corridor was a large room. The door was a heavy security door, but it had been battered and dented, the handle had been broken and the lock snapped off. The door hung open, no longer able to fit in its frame.

Malcolm wasn't afraid, he knew that nothing pleasant awaited him on the other side of the door, but his chances of encountering anything worse than what he had already seen were slim.

A security guard lay sprawled on the floor inside the room. He had put up a fight, two of the fingers on his right hand pointed in opposing directions; his nose had been broken and one of his top teeth poked through the flesh on his upper lip, the blood around the wound had dried into a thick, congealed mustache.

He had been beaten heavily, his face was swollen and his body bent at awkward angles, but it was the stab wounds that had finished him off. Malcolm side-stepped the blood on the floor, the room was small and—along two toppled chairs and some broken equipment—the body took up much of the floor space. Malcolm sat down on one of the chairs in front of a large bank of monitors, only then did he see the second corpse in the chair next to him. This security guard was fatter and older; it looked like he was only a few months away from a heart attack before a shape blade had carved a wide smile into his throat.

Malcolm turned away from the dead bodies and tried to ignore the heavy stench of blood and decay that clogged the unventilated room, a stench that he had become so accustomed to that his senses were already starting to ignore. He set his sights on the array of monitors in front of him. Some had been broken in the struggle and others had been ripped out of the wall, but a few of them still worked and in one of them he saw Darren and Eddie.

They were standing in the room he had just been inside, he was less than thirty feet away from them, but something stopped him from running out to greet them. Something worried him, and the longer he stared at the screen, the more worried he felt.

* * *

"Get up," Eddie ordered, gesturing with the knife, a reminder that he was armed and in control.

The youngster looked at the knife and then into Eddie's eyes. He shook his head and looked away.

"Get. The. Fuck. Up." Eddie said, taking a step towards him.

Still the kid didn't move, still he remained curled into a ball with his head buried in his knees, seemingly hoping that if he didn't see the world then it wouldn't see him.

Eddie kicked him, softly at first, aiming a toecap at his thighs, but when he didn't respond beyond a soft and muffled yelp, he kicked him harder, driving his foot into his stomach and forcing him to recoil. The youngster toppled sideways, kicked out his torso, and released a strangled cry. He righted himself instantly, threw out his arms in front of Eddie to deflect further blows and then rose to his feet, using the wall as a support and keeping his eyes on his attacker.

"What the fuck?" the youngster spat. "Who do you think you are?"

"Excuse me?" Eddie said.

"Kicking me like that," The boy spat. "You fucking ginger tosser. You think you're all that, but you're just a pathetic little prick."

Eddie's mouth hung open. He felt his hand tighten around the knife. Darren put a hand on Eddie's arm but Eddie flinched, backed away, and nearly swung for his friend.

"Calm down," Darren said.

"Calm down?" Eddie spat. "Did you hear this fucking cunt?"

The youngster was still murmuring; his words were rapid mumbles and his face was a mess of nervous tics. He looked like he was ready to cry, "I didn't say anything," he begged, his eyes pleading with Darren.

"I fucking heard you!" Eddie spat, pointing the knife at him and taking a step towards him. The youngster backed up until he was against the wall, Eddie had him cornered.

"I'll show you who's a ginger tosser," Eddie said.

The youngster looked appalled, a tear rolled down his cheek, his face was flustered, his head beading with sweat, his eyes ready to pop out of his skull. "I didn't—" he looked at Darren, begging. "I swear—"

"Kill him," Eddie heard Darren say.

Eddie turned to his friend. "What?"

"You heard me," Darren said. "He's mad. You'll be doing the world a favor. Kill him."

Eddie looked at the youngster again, he expected a startled response, expected him to be in tears over Darren's words, but he seemed to have settled, the words had seemingly calmed him down. Maybe he knew he was mad, Eddie thought, maybe he knew he was a danger to the world and maybe he knew there was only one way of fixing that.

"Okay," Eddie said with a nod, half to himself. "I guess there's nothing else for it."

* * *

Malcolm watched the scene unfold through the monitor. He saw Eddie talking to Neil and he knew something wasn't right with his friend. He no longer recognized the voice, the face, or the attitude of his former friend. He sensed something amiss with his tone and with the way his eyes darted around, as if they weren't even looking at the kid in front of him.

He was enthralled by what was happening on screen and, though he knew a storm was coming and he knew that he needed to stop it, he couldn't drag himself away. He didn't hear what Neil said to Eddie, but he heard the reaction and he heard Darren's intervention. Darren begged Eddie to leave the kid alone, trying to convince him that this feeble, frail youngster had done nothing wrong, but Eddie didn't seem to understand.

Malcolm knew something bad was about to happen and this time he managed to drag his eyes away from the screen. He took two strides before he burst into a run, heading for the room at full speed to save Neil's—and possibly Darren's—life.

33

Eddie picked the kid up by his collar. He felt light in his arms, nothing more than skin and bone. The heaviness that lurked in his soul, the evil that had murdered those people, didn't weigh a thing and didn't fight against him as Eddie lifted him up and rammed him against the wall.

The kid squealed like a stuck pig, his eyes opened wide and looking into Eddie's with horror. Eddie felt resistance on his shoulder and turned to see Darren tugging at him; he shrugged him off, dropped the kid and then waved the knife at his friend.

"I'm doing it!" Eddie yelled at him. "Leave me the fuck alone."

He turned back to the kid, in the split second that Eddie had looked away, he hadn't moved. He had a chance to run, but he hadn't budged an inch. The killer instinct in him was telling him to stay, he probably enjoyed the fight and the struggle as much as Eddie did, and even though he was going to be on the losing end of it this time, he clearly wanted to stay and experience it.

Eddie tossed the knife from his right hand to his left and then drove a fist across the other kid's face. He reveled in the feeling of his fist crunching against jawbone and grinned maliciously as the vibration reverberated through his knuckles and along his forearm.

The boy bounced backwards, his skull knocked against the solid wall, and then flopped forward, perfectly placed for Eddie to deliver another shift jab, this time to his nose. The appendage ruptured under the impact, following by a muffled whine as the kid crumpled in on himself.

"Hurry up!"

Eddie turned to see Darren yelling at him. He looked alarmed, desperate. Eddie could see the thirst for blood in his eyes; he was impressed and felt a newfound respect for his friend.

"Finish him!" Darren screamed.

Eddie nodded slowly, "Okay." He tossed the knife back to his right hand and looked down at the youngster, who was gazing up at him with defiance in his eyes.

"Kill me," the youngster said, echoing Darren's thoughts and Eddie's intentions. "Kill me."

* * *

"Please don't kill me. Please don't kill me."

When Malcolm burst into the room he saw Eddie looming over Neil, Neil was murmuring, repeating a succession of mumbled words, but this time Malcolm could make out what he was saying.

"Please don't kill me. Please don't kill me."

Darren was standing back, watching in horror and screaming at Eddie to stop, to leave Neil alone, but Eddie seemed lost in a world of his own. He picked Neil up with his free hand, whispered something to him and then prepared to drive the knife into his stomach. Malcolm tackled him before he had a chance.

He didn't think about consequences. He didn't think about the knife in Eddie's hands as he hit him and knocked him to the ground, but he felt the blade whip across his thigh when they fell, felt it cut through his jeans and open a small gash just above his knee.

He was lucky, but he didn't think about that. He let the adrenaline take over, let his anger—an anger that had been repressed, held deep down in the darkest pit of his conscious, for most of the day—take over. He rolled Eddie over and looked briefly into his eyes, there was no recognition there, no feeling, he didn't even look angry, he looked blank and apathetic. Malcolm hit him hard, so hard that he felt the floor beneath Eddie's skull as he forced the latter into the former. He hit him twice, three times, four times, driving his fist into a face that had been so familiar for so long.

Eddie didn't retaliate. His hands lay still by his side. He had lost control of the knife but he didn't even try to reach for it, nor did he try to punch back or to block his friend's punches.

Eventually Malcolm felt some resistance, some fight, but not from Eddie. Darren was behind him, pulling hard at his shoulders and his back, trying to yank him off their friend. He succeeded in the end, but only because Malcolm had exhausted himself. Darren dragged him off and they both fell to the floor, alongside Eddie who lay still—a smirk on his bloody face.

Eddie coughed, blood dripped from his mouth down his face. He laughed, a choking, warbling sound that filtered through the blood gushing from his nose his fat lip.

"Well then," he said with a snigger. "That was fun."

Malcolm shook his head. He looked at Darren who seemed less shocked with Eddie's indifference. He rose to his feet and looked down at Eddie who was also trying to climb to his.

"What the fuck is wrong with you?" he asked.

"Me?" Eddie coughed, wiping the blood from his mouth and inspecting the back of his sleeve. "*Me*? What the fuck is wrong with *you*?"

Malcolm didn't answer, he felt a pang of guilt, but that vanished when he looked at Neil and remembered how close Eddie had been to killing him. He felt the anger return and took a step towards Eddie, but Darren quickly jumped to his feet and moved forward to stop him.

"Leave him," Darren warned. "He ain't worth it."

Eddie looked at Darren and laughed. "You changed your mind so fast," he said.

"Changed my mind?" Darren snapped. "Are you fucking kidding? What the hell is going on inside that head of yours?"

Eddie didn't reply, he just stared.

"So, now what?" Eddie asked, his words slurred by his bleeding lip. He wiped the back of his hand across his mouth, smeared the blood across his chin and cheek. "Clearly you don't want me to come with you, so you could just kill me or . . ."

Darren turned to Malcolm and saw the concentration and determination on his friend's face as he glared at Eddie. They locked stares for a moment before Malcolm gave a shake of his head and lowered his eyes. "Just leave," he ordered. "Find your own way out."

"Really?" Darren asked.

"What else do you think we should do?" Malcolm wondered.

Darren thought about this for a moment. He knew they shouldn't split up, but he also knew that they weren't in it together anymore. They had been together as friends for a long time, but as strange as it felt, Eddie wasn't their friend anymore. Eddie was barely even Eddie anymore. They couldn't trust him if they went with him, and despite what Eddie had suggested, they couldn't kill him.

"We could tie him up," Darren offered. "We can always come back for him when we get help."

Malcolm quickly dismissed the idea. "This place is full of psychopaths, they'll find him. If we tie him up, then we might as well be killing him ourselves."

Darren nodded. He didn't like the idea of Eddie being loose in the hospital, he disliked the idea of Eddie sneaking up on them as much as if he were one of the crazies, but they had no other choice.

"Leave," Malcolm ordered. "Just . . . if you find a way out before us, make sure you get help."

Eddie nodded and held his friend's stare momentarily. Malcolm could see the apathy in his eyes and knew that if Eddie *did* find a way out, he wasn't going to get help. He would leave them to die in this place.

They both watched as Eddie departed, glaring back at Neil—still cowering in the corner—before he did so. When he was gone and they listened to the sound of his footfalls echoing down the corridor, Malcolm stared at his bloodied fists and slowly shook his head.

"You certainly gave him a beating," Darren noted. "I bet that felt good."

"I don't know what came over me," Malcolm said. "I just lost it. I've been angry all day, I nearly lost control earlier on, after we first came here, but . . ." he trailed off.

"I know what you mean," Darren said with a nostalgic tone. "I felt it too. I went crazy on Ian this morning and beat the shit out of him. I mean, the dickhead deserved it, but it's not like me."

Malcolm looked at his friend and nodded, he was right, it wasn't like him.

"It's this place," Darren said, looking around as if to emphasize his point. "It did something to us."

"And Eddie?" Malcolm said, asking the question on both of their minds.

Darren nodded. "Probably. He was already heading that way, but . . ." he finished with a shrug. "I don't know what happened to him. He wasn't listening to me; he didn't seem to be hearing what I was saying. I'm pretty sure he tried to kill me, he said he didn't know it was me, but he was looking right at me."

Malcolm nodded. "I saw him on the cameras; I saw the look in his eye earlier. Something's not right, something's snapped."

"He killed two people in the hallway," Darren said, remembering the violent slaughter. "They were staff, I'm sure of it. They were just scared, they weren't patients and they certainly weren't killers. I had the knife and I dropped it to show them I didn't mean any harm, then Eddie . . ." he shook his head, lowered his eyes to the floor. "He butchered them. I tried to stop him. I tried to tell him what he did was horrible, but he didn't seem to hear a word I said. He thought I was fucking praising him."

Malcolm patted his friend on the back, "It's okay," he said. "The psycho has gone now; we'll get out of here and leave him to rot." He looked around the hospital. "It's probably the best place for him."

34

Neil had stayed in his corner, watching the events unfold. His nose had stopped bleeding but the sleeve of his gown and his T-shirt underneath were both covered in blood; his lip was swelling and his eye blackening. He looked melancholic and was trying to keep a low profile, hoping that Malcolm and Darren would ignore him, even though they had probably saved his life.

Malcolm walked over to him, maintaining a smile and a calm exterior. He didn't want to scare him.

"Sorry about that," he said. "He used to be our friend but . . ." He struggled to finish his sentence.

"But now he's a fucking nutcase," Darren said.

"Sounds about right," Malcolm agreed. "But he's gone now and we need your help."

Neil looked up at him, he looked pitiful, like a beaten dog, but he also looked like he was ready to help.

"We need answers," Malcolm said. "What is going on here? What caused everyone to act like this?"

Neil shook his head slowly.

"You must know something," Darren begged. "Who started this?"

Neil shrugged again.

"Who's in charge?" Malcolm asked, before correcting himself, "Who *was* in charge?"

Neil sighed heavily. "Doctor Hildenberg. He's the head doctor."

Malcolm nodded, feeling like he was finally getting somewhere. "Is he still alive?"

Neil shrugged. "I'm not sure."

"What has he got to do with all of this?" Darren jumped in. "Is this some sort of sick experimenting thing?"

Neil frowned at him as if he was an idiot. In that moment, that brief expression, Darren and Malcolm saw a spark of intelligence, but it quickly faded and Neil lowered his head again. "I don't think so."

"Where is he?" Malcolm asked, frustrated. He checked over his shoulder, fearful that Eddie would return. He had no idea where his friend had gone, he might have been able to guess where the old Eddie would retreat to, they had been friends a long time and he knew him well, but he didn't know the new Eddie at all.

"You can check his office," Neil said.

"Where is it?"

Neil didn't answer; he merely glanced over Malcolm's shoulder, through the double doors which Eddie had retreated through.

"Okay," Malcolm said with a nod.

"You're not going to leave me, are you?"

Malcolm looked at Neil and saw the fear and desperation in his eyes. He didn't think that Eddie would return, but he knew that if he did, he would probably kill him. "I have no other choice," he said. "But you'll be okay, he's gone now. Just stay here, hide, and keep your head down."

Neil lowered his head immediately, digging his chin into his chest. He didn't look up at Malcolm or Darren and didn't utter anther word.

"We'll be back," Malcolm said, though he knew that he probably wouldn't be.

* * *

"They weren't the first he killed."

"How do you know?"

Darren shrugged. "There was something about him when I ran into him. He changed. God knows what he was doing before he bumped into me."

Malcolm thought about the recreational room, about the pregnant woman and her unborn baby at her feet; he thought about the woman slumped in the hallway and the man disassembled in the kitchen. Was Eddie capable of murder? The same kid who had played football with him in the street, the same kid who he used to watch cartoons with, was he capable of that kind of brutality?

He tried to give Eddie the benefit of the doubt, tried not to imagine what he might have done, but it preyed on his mind. As they walked back through the hospital corridors he took every corner with caution, wondering if his friend was waiting around one of them, ready to do to him and Darren what he had probably done to others.

Darren asked, "Do you think he led us here on purpose?"

Malcolm looked at him and then back down the long and empty corridor. He shrugged. He had been thinking the same thing, Eddie was the reason they were there after all, but he had nothing to gain by getting them there.

"No," he said. "This place does something to people. It did something to the patients and it's done something to us. We managed to suppress it, but Eddie and the patients . . ." he trailed off.

"Patients?" Darren quizzed.

Malcolm nodded slowly. "This isn't a clinic for rich drug addicts; it's a looney bin, a mental hospital, whatever you want to call it."

"Holy shit."

"Yep."

"Do you think Eddie knew?"

Malcolm stopped and stared. "Look, it doesn't matter if Eddie knew or not, it doesn't matter if he lured us here. What matters is that we find out what the fuck is going on and then get the hell out of here. Agreed?"

"Do we need to find out what's going on?" Darren wondered. "I'm all for breaking a window, yanking out the bars, and jumping. The sooner we get the fuck out of here, the better."

Malcolm shook his head. He thought about all the murder and the carnage. He also thought about Nell and about other innocent people who might be hiding out in the hospital. "We need answers," he said eventually, "we need to do what we can to help these people and bring justice to those we can't help."

Darren agreed, but he still felt the urge to run or hide, "And you think we'll find it with this doctor?"

Malcolm shrugged. He checked down the corridor and spotted the doctor's room on the right, hiding under a flickering fluorescent, the nameplate glistening in the stuttering light. "We're about to find out."

35

The doors shut with a bang, startling the teenagers who turned around so quickly that they nearly lost their footing. It was pitch black inside the room, broken only by a thin stream of stuttering light that crept underneath the door and illuminated their feet. They felt the rush of air from the door as it shut. They froze. Darren stretched out his arm and grasped at Malcolm's sleeve, holding it tighter, feeling comfort in knowing that his friend was so close, even though he couldn't see him.

He heard a noise in the darkness, a muffled noise that came from the other end of the room.

"Was that you?" Darren asked, hearing the hiss of his whisper as it reverberated throughout the room.

Malcolm answered softly and simply, "No."

Darren held onto his friend tighter, his fingertips brushing the flesh of his arm, his hand nearly wrapping around his wrist. He sidestepped closer, until he felt the comfort of his friend's body heat.

He felt his heart beat quickly in his chest and held tighter onto Malcolm's arm as his palms moistened with sweat and his grip loosened.

"I don't like this" Darren said. "I don't—"

His throat turned bone-dry. He could sense someone else nearby. He had a feeling they were being watched. He knew something wasn't right.

He held Malcolm tighter, moved even closer. He didn't feel embarrassed; Malcolm was bigger, stronger, and more confident than him. Malcolm had always been the leader of their group; he'd always protected them, Darren was just the funny one.

"It's okay," Malcolm said. "I'll find a light switch."

"Okay, be—" Darren paused, the words were stuck in his throat. He turned to his right, towards the source of Malcolm's voice. He felt him move beside him as he searched for the light switch. He turned to his left, towards the arm he had been holding. He loosened his grip and steadily pulled away, staring upwards, towards where their face would be, and his heart dropped to his stomach.

When Malcolm found the light switch and flicked it on, a big man grinned down at Darren, who quickly let go of the arm he had been holding.

"Shit," Darren croaked.

He saw the punch coming as it cut through the air and headed straight for his face, but he couldn't move in time to stop it. His breath caught, his heart stopped, and his brain froze in anticipation, then the punch landed and everything exploded. A bolt of pain raced through his body, he lost control of his senses, lost his ability to stand and to see. He toppled backwards, tripping over his legs and an unseen piece of furniture. His back and his skull collided with the floor and with whatever else managed to get in his way. He was dazed and semi-comatose. He tried to right himself, listening to a primal instinct that warned him to stand and fight or face certain death, but he couldn't drag himself to his feet. He couldn't concentrate his eyes on his attacker. He was slipping further and further out of reality.

Malcolm managed to dodge out of the way of his own attacker, he felt the rush of air as Darren took the blow, saw his friend propelled backwards under the incredible force of the impact, but he tried not to concentrate on it, tried to keep his mind on the man in front of him. After ducking out of the way of the first blow, he waited for a second. The man was bigger than him, but he was also slower.

The second was a low shot, which Malcolm hadn't been expecting. He tried to shift out of the way but his space was limited and there was nowhere for his body to move. He cornered himself against the wall, felt his attacker's fist against his stomach and then watched, helplessly, as he threw another low punch. He couldn't back up anymore and didn't possess the power to block the punch, so instead he braced himself. The punch sucked the air out of his lungs and forced all his oxygen and blood into his head. He recoiled, bent forward and then immediately wished he hadn't. He was exposed, waiting for a shot to his forehead, a punch that could knock him unconscious or kill him, but rather than a forceful fist against his exposed temple, he felt a hand on his shoulder, felt his attacker shove him upright and back against the wall. Then he felt a sharp prick in his neck. He didn't see the syringe in his attacker's hand. He didn't feel the drug enter his bloodstream, but in moments, before the needle was pulled out of his flesh, he felt the effects.

Malcolm lost his balance and fell to his knees, struggling to stay awake. His attacker calmly stepped over him and injected Darren with the same needle. The drug took away the pain and the fear, replacing it with a calm and empty void.

36

Malcolm remembered a struggle. He remembered fighting someone who had complete control over him; remembered being helpless as they lifted him, twisted him and moved him against his will as if he were a piece of clay that they could mold as they saw fit. He remembered trying to punch, trying to kick, and trying to squirm, but managing nothing more than a tremble; he remembered trying to shout, trying to scream and to bite, but managing nothing more than a drooling mumble.

He slipped in and out of consciousness. He woke up a few times, opening his eyes to see his attackers grinning, chatting, and laughing. He also remembered seeing someone else, the men that had attacked him and Darren had gone and were replaced by a wizened man with a curious expression. He also remembered seeing Darren—his head slumped over the back of a chair—and he even remembered seeing Eddie, who had a curious expression of delight and intrigue on his face.

Malcolm wasn't sure which of his memories had been real and which ones were dreams, but he continued to remember, continued to experience, until he eventually experienced a flash of reality and he returned to the world of the living. He opened his eyes for what felt like the hundredth time and knew they were going to stay open. He could still feel the drug in his system, the effect it had on his muscles, his nerves, and his mind. He was weak, sedate, and he struggled to think or move, but he was regaining control with every passing moment.

His vision was still struggling and he couldn't see anything but bright lights beaming into his eyes and causing a painful throbbing in his skull. He wanted to close his eyes and avoid the pain, but he didn't want to slip into unconsciousness again so he kept them open and tried his best to ignore it.

He heard voices behind him, there were at least two of them. One of them sounded old and calm, the other sounded young and excited. And although he didn't think they were the attackers, they sounded strangely familiar.

He managed to turn his head, edging his neck muscles incrementally and feeling the strain on his neck, his head, and his back. He saw a shape next to him, a slumped form sitting, hunched over in a chair. He knew it was Darren and he could tell that his friend hadn't woken up yet.

Like his friend next to him, Malcolm had also been restrained. The ropes tied his ankles and wrists tightly to the chair; he could feel the abrasive material cutting into his flesh. He didn't know how long he had been out, had no way of telling, but he was slumped forward with his back arched and he had seemingly been in that position for a while, because his back was aching and felt stiff.

His muscles were waking up, tingling with pins and needles as the blood flow was restored. He felt the fogginess in his mind subside, felt rational thought and common sense return. He could see more now. He was sitting on some sort of raised platform with a reflective laminate floor beneath him and pitch black beyond, but there were spotlights aimed at and around him; the glare stopped him from making anything out.

"He's awake." He heard the voice behind him say. "Should we begin?"

"Give him time."

"What about Darren? Are you sure he's not dead?"

Malcolm felt his heart rap against his chest, he turned quickly towards his friend, quick enough for a bolt of pain to shoot up his spine and explode inside his skull. His sight turned fuzzy, a myriad of dancing stars covered everything he saw for a split second, but when the stars faded and the pain subsided, he saw that Darren was still slumped over, and not responding.

"He'll be fine," the other voice said eventually.

"Should I give him a slap?"

"If you must."

Malcolm watched as someone walked in-between him and his friend. He heard a smack, followed by a snicker from the attacker and a yelp from Darren. Malcolm breathed a sigh of relief, happy that Darren was still alive, but the relief didn't last. He recognized the person standing in front of him, he'd thought he recognized his voice and now, he knew who it was.

Before Malcolm could say anything, Darren squirmed upright, glared at his attacker and blurted, "*Eddie*? What the fuck are you doing?"

37

Eddie's response was a boorish laugh. He threw his head back, his eyes to the spotlights above, and roared hysterically.

"You always were the clown," he said when the laughter had faded to an echo that bounced solemnly in and around the large room. "But I don't think you'll find any of this funny, *buddy.*" His distaste at referring to Darren as his friend was evident, the word curled off his lip like menace from a snake's hiss.

He turned around and looked at Malcolm. Malcolm could see him fully now that his eyes had adjusted to the bright lights.

"Hello again, Malcolm," Eddie said.

Malcolm didn't reply, he stared into his friend's eyes, into the evil and corruption that lay within his soul.

"Not feeling very talkative?" Eddie asked.

Still Malcolm stared.

"Well then," Eddie said, moving aside and drawing the attention of both of his old friends as he walked to the back of the room. "Maybe this will change your mind."

They strained to see what he was doing, but couldn't turn around enough on their chairs. They heard a loud mechanical click and saw the spotlights turn. They both turned back around sharply to see that they were on a stage, now illuminated from above. The spotlights had been turned on and they could now see the empty seats in front of them, with two men standing at the front of the stage.

As their eyes adjusted to the change in light, they noticed that not all the seats in the house were empty. Two rows back, with a perfect view of the stage, sat Malcolm's mother, Darren's mother, and his stepdad, Ian. They all squinted at the stage, their mouths had been wrapped in tape and their hands had been bound behind their backs.

"Welcome to the show!" Someone announced in a grand and proud voice.

Malcolm and Darren both turned to see a tall man in a white doctor's coat striding past them. He stopped in the center to stare at them and to let them see him. He had a gaunt and intelligent face, a white beard tufting out of his long chin, and receding grey hair that stretched away from an elongated forehead. He was thin, but he looked proud and wise. Both Darren and Malcolm also noticed something in his eyes, the way he moved and the way he smiled, a resemblance that was hard to miss.

"Malcolm, Darren," he announced, waving his hand around before placing it behind his back with his other hand. "I'm sure you're familiar with your audience tonight. Please ignore the two goons on the stage, they're with me."

The two patients didn't flinch at the comment, they continued to stare, looking like doormen at the head of the stage but with an expectant and excited look in their eyes, as if they were about to tuck into a super-sized bag of popcorn and watch the latest blockbuster.

"My name is Doctor Hildenberg; you probably have a few questions for me." He concentrated his expression, one of devilment, on Malcolm. "And this," he held out his hand, pointing to Eddie who strode forward to stand by his side, looking happier than he had ever been. "Is my son, Marshall."

"What the fuck?" Darren spat, feeling a surge of anger that fused with his confusion and fear. "That ginger-fucking-psycho is not your son and his name is not Marshall."

Marshall turned towards Darren, he looked like he was about to run over to him and throttle him, but a look from the doctor restrained him. "You may know him as Eddie, but I assure you, that is not his name and those people he had been living with were not his parents."

"You're mental," Darren noted. He knew he should keep his thoughts to himself, but his anger was getting the better of him. The fact that his friend—someone who he had played with as a child, someone who he had sleepovers with and grown up with—

was siding with this psycho over him made him even angrier. "You're just like all these other psychos. Who did you steal that coat from? Where's the real doctor?"

Darren felt the way he did before he'd attacked Ian. He could feel his anger taking over him and it only grew stronger every time he looked at the doctor and even more when he saw his mother in the audience. He preferred this aggression to the paralyzing fear he'd felt before, so he didn't try to suppress it.

"I assure you, I am a real doctor."

"Fuck off."

The doctor sighed and turned to Malcolm. "You're taking this much better than I expected, if I may say so."

Malcolm didn't reply straight away. He looked from the doctor to Eddie and then back again. He looked towards his mother, the woman who had abandoned him.

"What the fuck is going on?" he asked.

The doctor laughed, a laugh that Malcolm had witnessed in Eddie just a few moments earlier. "Okay," he said eventually, raising his hand. "I'll explain."

He paused for breath, to let everyone know that he needed their attention, this was his show, after all.

"You three; Darren, Malcolm, and Marshall, were all born here." He paused to study their reactions; Darren's face creased, Malcolm gave a blank stare, Marshall had clearly heard it all before.

"As I have been explaining to my son here," the doctor said, patting Marshall on the head in the manner of a man who has no idea how to act around children. "This is your place of birth and, using the techniques I have honed over the years," he added with pride, "I have managed to bring you all back here."

"What the fuck are you talking about?" Darren spat. "What is that ginger asshole doing with you?" he nodded towards Eddie. "What does he have to do with any of this?"

"He's my son."

"Bullshit!"

The doctor sighed and gave a gentle and patient shake of his head.

"How did he get here so fast?" Malcolm quizzed. "Was this all a setup, did he lure us here?" he referred to Eddie with bitterness, as if he couldn't speak his name.

The doctor shook his head. "He was as oblivious as you were. It's his *uncle* who brought you here," he announced, adding emphasis to suggest that he wasn't really his uncle. "He was a former patient of mine, easy to manipulate. Marshall had nothing to do with it, but of course, he will be involved from now on." He smiled. "You've been out for a long time boys, hours, we've been catching up. We had a lot to catch up on." He put his arm lovingly around Marshall's shoulders.

"This is all bollocks," Darren said, still riding the tide of anger.

The doctor shook his head, as calm as ever. "You have memories of this place," he said. "You all do. It affects you, it makes you angry, it changes you. You're frustrated because you remember this place; you remember the hatred, the anger, and the terrible things that took place here. You all remember being born here, suffering here and watching your parents suffer here. But you repressed those memories, you were young enough to do so and you fed off of each other, when one of you began to repress, the others followed. You three were practically brothers, you helped each other." He nodded slowly, an expression of pride and admiration on his face. "It's commendable really; the power of the subconscious really is an amazing thing."

"Shit," Darren said, but he had a feeling that the doctor was telling the truth. He hadn't remembered any of the hospital, but he remembered the feelings he had, the creeping sensation that something wasn't right. He didn't want to believe a word that the psychopathic doctor said, but he didn't doubt that he could be telling the truth.

"My son handled things a little differently than you," the doctor continued. "But his life in this hospital was much more difficult than yours." He put his hand around Marshall and smiled happily at him. "His mother was a patient here, her and I . . ." he tilted his head this way and that, "well, they said I raped her. But they said a lot of things that weren't true. The truth is she probably wasn't capable of ever consenting to anything, but what we did certainly wasn't rape. By the time she was ready to give birth, they found out about my experiments here at the hospital. They said I was trying to manipulate the patients, that I was trying to mold their minds—"

"Were you?" Darren cut in.

Hildenberg nodded, "Of course I was. I am a psychologist, a proponent of the art of the psychosis. I could hardly advance my understanding and my effectiveness in the field by merely helping people, now could I?"

"Of course not," Darren said. "That would be stupid."

Hildenberg made a "hmm" sound before continuing. "They stripped me of my role and they said I was mad, me, mad."

"Can you imagine that?" Darren mocked.

"They then found out about Marshall here," he continued, unperturbed by Darren's comment. "I told them the baby was mine, I wanted to look after him, but before he was born they locked me up. They stopped me going near him."

The doctor moved his arm away from Marshall and turned around to stare at the audience, to take in the parents and the children. "You two were born at the same time, to equally psychotic mothers."

The mothers in the audience tried to respond, but their words were muffled by their gags. Hildenberg waved a hand at his goons and they stood up and began to make their way towards the parents who squirmed when they saw them approach.

"They got to keep their babies, you stayed here and waited for them to be released, at which point they took you with them. But I lost my Marshall. They refused to let me keep him, refused to even let his mother keep him. Your parents, these *scoundrels*," he said with a dismissive wave of his hand, "helped Marshall get out; they kept him until he found a foster home." He shook his head. "Of course your fathers had nothing to do with it, they weren't even patients here. As for your stepfather," he said, looking towards Darren and then at Ian before shrugging. "He got in the way. I figured I'd bring him along."

The goons stripped the gags from the parents, each of them gasped and shouted in turn. The obscenities, the screams. They were cut short by the goons who threatened them. Ian, the loudest of the three—screaming at the doctor and threatening to tear out his throat—received a slap across his face for his trouble. When they were silent, Hildenberg raised his head and looked at Darren's mother.

"Tell him," he said.

Darren saw a tear roll down his mother's cheek, saw the expression on her face. He had seen her unhappy before, but this was different. The depression was deep on her face, from her glassy eyes to the wrinkles that creased on her chin and forehead. For the first time in years she was being genuine.

"I'm so sorry," she said, stumbling over her words as tears took over. "He's telling the truth, it's all true."

Darren felt angry. He was angry that his life had been a lie, that it took one madman and his psycho son to inform him of something he should have known all along, but when he looked into his mother's eyes, when he saw the sincerity and the pain on her face, he struggled to express that anger. Instead he gave her a warm smile, letting her know that he didn't mind, that he understood.

"Aww," the doctor called, throwing his voice like an actor in a proud role. "Isn't that sweet, eh, son?" Beside him, Eddie nodded exaggeratedly, standing tall and proud, proud to be next to his father, proud to be next to someone who was just like him. "But don't forget," he said with a sly smile, "not only is it all her fault that you were born here, *and* her fault that you're here now, but it's also her fault that your father left."

Darren shot an angry glance at the doctor. "What do you mean?"

He heard his mother begin to blubber, but he kept his attention on the doctor, on the wicked smile that curled the corner of his wizened face.

"I'm so sorry," his mother mumbled, before the doctor had a chance to speak. "I was in a horrible place, that's why they put me here. I was down, I was doing some really bad things, I—" she struggled to finish.

"She didn't want you," the doctor announced. "You were nothing to her, yet . . ." he thrust out a wagging finger, "*she* still got to keep you. Where's the justice in that, eh?"

Beside him Eddie shrugged and shook his head, agreeing with his father. "Your father had a little more respect for you," he continued, "but only enough to walk away from your mother, not enough to stick around to see how you turned out."

38

Malcolm locked eyes with his mother, exchanging things that couldn't be expressed with words. He had always been disappointed in her, he hated her for running away, hated her for leaving him in such a precarious position. There was a good chance he would have been forced to live on the streets, forced to go hungry, and she knew that, yet she did nothing to stop it. But, she let him live in the house and he knew that she could have taken everything, could have stripped the house of its furniture, or demanded that he move out. He didn't care about that though, the fact that she hadn't done anything, hadn't even said goodbye, was worse than anything else she could have done.

The fact that she had mental health issues also wasn't much of a surprise, she had never been the most stable woman, but the fact that she had hid the truth from him all these years was a surprise. She was useless at keeping secrets, she loved gossip and had never been able to keep her mouth shut, so to keep something like this from him throughout his life was hard to believe, yet, he knew it was true.

"So, this was all a setup?" Darren asked, grimacing towards the doctor. "You lured us out here to kill us?"

"He catches on quick, doesn't he?" Marshall mocked, grinning at his father.

"Why?" Darren asked, ignoring his former friend.

The doctor took a proud step forward, back into his showman role. "This is about justice," he announced. "I have my son back after all these years, but this place, these people," he said bitterly, looking at small audience, "took him away from me and they need to know what that feels like."

"We didn't take him away from you," Malcolm's mother piped up, shifting her gaze from her son for the first time. "It was the hospital, not us."

Doctor Hildenberg grinned and looked at Darren and Malcolm. "Believe me, the hospital and its staff has had its punishment. Isn't that right kids?"

Neither of them answered but they knew he was right. The hospital had been torn apart from the inside out; the staff had been tortured, scared out of their wits, and then slaughtered. The hospital would never recover from an incident like this and the teenagers knew it, as did the doctor.

"They sent me to an asylum, sent me away from my child," he continued. "But I came back. I changed my name, applied for a job, and these idiots took me. Within weeks I was working on my old experiments, manipulating the patients to my will." He looked proud of himself, almost giddy as he relayed his accomplishments. "I created a Trojan horse in the mind of the patients. They were weak and susceptible; it didn't take much. I gave them a trigger and released them all at once."

"I don't get it," Darren jumped in. "If you wanted us alive, why did they try to kill us?"

The doctor shrugged casually. "A minor mishap. I couldn't make them as selective as I thought, but," he looked to the front of the stage, to where the two goons had returned to wait for their part in this sickening spectacle. "I drafted in a few bodyguards to help keep you alive, to guide you and bring you to me when everything was ready."

The doctor turned to Malcolm and grinned widely, he was silent, as if waiting for Malcolm to speak, to admit; eventually he said, "Although it seems the patients weren't the only murderers here. You killed one of my men, didn't you?"

Malcolm glared. "It's hard to tell the psychos apart in this place. They all wear the same clothes: pajamas, dressing gowns . . ." he paused to look the doctor up and down, "white coats."

The doctor stared at Malcolm, lost in thought, a touch of awe on his smile.

"What about *Red* here," Darren asked, nodding towards Marshall. "Why did he go all psycho, was that you as well?"

The doctor didn't look towards Darren; he didn't seem to want to peel his eyes away from Malcolm. Marshall took the lead instead, an expression of devilment on his face as he strode towards his former friend and watched him twitch and squirm in his seat.

"For years you've mocked me, toyed with me—"

"We were friends," Darren spat, annoyed. "*Mocking* and *toying* was exactly what it was. It was harmless. You knew that then and you accepted it, but now," he looked to the doctor and back again. "Now that Dr. Evil is on the scene; you've lost your shit."

"He's my dad."

"What about your other parents, eh? They looked after you for years; they let you get away with murder."

Marshall threw his head back and laughed. The doctor broke his stare with Malcolm and turned to grin at his son and then at Darren.

"Funny you should say that," Marshall said eventually, the humor in his laugh was fake, so contrived and unnatural that it sent a chill up Darren's spine. Something wasn't right, whatever had once existed inside Eddie, whatever had once made him their friend and their companion, had gone—replaced by a soulless void, Marshall.

Darren waited for Marshall to elaborate, but no explanation came. "Why?" he asked, his voice croaked and he repeated himself, trying to hide the obvious fear that trembled through his words.

"Because I killed them," Marshall shrugged as he spoke, as if the act had been easy and had meant nothing to him."

"Bullshit," Darren said.

"It's true." Hildenberg stepped forward, looking proudly at his son. "A little unexpected, but my son was feeling a lot of repressed rage, rather like you two were, only more so."

"You brought them here, too?" Darren asked. "Why? What—"

Eddie was shaking his head, he held up a finger and Darren stopped speaking. "I killed them before we came here, *before* we left."

Darren remembered Eddie waiting for them outside his house, he remembered the expression on his face, the glint in his eye; he remembered the way he had shifted from foot to foot, looking up and down the street with the suspicion of a criminal.

"Holy shit," he said softly. "You knew all this time?"

Marshall shook his head. "Maybe deep down. But not really."

"My son has gone through a lot, we both have," the doctor clarified. "I didn't ask him to kill his parents, but he did it and I'll stand by him. He was acting on his own urges. He was drawn to kill them just like he was drawn here, just like he was drawn to kill some of the people in the hospital, people who had wronged me and, by definition, him. He did well. I guess I underestimated him," he said softly, patting his child awkwardly on the back.

"This is like a Bates' family reunion," Darren said, shaking his head.

The smile vanished from the doctor's face; he turned away from Darren, glanced briefly at Malcolm, and then addressed the small crowd, the waiting parents who had come to watch their children die. "I think we've done enough talking. I've been waiting a long time for this, what do you say we get this show on the road?"

Horrified faces stared back at him; the only one that agreed was Marshall, who was nodding with glee beside his newfound father.

39

"There was really only one way I could do this," Hildenberg announced, soaking in the apprehension at the end of his sentence. "Death can be quick, it can also be messy, but I want it to be slow." He addressed the parents in the audience. "I want you to suffer as I suffered, I want you to know what it's like to be unable to help your child, to be unable to protect them, or to take away their pain."

He moved to the side of the stage, Malcolm twisted his neck and watched him out of the corner of his eye. His heart was beating ferociously in his chest; it sank into his stomach when he saw the can of petrol in the doctor's hands.

"You're going to burn," he told Malcolm and Darren matter-of-factly, before turning to the parents. "And you're going to watch."

"This is not the answer!" Malcolm's mother shouted. "We had nothing to do with what happened to you, we're sorry, but please . . . don't do this to my boy."

"Your boy?" He raised an eyebrow at her, Malcolm knew what he was thinking; he was thinking the same. "Is this the same boy that you abandoned for a cheap affair with a degenerate?" He shook his head. "People like you both amaze and sicken me."

He turned to his bodyguards and gestured towards the parents. "Gag them again," he ordered, just as Malcolm's mother released a torrent of abuse towards the doctor, "I don't want to be interrupted by their screaming."

The bodyguards acknowledged the order and slowly moved to the end of the stage in tandem, a Laurel and Hardy double act, just as the doctor had ordered. He grinned at his creations. That grin disappeared when the spotlights crashed down on top of the two men.

They crumpled under the thunderous impact. The lights shattered on one of their skulls, showering splinters of glass down his face and spraying them across the stage. The second was hit by the pole that held the two lights together, it was a heavy, solid steel support and the impact was enough to crush his skull. They were both dead before they hit the floor.

The lights flickered madly on top of the two bodies as everyone in the room stared in disbelief. It was sudden, it was loud and it was deadly. They had fallen on top of each other, their limp bodies overlapping. A pool of blood spread around them, slowly oozing over the stage.

The doctor looked up to the rafters and then towards Marshall who was still staring at the two dead patients. "Go and check it out," he ordered.

"What?" Marshall said, turning towards his father, a look of bewilderment on his face.

"That wasn't an accident," he said, hiding the trepidation in his voice. "Go backstage and check it out."

Marshall turned towards the backstage area. It was unlit and fed off the light from the main stage, but after a certain point the darkness seemed impenetrable and the turnoffs—into the dressing rooms and storerooms—looked menacing. He looked back at his father, uncertainty on his face and in his voice. "Are you sure?"

"Yes, I'm fucking sure," Hildenberg snapped. "*Look at them*!" he said, gesticulating madly towards the murdered henchmen. The spotlight was still connected to the mains and was flickering and fizzing on top of them, one of their legs was twitching madly, as if trying to tap out a tune to the rhythm of the hissing electricity. "That wasn't a fucking accident," he repeated.

"Okay," Marshall nodded, hiding the apprehension on his face. He straightened his back and puffed out his chest. "You're right. Someone's fucking with us. I'll go and check it out," he said proudly, the tone of a kid trying to impress his dad.

Hildenberg smiled disingenuously, hiding his frustration. He waited until his son strode confidently into the darkness before he turned towards his audience. "A minor mishap," he assured them.

"You call *that* minor?" Darren mocked, nodding towards the twitching leg of the dead bodyguard.

Hildenberg followed Darren's eyes, he prepared a rebuttal, prepared to intimidate Darren and to remind him of what awaited him, but when his eyes fell upon the two dead guards his words caught in his throat. Inside he prayed that it *was* minor and that he hadn't just sent his son to his death.

* * *

Marshall slowed as he entered the darkness. He slapped the wall, looking for a switch, but he failed to find one. He ventured onwards regardless, into the encroaching darkness, relying on a quickly developing night vision and the knowledge that if someone was waiting for him, they would be at just as much of a disadvantage as he was.

He heard the calls from the audience as the parents shouted at the doctor, abusing him. Marshall found them sickening, they were horrible people and they deserved to suffer; they deserved to die just as much as Malcolm and Darren did. He was indifferent to the deaths of his former friends—though he understood the reasons that they had to die—but he would happily watch the parents die. They deserved it more. He knew that they would be next, knew that after they had watched their sons being burned alive, they would be killed. His father would enjoy their pain for a while, he would revel in their agony, but then he would kill them in the same way.

He grinned in anticipation as he walked backstage. He walked past the suits and costumes, used for drama therapy by patients that were now dead or insane. He was so lost in his own head, wrapped in his thoughts, that he didn't see the figure stepping out from behind the clothes. He didn't see it raise the fire extinguisher and didn't see it swinging down toward him.

40

Malcolm enjoyed the expression on the doctor's face. He had watched and listened as the smug madman had recounted his story with the glee of a James Bond villain; he had suffered under his ego, listened to his stories of redemption and been forced to sit there as he told Malcolm he was going to torture him and kill him, but now the doctor looked terrified and that brought a smile to Malcolm's face.

Malcolm had nearly jumped out of his skin when the spotlights fell on the bodyguards. He hadn't been watching them at the time and had only seen the falling lights out of the corner of his eye—the noise had been alarming and the result was catastrophic. He had also heard the noise backstage: the grunt and the bang. He didn't expect anything from it; he didn't expect to be saved. There was no one else in the hospital that knew they were there, no one on their side ready to save the day. He knew there was no hope for him or Darren, but the doctor didn't know that and Malcolm enjoyed the fear on his face as he pondered the possibilities on his night of vengeance being ruined.

Malcolm heard a shuffling sound. A slow, staggering sound that grew in volume with each ominous shuffle. It sounded like something heavy being dragged across a wooden floor and it was getting closer and closer. Malcolm stopped smiling and turned towards the backstage area, towards the darkness, wondering what would emerge.

The shuffling continued, capturing the attention of the entire room. Everyone was silent as they listened and waited, the fizz from the buzzing lights and half a dozen heavy breaths were the only accompanying noises as the shuffling increased.

When the source of the noise emerged, Malcolm realized that there *was* one person in the hospital that he knew, one person that knew he was there and might look upon him favorably, but he was the last person he had expected to see, the last person he would ever expect to see striding onto the stage with a knife in one hand and Marshall's unconscious body being dragged in the other.

"Who the fuck are you?" Hildenberg said, staring at the newcomer as he made his way straight towards the doctor before stopping, dropping Marshall's body behind him, and then planting a foot on his neck.

"I suppose I shouldn't be surprised that you don't recognize me," he said, grinning madly, the same grin that had been displayed on Marshall's face for most of the night, the same grin that the doctor himself had expressed during his gleeful act. "Although I'm amazed you don't see the similarities."

The doctor shook his head. "I don't . . ." He couldn't find the words and seemed lost in the newcomer's eyes.

"*Neil*?" Malcolm said, speaking for him. "What are you doing?"

"I'm sorry I'm late," Neil said, glancing towards Malcolm but still trying to maintain eye contact with Hildenberg. "I was just waiting for the right time," he added, nodding towards the two bodies at the edge of the stage.

"I don't understand," Malcolm said. The Neil he saw now wasn't the same scared kid he had seen earlier. This one looked vibrant, mad. He looked stronger than he was before, much more confident. He seemed at ease with himself and with the world around him. Malcolm hadn't seen the resemblance before but he saw it now. He didn't look like him, his hair was a different color, he was a different build, but he saw it in the way he smiled, the way he stood. He looked like Marshall.

"There's a lot to explain," Neil said. "But, unlike the good doctor here, I'm not one for big explanations so I'll keep it simple."

He reached down and grabbed Marshall by the hair, yanking him upright. Marshall stirred, bringing a look of relief to his father's face—who had considered that he might be dead—until Neil brought the knife to Marshall's throat.

"This little prick here, is my brother," Neil said, pressing the knife into Marshall's throat, as if a mere mention of the fraternal link disgusted him. "You see, his mother, *my* mother, didn't have just one baby. She had twins." He told the doctor. "If you'd have stuck around a bit longer, you might have learned that."

The doctor put a hand to his head, ran it through his hair. "This can't be. . ."

"Ah, but it is. Not identical of course, I clearly got all the looks, but we're twins." He yanked Marshall harder by the hair, caused him to moan; his eyes fluttered, as if he was about to open them, but they remained closed.

The doctor was shaking his head, "But there was only one adoption certificate."

"Because I wasn't adopted. This one was lucky," he said, yanking Marshall's hair again, grimacing through gritted teeth as he did so. "I was sent to a home. I was a sweet little baby, I stood every chance of being adopted like him, but then word got out about my father and my mother." He paused to stare at the doctor. "No one wants a psycho kid from a psycho family."

Marshall stirred again; Neil kicked him hard in the ribs, a cathartic release of some inner angst.

"I spent my infancy in an orphanage and my childhood in a psychiatric hospital," he shrugged. "Schizophrenic they said, I guess I'm a product of my father's creation. *You* made me like this. *You* ruined my life. *You* raped my mother, ignored my existence, and then had the nerve to try to fuck with me. I was transferred here when I heard you had returned, I managed to fiddle the files, to make sure I came here. I was hoping for some recognition, I was hoping that you would at least remember me before I killed you, but not only didn't you recognize me, you actually had the nerve to try to mold my mind like one of your psychotic fucking patients."

"Remember you? But I didn't know, I didn't—"

"Shut up!" Neil screamed, his voice breaking. "What about this piece of shit?" he said, his voice loud enough to tear his own throat. "You remembered him. You engineered your entire career to get him back. What about me, eh? Where the fuck did I fit into your plans?"

"I honestly didn't know, I thought—"

"You thought *nothing*," Neil snapped. He lifted Marshall up, pressed him against his torso, pointing him towards his father, and pressing the knife against his throat. Marshall opened his eyes and looked at his father, he looked confused, dazed.

"What do you want?" Hildenberg asked, switching his worried expression between his two sons. "I'll give you whatever you want, just don't hurt him."

Neil laughed. A laugh that sent a chill through Malcolm and Darren, they had heard the same callous cacophony spew from Marshall's lungs only moments earlier. "You don't understand," he said, staring at his estranged father over his brother's shoulder. "*This* is what I want. I'm not here to negotiate; I'm here to see the expression on your face as I kill your precious little boy."

Hildenberg's eyes opened wide, he made a move forward, to dive at his sons and save Marshall, but Neil moved before he could. He dragged the blade across his brother's throat, opening a large wound which immediately showered blood down his torso. Marshall's eyes continued to stare into his father's, continued to try to grasp what he had woken up to. He looked down, at the blood spewing from the hole in his throat, he tried to cup it, tried to lap at it, but the torrent continued. Eventually, with one last glance at his father—a trembling mess of rage and despair— Marshall slumped forward, facedown into a pool of his own blood.

Neil didn't remove his eyes from his father. He seemed delighted with the despair he had created. "You are sick," he said.

"You and him," he drove a toe into Marshall's bleeding corpse, "and this whole building needs to be destroyed."

Hildenberg stared back. He was breathing heavily, panting like an animal. His face was red, tears welled up in his eyes and threatened to stream down his face. He opened his mouth to retaliate, but the words refused to form. He shook them away, clenched his fists and then charged at his son, with an animalistic roar.

41

Neil enjoyed the anger in his father's eyes and seemed to allow the attack. Hildenberg tackled him to the ground, knocking the knife from his grasp and crashed down on top of his spurned son. Neil was still smiling when Hildenberg pulled back to look at him, to spit a frothy stare at his contented grin.

"You want to *eradicate* me?" Hildenberg spat, spraying Neil with angry spittle. "I'm not a fucking pawn. I'm not a nobody that you can walk all over."

"Like your son you mean?" Neil laughed.

Hildenberg drove a knee into Neil's groin, wiping the smile from his face. He thrust his hands against his neck, pinned his head to the floor and began to squeeze. At first Neil didn't respond, he allowed his father to increase the pressure on his neck, and stared into his angry eyes as he attempted to choke the life out of him.

"You're not my son," Hildenberg hissed. "You'll never be my son."

Neil continued to stare back, enjoying the moment, the despair and the anger in his father's eyes.

Malcolm and Darren watched the spectacle in disbelief, swapping stares between each other and the scrap on the floor. They were helpless and didn't know who to help even if they weren't. Malcolm tried to squirm free, tried to work his hands out of the ropes, but they were tied too tight, the material sunk into his flesh with every movement, every twitch.

On the edge of the stage, where the dead bodies of the two bodyguards lay, the spotlight continued to fizz. It began to spit like a Roman Candle, spraying bright sparks over the stage and over the bodies. Eventually the sparks landed on a dry spot of clothing, catching fire. More sparks fired, more ambers caught, and before long the two bodies at the foot of the stage began to burn; the scent of singed flesh filled the room.

"Are you just going to lie there?" Hildenberg roared at his son.

Neil's face was turning from red to blue but he still didn't move. Hildenberg's face was flush with exertion. He thought he was going to kill him without a struggle and he considered reducing the pressure, removing his hands and waiting for an answer, but the anger and the adrenaline was too high. He continued to squeeze.

Finally, Neil reacted. He bucked out like an animal, catching Hildenberg by surprise. The doctor released his grasp on his son's neck and steadied himself, stopping himself from failing over. Neil bucked again and again, he drove his knee upwards, into the small of Hildenberg's back and then, when the doctor was about to fall, he drove both of his hands upwards, hitting the doctor in his chest and knocking him backwards.

Neil scrambled upright and placed a boot down on the doctor's throat, like he had done to Marshall. The doctor wrapped his hands around it and tried to pry it away, but that only caused Neil to apply more pressure.

"Did you enjoy that?" Neil asked, grinning. "I wanted to see the look in your eyes as you killed me. You brought me into this world, you gave me life, you destroyed my life, and now, you've nearly ended my life. Fitting, wouldn't you say?"

Hildenberg tried to reply, but his voice choked out of his mouth; he tried to kick out, but his legs couldn't reach his attacker; he tried to punch, to grasp Neil's legs, but he needed his hands to relieve the pressure of Neil's foot on his neck.

Neil didn't shift his gaze from his father, didn't look up to the edge of the stage to see that the fire had spread from the two bodies—their flesh hissing and welting under the intense heat—towards the stage curtains. The flames climbed the fabric in an instant, whipping up the curtains and coating the entire stage in the intense light and heat of an inferno.

Neil felt the heat on his skin, he smelled the burnt flesh in his nostrils, cloying at the back of his throat, but he ignored it and concentrated on his father, on the man he had been hunting for most of his life.

"I feel like this should be prolonged somehow," Neil explained, watching as Hildenberg's eyes bulged, as the kicking and squirming reduced, as his face turned blue. "I feel that I should be able to enjoy this more, like I should make you suffer like you were going to make these two suffer, but . . ." he shook his head, "The sooner I kill you, the better."

Hildenberg's eyes were losing focus; his grip on Neil's foot was diminishing.

Malcolm and Darren watched in horror. Malcolm opened his mouth to say something, to tell Neil to stop, an instinct in him that wanted to save human life, but something stopped him. He knew that if the doctor's life was spared, then his own life was at risk; he knew that his only chance of making it out of the building alive was if Neil killed his father.

"Any last words?" Neil asked, mocking the dying man who couldn't speak.

Hildenberg's hands were by his side; his feet were flat against the floor. He had given up but his eyes still twitched, his body was still alive. He looked up at his grinning son, stared into his maddened eyes; he saw the anger, the madness, the depravity, and the timidity, and then he saw nothing.

* * *

The fire was in full flow, the curtains ablaze with a ferocious wave of flames, reaching skyward, licking at the ceiling and lapping at the electrical equipment.

Neil stood in the center, looking down at his dead father and brother. His hair was matted with sweat from exertion and heat. He wiped a hand across his brow, let out a long sigh and then turned to Darren and Malcolm. "I suppose you'll be wanting me to help you?" he asked.

Darren's jaw dropped open in disbelief; Malcolm didn't waste time in answering, "Yes! Please." He could feel the heat, from the inferno above him. Parts of scenery were dropping around him, singed and charred pieces of material floated in the air which was thick with heat and smoke. He flinched when he heard a loud crash behind him as a lighting rig fell, making a hole in the stage and spreading the flames into the foundations of the theatre.

Neil untied Malcolm and then worked on Darren. He took his time; Darren thought he heard the sound of him whistling to himself above the chaos around them.

"Now what?" Malcolm asked, rubbing his hands where the ropes had chafed his wrists and directing his attention towards Neil. He ducked instinctively as another rig crashed down behind him, the entire backstage was ablaze and the flames were fanning, about to envelope them.

Neil shrugged. "You leave. Do what you want."

"And you?" Malcolm asked, already edging away, feeling the intense heat scorch his flesh.

Neil shrugged again and turned to the bodies at his feet. Their flesh was melting; Eddie's hair had caught a spark from the fire and was beginning to burn, the sickening smell of burnt hair and flesh washed over the stage. "There's nothing here for me," Neil said. "I've done what I needed to do."

"You can leave, you can—" Malcolm shrugged off Darren who was trying to tug him off the stage. He glared at him, watched him leave the stage and then turned back to Neil. "—You can be free. You can—"

"I need to see this place burn," Neil said simply, "and I need to burn with it."

"Are you fucking kidding me?" Malcolm said, his desperation and his anger rising as the fire raged around him. "Don't die here like those two."

Neil didn't seem convinced. "I have nothing beyond this."

Malcolm could feel the searing heat. He could feel Darren getting desperate, tugging him. "You have life. You have the knowledge that you can go on living while these fuckers rot."

"I already outlived them," Neil said. "I don't need anything else."

"But—"

Neil stepped forward, sensing the desperation in Malcolm's voice. He was smiling. He was content, seemingly welcoming of the roaring flames and his impending death. He extended his hand, took Malcolm's in his. "You're a good man," he said. "Thank you for trying to help me. Thank you for caring. But . . ." he shook his head, "you're not going to win this battle."

Malcolm gripped Neil's hand tightly. "You sure?"

"Go," Neil said.

"Yes," Darren called from behind, tugging his friend and forcing him to break free from Neil's grasp. "Let's get the fuck out of here!"

Malcolm coughed as a rush of hot and toxic smoke passed into his lungs. He took a step back, having to shield his eyes from the intense light and sweating under the intense heat.

"Come on!" Darren screamed behind him.

Neil was so close to the inferno that Malcolm knew he could feel it, he was close enough to burn, yet he didn't move an inch. Malcolm watched as Neil opened his arms spread eagle and then threw his head to the ceiling. He shouted something, but Malcolm couldn't make it out. He took another few steps back, allowed

Darren to tug him further away, then he watched as the flames engulfed Neil, as the man that had saved his life disappeared in a wash of angry yellow and red.

Darren rushed down the aisle, towards his mother. He rushed to get her untied as Malcolm untied his own mother.

"I'm so sorry!" she yelled, her eyes streaming with tears. "I just . . . I'm—" she was stuttering, struggling to speak. Darren held up a hand to silence her, he pointed to the end of the aisle and told her to wait. He watched as Malcolm untied his mother to similar teary scenes—which Malcolm regarded with apathy—then he turned to Ian who wasn't crying or mumbling. He regarded Darren warily as Darren studied his restraints.

"If you were to leave me here," Ian said simply. "I'd understand."

Darren frowned. The idea had occurred to him, but at that moment he felt indebted to Ian. He felt sorry for what he had done earlier in the day, even if he'd had good reason. He shook his head and untied the ropes around Ian's hand, allowing him to untie his ankles himself. When he was free they stared at each other for a moment, Darren saw the gratitude in his stepfather's eyes, he saw a humanity that he had never seen before.

"Come on!" his mother screamed from the edge of the aisle, let's go!"

The fire was creeping up the aisle, washing over the seats like a wave. The stage was gone, Neil, his father, his twin, and the two bodyguards were now just a part of the epicenter, their bodies extra fuel for the fire.

42

They exited the double doors to the sound of chaos behind them. The fire was spreading quickly; it had already made light work of the hall and was expanding to the upper levels as well as breaking out through the door, encroaching on the corridor.

The group didn't know where they were, but they didn't have time to figure it out. They ran down the nearest corridor. Ian went first, but he kept an eye over his shoulder, watching his lover and her son who followed close behind. Malcolm half-carried his mother down the hallway, making sure she kept up with him and the others as they all ran as fast as their weary legs could carry them. Their feet slapped against the hard floor, echoing throughout the building, but they no longer feared the patients, no longer cared about being heard or seen, they were running away from bigger things now.

They didn't stop when they raced past a pile of dead bodies, propped up against the wall like some macabre art installation; they didn't stop when they heard screaming from a nearby room, or when they heard someone shouting to them from the other end of the corridor. They all pushed on, and when any one of them slowed, the others yelled at them to continue.

They ran down endless corridors, until they all started to look the same, then they realized they were running in circles, and that the corridors were the same. The fire had torn through the building and destroyed much of their path. They could feel its heat all around them, could see the thick smoke flowing down the corridors and could feel it in their lungs. Eventually, Malcolm yelled at them to stop. They were breathless, panting. Darren's mother looked like she was on her last legs, she was coughing violently, her eyes ablaze with terror; his own mother looked despaired and lost, her pleading eyes were fixed on him. He moved to the head of the group and led them at a steady pace in the opposite direction.

They walked until things started to look familiar, until he saw the same horrors that he had already seen, until he felt the same dread that he had already felt. He saw the bodies, the doors that led to the slaughter. He felt a sense of urgency when he knew where he was, felt the heat in his lungs as the fire continued to rush through the building.

"Where are we going?" Ian asked, the first to speak since their escape.

Malcolm looked at him for a moment and then turned back down the corridor and continued walking "We're getting the fuck out of here," he said. "The entrance is this way."

* * *

The front door was still locked, a part of him had hoped that the others had used it to escape the fire, but no one had gone through. He guessed that they were still fighting, still torturing, still prowling, still doing what the doctor had manipulated them into doing, despite the fact that half of the building was on fire.

Darren's mother was still coughing madly; her weak lungs struggled with the smoke. Ian put his arm around her and looked into her eyes. He looked concerned; Darren had never seen such a sincere, honest, and human expression on his face. He wondered if Ian's concern was for his own safety, but he saw the way he looked at her, the gentle way that his hand rested on her back.

The flames were tearing through the building and had followed the group into the entrance way, rushing down the hallways after them like the patients had done hours before. The building was falling down around them, the coughing, the worry, and the stress was punctuated by the heavy sound of falling masonry. The building had stood for over a hundred years, but tonight it was going to fall.

Malcolm kicked the door hard; the impact reverberated through his ankle, through his calf, and threatened to explode out of his knee. He winced and pulled his foot back, hopping backwards and grimacing towards Darren who shared his pain. Darren tried to run at the door, to charge through, but the door was strong, the lock was fit to withstand anything that a tired, hungry, and scared kid could throw at it. Ian also tried to open it and before long they were all battering it, hoping to crack the lock or to bring the door down.

Malcolm's mother began shouting, pleading with whoever might be within earshot, to go and get help. Her pleas fell on deaf ears; there was no one around for miles, no one to see the flames engulf the building, certainly no one to hear the tired and desperate screams of one woman. In the dark they might have stood a chance, a blaze in such a large building would have lit up the night sky, but it was afternoon, hours had passed since they had entered the building, and it was bright outside.

Eventually they stopped, Malcolm held an arm up to stop Darren who continued to kick, punch, and charge the door when the others had given up. He took a step back, fired a worried glance over his shoulder, at the advancing flames, and then back at the door. He looked around the room, knowing that everything he saw would soon be engulfed by flames. The heat was getting unbearable and debris was raining down around them.

He heard screaming coming from deep inside the building. He turned to look down the hallways, but couldn't see much through the blinding light. The voices continued, all screeching through the roaring fire. He looked to see that the others had heard it too, his mother was staring at him with pleading eyes, she sensed her time was up and she was begging her son to help her, knowing that she had failed to help him on so many occasions in the past.

Malcolm felt a stab of hope when he spotted something behind the reception desk. He raced over, ignoring his mother who seemed to think he was about to abandon her, about to run back into the flames. He hopped the desk, picked up a chair and drove it into the glass case that held the fire-axe. He stared at it for a moment longer and then vaulted back over the desk and raced to the door.

The others watched as he hacked his way through the thick wood, straining and moaning with every swing. The screams were increasing behind them and the fire continued to rip through the building, firing up the room with an unbearable heat, but Malcolm ignored everything else and concentrated on the task ahead of him.

He was unable to hide his excitement when he punctured a hole through to the outside. The cool wind that rushed in, sucking out some of the toxic fumes, was almost orgasmic. It spurred him on, kick-started his adrenaline. He continued until he made the hole big enough to crawl through, then he threw the axe to the side.

He turned around, ready to order the others through. They all look relieved, happy to see the gap to the outside, but that relief quickly vanished when they saw the look of horror on Malcolm's face. He was looking over their shoulders, towards the hallway that they had all raced down. Three patients were running into the room, heading directly for Malcolm and the others.

43

Malcolm hoped that the screaming, running patients were just trying to escape. He hoped that they had come to their senses and that when he saw them, they would have expressions of fear and desperation, and not murderous intent. But they weren't scared, and judging by the large butcher knife held by one and what seemed to be a chair leg held by another, they didn't have escape on their minds.

Malcolm's arms were tired, his muscles burning from chopping the door and everything that had preceded it. Darren was just as helpless, which is why neither of them reacted. They didn't know what to do, didn't know which way to turn, whether to charge and fight with what little they had left or to slip out of the gap in the door and run. But before they could come up with a plan, Ian made up their minds for them. The drug addict had picked up the axe and ran to meet the patients before any of the others could move.

Ian stopped in the middle of the entrance, between the metal railings, ready to block the screaming attackers. He turned to look over his shoulder and shouted through the noise, his voice thick with emotion and smoke. "Get them out!" he ordered. "Quickly."

As soon as he turned back to his attackers they were upon him. The first one ran with his arm behind his back, ready to throw a punch. When he was in touching distance he launched the attack but Ian saw it coming. He stepped to the side and drove the handle of the axe into the side of his head. The attacker lost his balance and collapsed, hitting the railing on his way down. The resulting crack echoed throughout the room and the attacker slumped, unconscious, his body and head at unnatural angles.

Ian turned to the others who had both paused and were standing in front of him like dogs, grimacing and growling, ready to pounce.

"Who's next?" Ian asked, feeling like the hero.

Darren was baffled as he stared at his stepfather, wondering what had happened to the abusive dick that had stayed in his house for the last few months. He was still wondering when Malcolm began ushering the others outside, one at a time. He started with his own mother who was more than happy to go first. He helped her up and out, practically pushing her through the gap. She fell on the other side, ran a few paces away, and then looked back, waiting for the others to follow.

"I can't leave him!" Darren's mother pleaded, staring at her lover.

"You need to," Malcolm said.

She shook her head and seemed caught in a dilemma. She looked at Ian. The other two attackers had swarmed him now. He swiped the axe in front of one of them, threatening to hack off his leg, but he moved away just in time and then took advantage of the fact that Ian was off balance. He charged at him and drove a makeshift wooden bat across his face. Ian stumbled back and swung madly with the axe, but the attacker moved away again.

"Come on!" Malcolm yelled, watching the action and wondering how much fight Ian had left.

Darren reached out and grabbed his mother roughly by the shoulders. She stared blankly into his eyes, her mind was so used to the intoxicating comfort of chemicals that it didn't know how to react when it had been without them for hours. "You need to go," he said. "We need to get out of here. Ian will be fine."

He wanted to lose his patience with her, he felt like screaming at her. She was putting his life at risk, putting Malcolm's life at risk, and she didn't seem to care. He was as frustrated with her as he had always been, but he kept his patience. "Please," he added, hoping to appeal to whatever motherly instinct remained in her. "Please, Mum."

She looked him, and then at Ian one last time and then turned and crawled through the hole. Malcolm helped her through, it was a struggle, he could feel her trembling, feel her whole body shaking; she was sweaty and sticky, but she eventually made it through.

"You next," Malcolm said to Darren.

Ian was struggling now. He was still holding onto the axe, but the cumbersome weapon wasn't doing him any favors. One of the attackers had backed off and was toying with him, swinging madly and using his bat to try and knock the axe out of Ian's hand. The other was approaching with a knife, looking for a way in while avoiding swings from the axe.

"You first," Darren said.

"But—"

"Please," Darren cut in.

Malcolm stared at his friend for a moment. He heard his mother screaming to them through the wall behind him, heard Darren's mother crying. He looked to Ian who was still standing tall, holding onto the axe, despite the desperate attempts by his attackers to bring him down.

He nodded softly to Darren and then climbed through the gap. He turned around on the other side and waited to help his friend through.

"Come on!" he yelled.

Darren was staring at Ian and Malcolm could sense his dilemma as he watched. Ian had been nothing to him, *worse* than nothing, but now he had helped him, he had saved his mother's life and was about to save his. Darren knew that he couldn't just watch him die; he knew that he couldn't leave him to the mercy of his two attackers.

The heat was unbearable; the fire was at its peak and the building was on its last legs. The hallway through which they had all come, including the men that attacked the Ian, was engulfed; there was no escape through there and it was a matter of time before the fire took over the entire building.

Darren moved forward, ready to help. He stopped when Ian turned around, the two men still clinging on. He saw the look on Ian's face and was surprised to see that he didn't look afraid. He was struggling, and it showed, but he looked confident and strong.

"Go!" He yelled to Darren. "I've got this."

"But—"

"Go!" he shouted. He managed to throw one of them off him and squirm out of the range of the other. Darren watched for a moment. He expressed his gratitude with a sincere smile and then turned and vaulted through the hole, with Malcolm dragging him through.

They both ran to join their parents, a dozen feet or more from the building. They all watched from there, riveted by the flames. They couldn't see what was happening through the gap, but they all stared at that small hole, hoping that at any moment Ian would step through and join them.

They watched in silence for several minutes. They watched as the rubble fell, as the windows broke and shattered; they watched as the building, once glorious and intimidating, became a fiery shell of its former self. A spiral of thick black smoke was being pumped into the air, the crackling and crashing of the fire and the damage that it caused erupted into the bright afternoon.

The four of them watched and waited, until eventually the hole became part of the fire, as did the rest of the building. They never saw Ian leave.

Darren consoled his mother, wrapping his arm around her feeble frame as his stepfather had once done. He smiled, nodded in respect towards the burning building, knowing that Ian's last act in life was probably his most rewarding.

Epilogue

Malcolm looked down at his hands and sighed. It was a tired, worried sigh. He shifted his backside, trying to find a comfortable position—one that didn't dig into his buttocks or send shooting pains up his spine—but it was impossible, such a position didn't seem to exist here. The floor beneath him was cold, hard, and dusty. It had been trod by many solemn feet, sat on by many lonely backsides.

In the silence, listening to his own breath and that of his current cellmate, he thought about Eddie and Darren. It had been a year since he had last seen the former and not a day went by when he didn't think about him, when he didn't think what went wrong and what he could have done to change things. Of course, he didn't voice those thoughts, Eddie didn't exist outside of his head.

A line of bars surrounded him, a mesh of metal that colored the cell walls in a latticework of shadows cast from the light in the room beyond. He sighed again as he looked at the bars. He thought about the route that his life could have taken. It's funny how one small thing can have such a dramatic impact.

If he hadn't gone to the hospital that night.

If he hadn't listened to Eddie.

If he had stuck to stealing from houses.

The past was a series of questions, a list of regrets, buts, and what-ifs, but there was no turning back, no changing what had happened. He knew that all too well.

This building was his home now. He didn't mind thinking about it that way. He quite liked it, he liked the solitude and he liked the company. His life had once revolved around crime, around getting drunk, smoking dope, and stealing, he did none of those things now, he did nothing that could give him a high—natural or not—but he preferred his life now to the way it was.

He looked over to his cellmate and smiled before carefully rising, he didn't want to alert him, nor did he want to send his back into spasms. He stretched, yawned, and then grinned through the bars.

"He's settled now," he said. "Let me out of the cell."

Petti sighed and gave a joking shake of her head. "Mal, I've told you before to stop calling it a cell."

"Why, you worried the dogs will feel self-conscious?"

Petti grinned and stood up. She opened the latch and the door swung open. Malcolm glanced back at the dog he had shared the better part of an hour with. He was still scared, still curled into a ball at the back of the cell, but he looked more comfortable than he had been and it looked like he was trying to sleep.

"You did a good thing," Petti said. "You went beyond the call of duty," she added with a wink.

The dog had lived a horrid life. Its first owner had been a drunk and a madman who took out his frustrations and hatred on him. He had probably been a bright and energetic puppy before then, but his owner dragged him down and he turned into a timid, shy dog. He was eventually rescued and found a loving foster family, but they tired of him; the husband and wife divorced, the family split under bad terms and they tried to use the dog as an emotional bargaining tool, before deciding that neither of them wanted him.

He had been admitted into the shelter that morning and Malcolm had been drawn to him instantly. He felt a kinship. He was alone and needy, desperate for human support. He cried when they left him in the kennel alone, he refused to eat and, despite looking like he was desperate for sleep, he refused to even close his eyes when he was on his own—as if he was afraid of what the darkness would bring.

"I like him," Malcolm said, smiling as the dog closed his eyes and nestled his head between his front two paws. "I think I'll adopt him."

"That's sweet." Petti turned to the dog and spoke softly in case she woke him up, "You hear that Rex? Malcolm wants to keep you."

"No," Malcolm said sternly, "not Rex. This is a new start for him, he needs a new name."

"Okay," Petti said, straightening up and putting her hands on her hips. "What have you got in mind?"

Malcolm stared at the dog for a while as if deep in thought, but he had already thought of a name. "Eddie," he said.

"Eddie?"

"Yeah. Like an old friend of mine. He turned out to be a bit of a dick, but we had some good times." He smiled at the dog. "My friend had a chance at a good life and he blew it in a big way, but I have high hopes for this Eddie."

"For Eddie the dog?" Petti said, looking slightly perplexed but retaining a cheeky smile as she stared at her colleague.

"Yeah."

"Okay then." She laughed softly, reached out and grabbed at his face. She wrapped her hand around his mouth, squeezed her fingers until his lips puckered like a fish, and then leaned in and gave him a kiss. "Eddie it is," she said, pulling back. "Our new pet."

Malcolm grinned and moved in for a deeper, longer kiss. He hadn't been able to keep his hands off Petti since they had been together. He had finally plucked up the courage to ask her out just a few weeks after the incident at the hospital. He had felt renewed and had a new lease on life. He was also desperate and didn't have a place to go, he spent the first few weeks living in his house but eventually he was evicted. He had lost everything and felt he had nothing more to lose, then Petti agreed to go out on a date with him and the rest, including a full-time job at the shelter and moving into her house with her, was history.

"For fuck's sake, get a room."

The embracing couple pulled apart when they heard the door slam shut. They both turned towards the newcomer.

"We *did* get a room," Petti announced, grinning, "but then we invited some dickhead to live with us and we haven't had a moment's peace since."

Darren stopped in the middle of the floor; he frowned and looked at them both suspiciously. "What dickhead?" he asked. "I thought it was only us three living there . . . you're not talking about Malcolm, are you? Because I resent that remark. He's my friend and I won't stand here while you talk about him like that."

"Fuck off," Petti said, striding forward to punch Darren playfully on the shoulder. She brushed past him, leaving him rubbing his shoulder as she entered the back room to a chorus of barking from the many kenneled dogs that waited to be fed.

"So," Malcolm said, looking around with his hands in his pockets. "How's the job hunt?"

Darren shrugged, "Nothing yet. I applied for a few, but I'm not holding my breath. You'd think that with my skills I'd have a crowd of employers lining up at my door."

"I guess there isn't much need for burglars these days."

Darren shook his head. "I was never much good at that anyway. It's a miracle we never got caught to be honest. It's a good thing we got out when we did."

"Agreed."

The two locked stares for a moment, a wealth of questions and conversations passed between them but neither of them uttered a word. They didn't talk about Eddie, had barely spoken of him since the incident at the hospital. They didn't want their names linked to what had happened so they didn't report it to the police and they let the story unfold by itself. Malcolm's mother returned to her lover, abandoning Malcolm again, but this time at his request; Darren's mother returned to her drugs and her drink, slipping back into an oblivion that she was never going to leave. With Ian dead, she didn't have anyone to facilitate her addictions. Darren thought that she would be healthier without Ian. But that didn't seem to be the case. Whether she had been traumatized by his passing or whether he had actually been reining in her reckless behavior he didn't know, but she was worse than she had ever been.

There were a few other survivors: two patients and a staff member. The patients had managed to get out through a back door and were found wandering the fields covered in blood. They put up a fight with the fire brigade and the police, but they didn't hurt anyone. The staff member had hidden in a shower stall in the changing rooms before clambering out of an unbarred window when the fire started. The survivors had achieved fame and infamy, the former had been arrested, charged, and moved to a different facility, the latter had spent three months giving interviews and was now rumored to be writing a book.

Malcolm and Darren had been questioned by the police, but other than their links to one of the victims, there was nothing to place them at the scene. The building had been demolished; the surveillance equipment and any fingerprints or DNA they had left behind was destroyed. They identified Eddie and Hildenberg from their dental records, they never identified Neil.

"So who's this fella," Darren said, nodding towards the sleeping dog. "I've never seen a ginger dog before."

"Then you haven't seen many dogs. It's a red setter. Quite common."

Darren nodded, a glint in his eye as he admired the sleeping canine. "He's cute."

"He's ours now."

"What's his name?"

Malcolm paused, waiting for Darren to make eye contact. "Eddie."

He saw the memories flash across his friend's face, but they weren't fearful or angry. Malcolm hadn't had nightmares about Eddie and he rarely thought about the horrific things he did on that night, when he thought about him he thought about the Eddie that had been his friend for so long, he thought about the kid that he had grown up with and, as he looked at Darren, he knew that Darren remembered him the same way.

"That's a nice name," Darren said after a long pause, a silence interrupted only by the sporadic barking of dogs in the back room and the cheerful cooing of Petti as she fed them one by one. "I like that name."

"Me too," Malcolm agreed after a while.

Darren stared at the dog again; he paused, protracting another silence, before adding, "Better than fucking *Marshall.*"

Acknowledgments

To my agent, Peter Beren and my editors, Emily Shields and Nicole Frail. To Yiota, my partner, for her unending support; to my dad for being one of my biggest fans and my strongest advocates; to my brother, Gary, who will probably never see this, but definitely deserves to be part of it.

To Josh, for being a tutor, mentor, and friend; to Anthony, Jon, Debbie, and Ben for help-ing to make sure these words don't go unread; to Mike for continuing to read and support my work in all its many guises; to Shana, Alfonso, and Megan for their dedication and hard work; to Steve for reducing my tax-time headaches.

A list of acknowledgements wouldn't be complete with mentioning Alan, Carl, Gary, and everyone else who has helped and supported me over the years.

Made in United States
Orlando, FL
23 March 2023

31335244R00131